The King Bird had always escaped the traps set for him. He had defied posses to capture him, knowing he had the advantages of skill and guts. But now, trapped in this room, with men outside ready to kill him and a gun trained on his back, he felt that he had finally come to the end of his trail. This was one ambush he couldn't ride away from.

The voice behind the door mocked him. "Good-bye, King. Sorry to be so rough. Ready, boys! Let it go!"

The King Bird knew after an instant, when he smelled the odor of smoke and heard the crackling of flames on dry wood, that whatever hope there might be, there was none for him in this room. His only chance was to go outside and face those waiting guns. . . .

Warner Books
By Max Brand

Man From Savage Creek
Trouble Trail
Rustlers of Beacon Creek
Flaming Irons
The Gambler
The Guns of Dorking Hollow
The Gentle Gunman
Dan Barry's Daughter
The Stranger
Mystery Ranch
Frontier Feud
The Garden of Eden
Cheyenne Gold
Golden Lightning
Lucky Larribee
Border Guns
Mighty Lobo
Torture Trail
Tamer of the Wild
The Long Chase
Devil Horse
The White Wolf
Drifter's Vengeance
Trailin'
Gunman's Gold
Timbal Gulch Trail
Seventh Man
Speedy

Galloping Broncos
Fire Brain
The Big Trail
The White Cheyenne
Trail Partners
Outlaw Breed
The Smiling Desperado
The Invisible Outlaw
Silvertip's Strike
Silvertip's Chase
Silvertip
The Sheriff Rides
Valley Vultures
Marbleface
The Return of the Rancher
Mountain Riders
Slow Joe
Happy Jack
Brothers on the Trail
The Happy Valley
The King Bird Rides
The Long Chance
Mistral
Smiling Charlie
The Rancher's Revenge
The Dude
Silvertip's Roundup

MAX BRAND

The King Bird Rides

WARNER BOOKS

A Warner Communications Company

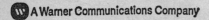

CONTENTS

CHAPTER I

THE HUNT

IT WAS not a great eminence that they stood on, but the air was so dry and clear that the eye could wander from the height, like a lord of space. Marshal Jim Hampton removed the field glasses from his eyes and handed them to his companion. The latter swung them up and caught in the field, first, a range of mountains, brown in the lower foothills, and sloping back rapidly to summits blue with distance and pale with ice. Then, to the side, he found straggling groups of mesas, their western sides gilded by the sun, which had almost set. Long shadows were painted black on their eastern sides, and black covered the canyons.

Then, in an open gorge, he found what he wanted, a rolling cloud of dust that pursued a smaller cloud that moved in advance of the first, like two of those little misty whirlpools that will go running down a hot street on a windless day.

He changed the focus of the glasses a little, and could make out the dark, faint forms of riders behind, and a single horseman in front. Even as he looked, down the side of the canyon streaked a quintet of fresh riders.

At least, by the dust they raised they seemed to be traveling fast, but though they aimed at the leading horseman, they did not quite cut him off.

"They've got him!" he shouted.

"I don't believe it," said Marshal Jim. "Look again."

"Almost," said "Tug" Ramsay. "They'll have him soon. They've got horses that are pretty fresh."

"That all depends," said the marshal. "The black mare

7

usually has a coupla more links that she can let out, in a pinch."

Tug Ramsay steadied the glasses at his eyes, and gasped.

"There's still the same distance between 'em—still the same—still the same——"

He groaned with eagerness. Then, lowering the glasses with a jerk, he exclaimed:

"They *got* to get him, this time!"

The lean and ugly face of the marshal puckered with a grin.

"Want 'em to catch him pretty bad, don't you, Tug?"

"Why, sure I do," said Tug Ramsay. "Don't you?"

"I dunno," said the marshal. "It's the third time in two years that I've got together every man that I could muster and gone after him. He's beaten me so many times that I dunno how it would feel to have him out of the field. The world'd seem sort of empty."

Tug Ramsay, in amazement, stared at his companion, and looked blankly away from him toward the ruins of the old Spanish fort that were scattered about them on top of the mesa.

"Yeah, I guess you'd appreciate that much more space, marshal," said he. "He's a devil, is what he is. I'd like to sink a chunk of lead in him."

"He ain't a devil," said the marshal. "You dunno him very well, do you? You ain't been long enough out of the north to know him very well."

"I've heard the boys talk around the fire, by night," said Ramsay.

The marshal took the glasses and focused them on the distant dust clouds. There were three of them now. A distance was growing between the two to the rear; just a little ahead the leader remained, an almost indistinguishable spot, because the sun was down, and all the air began to fill with golden dust.

"He's not a devil," repeated the marshal.

"The King Bird ain't?" said Tug, his jaw falling as he gaped. He had a powerful face, not an intelligent one, though there was plenty of cunning packed away in his sloping forehead. "Why," he continued, "the boys've told me yarns every evening, this week while we been chasing him, and there he is out there still—still runnin'. Nobody but the devil himself could've kept away that long."

"Know what he looks like?" asked the marshal abruptly.

"Nope. I dunno that I do," said Tug. "Big devil, I reckon."

"Not more than five-ten. Not heavy, either," said the marshal. "Not a bit heavy."

"Where does he put his stuff then?" asked Tug Ramsay.

"Brain power, and nerve power," said the marshal. "That's the only explanation I know. It ain't size that counts. You could kill a grizzly with a little pinhead of a .22, if you hit the right spot."

"Yeah, I know all about that," said Tug Ramsay. But he shook his head in doubt.

"Ever read fairy tales, Tug?" asked the marshal slowly, for he was still studious, the field glasses at his eyes.

"Ain't they climbin' his frame by now?" broke in Tug.

"No, they're just as far behind him, and the light's getting pretty bad for seeing, even up here—bad for shooting, down there! Ever read fairy tales, Tug?"

"It's a fairy tale, if he gets away this time," said Tug.

He indicated the down-headed horses which some of the men were working over now. They had ridden hard in some of the earlier relays that day. They were still spent.

"Yeah," said Tug finally. "I've read a few fairy tales, I guess, when I was a fool kid."

"What kind of idea d'you have about the prince or the young king, when you was reading 'em?" asked the marshal.

"Me? Well, you know how a fool kid is," said Tug Ramsay. "Kind of a golden-haired, blue-eyed guy was what I always had in mind."

"That's the King Bird," said the marshal.

"Go on," said Ramsay incredulously.

"That's what the King Bird looks like," insisted the marshal. "Don't you doubt that. Oh, he's like a picture out of a book, and gilded in your own imagination, too. That's the way he is!"

He lowered the glasses.

"They've dropped into a canyon that's as black as night," he went on. "And I don't think that we're going to have the King Bird in our bag this time, either."

"Thirty men—a hundred hosses," said Tug Ramsay. "He *can't* get clean away from us!"

"It don't seem possible," murmured the marshal.

He looked wistfully toward the spot on which he had fixed the glasses. He was seeing only his own thoughts, and the purple and golden evening that moved out of the west in a wave and made all the distant country dim. One became suddenly conscious of the sky, and the star points that were pricked in it.

"We've done enough work to catch a gross of King Birds," growled Tug Ramsay. "Dog-gone me if I understand it."

"He's a cut above us," said the marshal curtly. "That's all. He's a cut above. And now I've gotta write that blasted report."

He turned on his heel and went back into the ruins to one of the few remaining habitable rooms. Even this had only a partial roof left on it. But it gave him a sense of privacy, and therefore he had thrown his blankets into a corner. Now he sat down and with straining eyes, and a bowed head, he wrote until the words grew dim before his eyes. At that point, he signed his name, and stood up with a slight shudder, as though he had caught a chill.

Slowly the men gathered back to the main camp. For three hours, they were coming in, for some had to walk and lead horses that were so worn out that little life remained in them.

Few words were spoken at that camp that night. And those words were mostly curses.

Of course, the marshal might decide to start the hunt again, but it was unlikely.

The trap he had laid had been sprung the week before, and since then, for seven days, with prepared relays, and over selected ground, the hunt had gone on with hardly a cessation. Now men and beasts were exhausted, and the "King Bird" was somewhere off there in the tangle of black ravines that split the more northerly landscape—still free!

The marshal came out from his room, and got a pan of mulligan stew and a lump of bread together with a dipper of coffee from the cook. He retired with those provisions, consumed them, and sat a while in the moonlight, smoking, and looking out over the country.

It was a hard blow, a shrewd blow. He had felt that the chances in his favor were a hundred to one at the start; ten to one, even, on the morning of that day.

The beauty of that wide scene could not soothe him. The report which he would have to mail on the morrow rankled like a poison in his mind. And so he rolled into his blankets with a groan, and finally slept.

He was wakened by a soft sound. Horses could have stamped and neighed all the night long, in the camp, without disturbing him, but this soft whisper sank at once through the profound deeps of his slumber and jerked him erect, reaching for the gun that was under his blanket.

He did not draw it out. For the silhouette of a man was before him, and the gleam of a gun was near his head.

"The King Bird!" breathed Marshal Jim Hampton.

CHAPTER II

LAWMAN AND OUTLAW

THE ROOM was composed of two wedges, one of black shadow, one of silver moonshine. In the shadow lay the marshal, and in the moonlight stood the King Bird.

"Get up," he said. "Get up and take your gun. Don't try a snap shot, though. I'm watching, Hampton."

"All right," said the marshal.

He picked the revolver from beneath the blanket, and stood up in his stockinged feet, and stared at the other. The

11

handsome face of the King Bird was faintly marked with shadow, for he was smiling, not broadly, but as one who feels a great inward delight.

"There's room in here," said the King Bird. "Unless you want more space. How about standing with our backs to the wall? That will give us four or five paces in between. That do you, marshal? Or would you like more space, still?"

The marshal turned his head from side to side and measured the distance between the walls.

His mind flashed far abroad. He could see the items in the newspaper. "Marshal killed by desperado." No, they would call him "celebrated marshal." He had done enough to deserve an adjective or two in front of his name. He could hear his friends speak. Judge Hooker would say: "Well, Martha, they got Jim at last. The King Bird got him. I always knew that the King Bird would get him. He was getting too old to go after that kind of game."

Not many comments would be made. He himself made few comments when his friends disappeared. The pain remained for a short time. Then the days covered it, and the world was as usual.

Now he was about to die. He knew that he could not match the merciless precision that was in the hand of the outlaw.

"All right, King," said he. "We'd better get the moon a little higher, though. That'll give us both a fair break."

"No," said the King Bird. "I'm not going to wait. I'll take the slant of it in my eyes."

The marshal managed a soft laugh.

"Is that it?" he said. "Not on your life, King. If you want this to be a fair match, have the moon square over us, or nearer in the middle of the sky than it is now. I've always known that I could beat you with a gun, boy. I don't want to spoil my party by thinking that you threw any chances away."

"Are you going to beat me, Hampton?" said the young man.

"I think so, King."

"You're a tough old codger," said the King Bird, smiling more broadly. "I'll tell you how we can manage. We can step outside into the moonlight. That do?"

"Why not?" said the marshal, though his heart sank, as he saw his chance to win time diminishing.

"Walk first, if you don't mind," said the King Bird. He stood at the broken doorway, and murmured: "You'll move slowly, Jim, won't you? I don't want this to seem like murder."

"No, you're pretty dog-gone careful about that, ain't you?" said the marshal. "You're always careful not to let it seem like murder?"

He stepped past the other at the doorway.

Just beyond was the ruins of a little patio. One end of it was smashed down, the wall quite flat, so that the eye could run out over the moon-drenched mesas and on to the mountains, softly modeled of thin lights and thinner shadows.

They were farther from the other men of the camp now and could speak more easily.

"This is better, anyway," said the young man. He seemed to be turning his head idly, carelessly, from side to side, considering the prospect and the immediate lay of the ground.

The revolver hung down in his right hand. The left hand drooped gracefully from the glistening silk scarf that was wound around his hips, Mexican style.

He was always one to pay the greatest attention to his clothes. He could come out of the wildest desert as out of a bandbox. Even his boots he had rubbed up—otherwise they would not have been gleaming, surely. He had taken care, in making this moonlight call, as though it had been upon a sweetheart.

"This is better," he repeated.

"Yeah, it's a lot better," said the marshal, trying to make his voice cheerful.

"We can back away to the walls. That would make about fifteen paces. Or as few as you please," said the King Bird.

"Why, the fewer the better," said the marshal. "It don't matter to me."

"Doesn't it?" said the other. "Oh, doesn't it?"

He smiled again, pleasantly, and ice slipped into the heart of the marshal.

13

What a waste he had made of life, riding, rushing, laboring, striving after fame and a little fortune, when this beautiful world can give so much happiness to those who are willing to sit patiently in the sun, harming no one, themselves unharmed!

"Well, then," said the young man, "we'll make it six or seven steps, say, and you jerk your gun on the sixth or the seventh step, just as you please. I suppose it would be a little more fun if we put the guns up?"

Fun? Was that what he called it? Fun?

Yes, it was only fun, perhaps, for this man with the hands of a conjurer, and the eye of a hawk.

Jim Hampton put up his Colt. Instantly the weapon disappeared from the grip of the King Bird. What other man in the world would have taken such a chance?

The marshal could not help exclaiming: "You beat me, King. You had me cold, and now you're throwing away your advantage!"

"I never took an advantage in my life," said the young man instantly.

"No?" murmured the marshal, glad of talk, glad of anything that would preserve a few more seconds of this dwindling existence.

"Never," said the King Bird.

"That ain't what people have heard," said Hampton.

"Who heard the opposite?" snapped the young man eagerly.

He came a half step closer. The marshal could see the sheen of his eyes, and through the shadow the dull gleam of that golden hair of his.

"Everybody's heard the opposite," said Hampton. "You've been in so dog-gone many gun plays, King, that you can't expect to get off with a good reputation."

"I can, and I shall," said the young man. "I'll find the hounds that dare to backbite. I'll find 'em, if they're a thousand, and teach 'em the *truth* about the way I fight."

"You're a cool kid, at that," said the marshal, almost forgetting his sense of personal danger, in his admiration of the calm poise and surety of the other. "You act like you were pretty satisfied with what you get out of life."

14

"Why not?" said the King Bird.

"Well, but why so?"

"Who would I change with?" asked the young man.

"With anybody that's got a decent home, a family, friends, and enough to live on without being a slave," said the marshal.

"Yes?" murmured the young man.

"Yeah," said the marshal. "That's the way it looks to me."

"I suppose it does," said the King Bird, a quiet wonder in his voice. "But for my part, I've always wondered at people like you, Hampton, with brains enough and strength enough to be free men—and instead of that, you're done in, like the rest of people, like almost all of 'em. You've got the whip on your back!"

"What whip?" asked Hampton.

"The whip of the driver. The man who sends you out on a trail—he's your driver. Every puppy of a reporter that comes and demands a story from you—he's your driver. Every fool of a lump-headed citizen is your driver and your master, too. You have to work for 'em. If they're not satisfied, they file a little complaint against you, and snap!—there's the end of your job! You're out on the street again, and your reputation isn't worth a rag!"

"Well," said the marshal, "I'll put something against that, King. I've got the respect of those citizens. There ain't many that don't trust me. Gents come a hundred miles on hossback to ask my opinion about things. Folks come and talk to me about the way to raise their kids—me that ain't never had none! The gents that write me up in the newspapers do me proud. There ain't a place in the world where I can't go and keep my head up. And here you are, run like a poor coyote through the hills, any time that a posse gets together."

The young man laughed. "That's part of the sport," he said. "It keeps my eyes open. It keeps me fit. Man, how would a fox feel, if it didn't take a run, now and then, just to sharpen its wits and lighten its heels? That's what creatures are on earth for, Hampton—to use their faculties! What are teeth in a wolf for? What are wings on a hawk for, and talons to strike with? And that's the life I want, mind you—space to range in, like the hawks, Hampton; and game to prey on, too; and if you fellows come out and give me a run through the blue, now and then, all the better. The harder you make me fly, the higher I'll get and the more I'll see of this little old world."

He stood there, laughing in the moonlight, as fine a picture as ever had filled the eyes of Marshal Jim Hampton.

He peered at the young man with a curious interest.

"I think you believe what you say. You're not a liar, as a rule."

"No, not as a rule," said the King Bird. "I'd sooner turn into a mole and live underground than live your life, Hampton. Honestly, it's more of a punishment to let you keep on dragging out your existence than to put an end to it. But this is the third time you've run me. And three times is enough. Three times brings the game around, full circle. I don't want people to begin to take me too lightly, you know."

He laughed again, very gently, and there was almost a caress in his eyes as they dwelt on the face of the marshal.

"You feel—well, like a king, eh?" said the marshal. "And yet you're not stupid. You know that sooner or later they'll get you. You'll trust a friend, and be snagged—even if I don't get you to-night."

"It's not a *long* life that I want," said the young man. "I have all that I want."

"Have you?" murmured the marshal.

"Yes, everything."

"What have you?"

"Freedom, the finest horse in the world, and the most beautiful girl!" said the young man.

"The freedom—the horse—the woman, eh?" said the marshal thoughtfully. "Well, I dunno that you can be blamed for being so wrong. You ain't lived long enough to find out any better."

"Am I wrong?" asked the young man, smiling contentedly in his surety.

"Wrong on all three counts," said the marshal.

"That so?" asked the young man cheerfully, still smiling.

"This here thing you call freedom—it's a coyote's sneaking

16

life. If you knew the real thing, you'd understand what I mean."

"That's a hard point to argue," said the young man calmly.

"The other two I could prove to you," said the marshal.

"Ah?" murmured the King Bird.

"As for the hoss," said the marshal, "it's a good mare. And it runs its heart out for you, free and willing. But take it by and large, it ain't a patch on Dick Macey's silver hoss."

"No?" The young man frowned. "I never heard of Macey's horse. Yes, I have, though," he added, his frown ceasing. "He's the half-breed with a gray stallion."

"That's it," said the marshal. "That hoss is so dog-gone fast and it's got such wind—why, man, I didn't mind hunting you three times, you and the mare. But one flyer at the half-breed and his gray, that was enough for me. It ain't alone that it's a faster hoss than the mare, but it can stay. Him that rides the gray, he don't need to turn and twist and double none. He can sit tight and ride right away from any man on earth."

"That's something to look into," said the young man sharply. "There's one thing left," he added.

"The girl?" said the marshal. "Oh, I can prove to you that she ain't what she seems!"

CHAPTER III

THE MARSHAL'S INFORMATION

THE KING BIRD strode suddenly close to him. "I'm going to cut your heart out for that, Hampton," said he, his eyes gleaming.

"You're going to back out of here a whipped dog," said the marshal. "Because I'm going to tell you something, before I put a bullet through you. You ain't going to die happy, brother."

Now, as the marshal spoke, he saw a head lift suddenly above the wall at the end of the patio. It was to Jim Hampton as though an angel had peered out of the highest heaven.

His eyes merely glanced toward it, but the head of the young man in front of him instantly flicked around. That silhouette, however, had disappeared!

The King Bird confronted the marshal again.

"It's time for you to say something," said the King Bird.

"About the little Mexican girl? About Inez?" asked the marshal.

The other started.

"It's all right," he said. "I'll hold myself now, but you're going to die for it, Hampton!"

"Let me tell you something," said the marshal. "If you're an open-minded young man, you'll listen to facts. I'm kind of sorry for you, King. You got some good qualities about you, and I'm kind of sorry. Inez is a pretty thing, but—— Well, will you listen to facts?"

"To *facts* I'll listen, for a moment or so," said the young man.

"Well," said the marshal, "ever strike you strange that we tried for you that night you went up the road out of town, and we jumped you crossing the bridge, a week ago?"

"Not strange," said the King Bird. "You're always ready to try for me."

"I can tell you why you were on that road," said the marshal.

"I don't believe it," said the King Bird, his face darkening cruelly with a frown.

"To meet Inez's brother."

"The devil!" whispered the young man under his breath.

"I wouldn't be telling you this," said the marshal truthfully, as he saw three heads, in place of one, appear above the patio wall, and begin to move slowly closer to the outlaw, "I wouldn't be telling you this, if I thought you were going to leave this patio alive. But since you ain't, I'll give you some information, son. The gent you were going to meet was Don Ramon, all right."

"You've said that," snapped the young man.

He stood straight, and the heaving of his chest was perceptible. He was much shorter than the marshal, but the greatness of his anger seemed to make him swell and grow in size.

"And I'll tell you another thing that maybe you don't know," said the marshal. "Even if you'd busted through us and gone on down the road you wouldn't 'a' found Ramon."

"Had you found him first?" asked the King Bird.

"No, but he wasn't there."

The young man made a light, brief humming sound. It was his breath forced through his compressed teeth and lips.

"Well, that's all right," he said steadily.

It was very easy for the marshal to understand how this youth had killed men, as he listened to that voice.

"May I ask how you knew that Ramon might have been down the road, waiting for me?" asked the King Bird.

"That's easy," said the marshal, seeing the drift of the silhouetted heads closer and closer to them. "Inez told me."

The young man gasped. The marshal could see the shock of the words, like the shock of a bullet. He could not help saying:

"I'm sorry for you, my lad. But there's the way things go, in this here world. You were sitting in the middle of the sky, a minute ago. And you were lookin' considerable down at the rest of us. And now you're in the dust, and a worm could crawl over you and not feel the bumps. You had the finest horse in the world, and I've named a better. And you were going to marry the most beautiful girl in the world, and you've found out about *her*."

"If I believed you," said the King Bird, and his voice was slightly tremulous, like a string vibrating, "I'd be the lowest hound in the world."

"And all your fine, free life, King," said the marshal, "will go out like a snuffed candle. And what's left of you? Just a vacant spot in the air. That's all."

He stepped back a little.

19

"I've heard enough talk," said the King Bird. "Afterward, I'll do a little investigating on my own account. Now for a touch of action, Hampton. Are you ready?"

"Readier than you are, my boy," said Hampton. "I'm kind of sorry about it, King. But the time never was when I was fit to stand up to you with a gun."

Then, suddenly lifting his voice, he shouted: "Shoot!"

It was as though the King Bird were actually a winged thing.

It seemed that the mere breath which the marshal used in shouting his command, thrust the young man backward and to the side, like a dead leaf caught by the air.

Certainly he had leaped before the three guns spoke from the top of the wall hardly ten paces behind him.

They fired again, but he was already through the door of the marshal's room.

"After him!" yelled the marshal, and he himself plunged valiantly, straight at that door, gun in hand.

He ran into an empty room.

The men who had so luckily seen the marshal's plight in the patio had tumbled over the wall and were sprinting behind him, yelling to rouse the camp, as though, in fact, the gunshots had not already brought every man out of his blankets!

The marshal, running out through his room from the opposite door, came to the old adobe wall of the fort, ten feet thick, and rushing through a place where the adobe had crumbled or been earthquake-shaken almost to the ground, he looked down the steep face of the mesa, and saw nothing but the white of the moonlight, that silvered the rock.

Eagerly he stared, like some mousing owl, when the sight of a field mouse brings the bird down close to the ground, and it searches a thicket carefully to find the game.

Still he saw nothing!

The three men who had followed him, whose two volleys had unfortunately missed the target, came stumbling out to join him.

"If he's not the devil in fact, and put on wings," said the marshal, "he's down there. He's gotta be down there somewhere. You could see him, if you used your eyes. Rub 'em open and take a look. You're a mile younger than me!"

Keenly they watched. There was enough reward for the first man to put a bullet in the King Bird to make them sharpen their eyes. But already the whole camp was swarming about them, before one of them saw a dark form slither down the face of one of the lower rocks, and emerge again, in the deep shadow at the base of the cliff.

He called out, and pointed his cry by shooting.

But that fugitive form had dipped at once into the shade, straight down under a bulge of the rocks.

"Horses! Horses!" yelled many voices.

The marshal, after a moment, shook his head.

He pointed, and those who looked with him, saw a slim shadow fleeing across the moon-whitened sands of the desert. It was a rider moving his horse at an easy gallop, like the flitting of the wings of a swallow, that carried him over rough and smooth.

"What's the use?" asked the marshal.

"We got him under our noses!" shouted a man at his ear, grasping him strongly by the shoulder. "Let's go down after him!"

"Why?" asked the marshal, with a sigh. "By the time that we got our hosses down the slope behind the mesas, he'll be a mile away. The black mare's beat us every time, and all day. D'you think that you can catch her now, when she has a decent head start?"

He shook his head. There was a general chorus of protest. Such a reward was on the head of the King Bird, that there would be plenty to divide even thirty ways. But in spite of that, they had other reasons to wish to catch him. He had avoided them for seven desperate days of riding, and there was not a man of the lot who would not have given blood to bring the outlaw to bay.

But still the marshal shook his head.

"We're beat," he said succinctly. The sense of time and of many years came down upon him. And he found himself saying to his second in command: "I'll tell you something, Bert."

21

"Well, you tell me, then," said Bert.

"You take a fellow like that," said the marshal, "and it's pretty hard for a crowd to beat him."

"What *will* beat him, then?" asked Bert.

"He might beat himself," said the marshal. "And I got an idea that I've put the crank in his head that'll break the machine."

CHAPTER IV

THE ANNOYING GIRL

FAR SOUTH, far south from the mesas, the King Bird sauntered down a blurred and ancient trail that had been laid out by the leisurely moving of herds coming up from the southland, in the days when the Apaches rode beneath the Mexican moon. The trail was so scattered with the bones of beasts and of men that it looked like a partly rubbed-out chalk mark, two hundred yards wide. From high places, one's eyes could follow it miles and miles into the horizon.

From this grim trail, the King Bird turned aside, and went over a hill, and down into a little valley—or, rather, a mere chance depression among the hills.

He was walking. And behind him came the black mare, with the saddle loosely girded upon her back, and no bridle on her head. She roamed as she pleased. She had had seven days of terrible work, that had ended not long before, and now she was resting on the trail with her master.

He had walked slowly all of the day before, while she moved from side to side, picking at the best grass, then trotting up to him. Sometimes she was as much as a quarter of a mile away, standing on a hilltop and scanning the landscape, with a more than human beauty, and what seemed a human understanding. And then she would come with a sweep and a scamper back to her master.

His eye of love and pride followed her constantly. Of the two things that the marshal had said to him, he hardly knew which hurt him more—the word of the girl's treachery, or the suggestion that there might be, in all the course of the mountains, a finer mount than this.

He denied both statements, and repaid the marshal with a liberal addition of personal hatred. That was a score which would be rubbed out, in the course of time. In the meanwhile, he intended to investigate matters.

From the next hilltop, he had a view of the little half-Mexican town of Valencia. The American part of the town was in the flat near the road—and business. The Mexican huts scrambled up the sides of the eminence whose flat top was crowned with trees, and the old house in which the Ramirez family lived. Inez would be there. He smiled as he thought of her. Then he remembered what the marshal had said, and gritted his teeth firmly together.

As he came down into the hollow again, he saw some one riding fence on a pinto mustang. The brim of the wide hat of the rider flared up in the wind, and he saw the glint of red hair. The King Bird nodded and smiled, and turned straight toward the other.

It was a girl. That was clear in spite of her man's overalls, and the bandanna around her neck, and the battered old sombrero on her head. It was clear even from a little distance; it was more than certain when one came close enough to see the brown of her arms, for she was working with her sleeves rolled up, tightening a sagging length of barbed wire with a lever. No man or boy ever had elbows turned in just this fashion, with such neatness and delicacy.

It was a hard tug for her to get the lever down and, holding it with one hand, nail the end of the wire with the other. She had just managed that when the King Bird came up.

"Hello, Brick," said he.

She was putting in another brad to hold the wire, swinging

23

the hammer with power and certainty, and she answered, without making a pause in the stroke:

"Hello, King. I thought you were dead."

"Not half," said he.

She straightened and turned to him. She shook off a heavy, buckskin glove, pulled out a handkerchief, and rubbed the moisture from her forehead. She was all brown, and pretty enough, except that her nose had been a little scanted in the making.

"Thought Jim Hampton was feeding all of you except the scalp to the coyotes, by this time," said she. "Glad to see you, King."

She shook hands with him.

"Don't let me interrupt you, Brick," said he. "Go right on working. It makes me feel pretty cool and comfortable to watch you tying into that fence."

He perched himself on a fence post, as he spoke.

"You lazy loafer!" said the girl. "Molly's tucked up a bit. She's had to do some running, eh?"

"Come here, Molly," said the King Bird.

The mare lifted her head, with a wisp of bunch grass in her teeth; she gathered it in and came over to him, munching, and stood before him with her short ears pricking.

"Stand around, girl," said the King Bird.

She turned at once to the side, obeying his gesture more than his words, while he looked critically at her.

"No, she's not tucked up. Just drawn a little fine," said the King Bird, at last.

"She *is* tucked up a bit," said the girl, shaking her head. "You took something out of her, King."

"I took something out of her, but she's getting it back again," he answered. "She's iron; she stands the hammering."

"She's all right so long as she only has to carry a boy," said the girl.

"Boy?" snapped the King Bird, frowning.

"What do you weigh, King?" she asked.

"Oh, a hundred and fifty or sixty," said he carelessly.

"A hundred and fifty—when you've got your winter fat on, and winter clothes, too," said "Brick."

24

He glared at her.

"You don't annoy me—much," said he.

"What's been happening?" she asked.

"Oh, a couple of things," said he. "What's going on around here, Brick?"

"Oh, a couple of things," said she.

He looked at her with angry, staring eyes. Impatiently, he made a cigarette, then seemed to remember himself, and offered her the "makings."

"I'm not smoking," said she.

"That's a surprise to me," said the King Bird. "You're like a half-grown freckle-faced brat of a pigeon-toed range kid, in every other way. You're just like a boy with his first six-shooter, and his first pair of boots, you're so full of yourself, and so fresh. You need a trimming, Brick."

"That's more than you can give me," she answered, giving glare for glare. "And just tell me, Mr. Solomon—how old are you, anyway?"

"Oh, I'm old enough, brother," said the King Bird. "I'm plenty old enough to tell you a few things."

"You tell everybody a few things, but nobody listens," said the girl. "Besides, you don't have to speak. I can easily guess your age within a year."

"Go right ahead," said he, sitting a trifle straighter.

"You're twenty years old to a day," said she.

He started.

"Twenty?" he repeated, flushing a little.

"Yeah. You're just out of your teens."

"Oh, am I?"

"Yes, just."

"You don't annoy me—much," he repeated. "As a matter of fact, I'll tell you something, Brick—I'm twenty-two. But I look older."

"Yeah, when you tie a white beard on your face you do," said she. "Are you all of twenty-two, or is that just bunk?"

He frowned, and eyed her narrowly.

"A lot of people take me for thirty," he ventured. At this she laughed.

"Thirty?" said she. "Thirty—with that baby face?"

He started again.

"Quit it, Brick, will you?" said the King Bird.

He stepped down from the post, and stood his full height.

"A whole *lot* of people take me for thirty, or even more," said he, with icy dignity.

"Stay on the post, King," said she. "It makes you look taller."

"You're not funny, Brick," he told her. "Not a bit. You're just dull. You used to be an amusing kid, but now you're just rude—and dull. It doesn't make any difference to me what you say and think."

"Doesn't it? I had to laugh the other day, though, at what a fellow said about you."

"What did he say?" asked the King Bird anxiously.

"He said what a beautiful girl was spoiled when you turned out to be a boy!" said Brick, laughing very heartily again.

She laughed so much that tears came into her eyes. The King Bird was white and hard as ice.

"Do something for me, will you, Brick?" he said.

"Yeah. What is it?"

"Tell me the name of the fellow who said that about me!"

"Why? I don't want to get you into any more trouble."

"Don't you?" he murmured.

He stepped closer, and laid a hand on her shoulder.

"Come on and be a good fellow. Tell me who said that!" pleaded the King Bird.

"Want him to say it to your face?" she asked.

"Yes, I'd like that a lot," said the King Bird.

"If you're bright and keep your little pink ears open," said she, "you'll hear the some thing said by others."

"Come here, Molly," he cried.

The mare came instantly, like an obedient and well-trained dog. Out of the saddlebag he drew a holster of soft leather. And from the holster he took a beautifully made, pearl-handled, .32-caliber revolver.

"Look at this, Brick," said he. "I was thinking of you, when I bought this."

"Jiminy!" said Brick. "What a howling beauty! Let me try the balance of it."

She stretched out her hand, took the gun, and weighed it.

A crow came over them, winging low and clumsily. She tried a snap shot, and the crow dodged in the air, and flew away, leaving a tuft of feathers behind it, gradually whirling about and settling toward the ground.

"You could shoot with your eyes closed—with this one!" said the girl.

"It's yours, Brick," said he. "It's yours if——"

"If what?" she asked eagerly.

"If you'll tell me the name of your friend who said I— er—you know what he said!"

She offered the gun back to him.

"The trouble with this," she said, "is that it's too light. Not enough weight in the heel of it; just the sort of a gun that a little boy would like."

"It's not right for you, eh?" said he. "Listen to me, Brick —you little liar!—you're aching to have it, and it's yours, if you'll tell me the name of that hombre."

He appealed to her with wistful eyes.

She shook her head.

"I've got a slick pair of silver spurs that you might want, too, Brick," said he.

"Thanks," said the girl. "Suppose I tell you the name, you might try to do something, and get a spanking."

He sighed. "All right," he said. "I give up. Nobody can beat you when it comes to meanness, Brick. You were born mean, and you've grown up mean. You're mean by nature, and you've educated yourself to be meaner. I give up. Hardtack is spoon bread, compared to you!"

"Here's the gun," she suggested.

"No, that's for you," he answered.

"I don't want to be pinched as a receiver of stolen goods," said Brick.

"Quit it!" he exclaimed loudly. "I'm getting tired of this! I bought that with honest money!"

"Who loaned you the honest money?" said she.

He stared at her grimly. And suddenly she laughed a little.

"Why, King," she said, "my heart would have broken right in two, if I couldn't have this little old gun. I'm thanking you a lot."

She offered her hand, and he took it gingerly.

"I hate to touch you," said the young man. "You're so full of thorns. What a tongue you have, Brick. You'd make a lawyer, you would. Any murderer would rather be hanged than have you unlimber your vocabulary on him. Now you tell me what's been happening around here, will you?"

"Oh, just a couple of things," said the girl.

He frowned again, and then he sighed.

"All right," he groaned. "I have to give up again. I always have to give up, when I meet you. Conversation is not your line. Five minutes talking with you is worse than five hours wrestling with a heavyweight professional champ. I'll tell you what happened. I was dropping up the road one night, week before last, just outside of Valencia, yonder, when the bushes turned into men and started shooting at me. Molly got me clear.

"At least, I thought I was clear, but I was wrong. For seven days I was wrong. Every time I turned around, it rained horses and rifles at me. Jim Hampton was playing all his cards at once, and I must say that it was quite a game that he showed me. Then the other night up in the mesa country they almost had me. I asked the last question of Molly—and she said, 'Yes!' Just barely was able to say it! Come here, Molly!"

The mare started back to him from her grazing, but the girl stopped her and putting an arm about the small of her neck, began to rub the little velvet square of the muzzle.

"Go on, King," said Brick, whose real name was Helena Blair.

"I got loose, and slipped back to pay a call on Hampton, who was perched with his gang on top of one of the mesas in the wreck of an old Spanish fort. I found him, and had a chat with him. We were going to have it out, you see? That was the third time that he'd given me the run, and three times is enough for soup. While we stood there, exchanging the time of the night, so to speak, the marshal gave me a few shots. He said I was leading a fool's life."

"Good for him," said Brick.

"Keep still," said the King Bird. "I told him that I have all I want—beginning with Molly, and winding up with Inez. They're the finest that I know. And he told me about a gray horse owned by a half-breed called Dick Macey——"

"That horse is a real one," said she. "That's the best horse I ever heard of."

He sighed, as he looked at her.

"We'll see about that later," said he. "The other thing he told me, I can't say even to you."

"You'll sleep better if you do," said the girl.

"I've always told you everything since you were a little bit of a mug," said the King Bird. "I don't know why, except that you keep your mouth shut, and you've got a head on your shoulders, too. But I can't tell you this."

"It's about Inez," said she.

He considered. Then the words burst out: "Hampton said that it was *she* who helped him lay the plan to catch me, when I went up the road that night from Valencia. D'you believe that she'd do that?"

The girl kicked at the ground with the toe of her boot for a moment.

"Mexicans can be pretty temperamental, King," said she. "And Inez might get tired waiting for you to catch a gold mine and square yourself with the law. Besides, it might sprain her dignity a good deal to marry anything less than a Don. You're only the King Bird, you know. What *is* your real name, King? After four years of knowing you, I ought to be trusted with that, oughtn't I?"

He shook his head gravely.

"That's where I stop," said he. "But about Inez—you know her."

"As well as she'll let me," said Brick. "A poor little country cowgirl like me, King, can't get very far with her. What would you do, anyway? What if she *had* double-crossed you?"

He put back his head, and smiled faintly, his eyes half closed, his nostrils quivering.

"She has brothers. There's Don Ramon, for instance," he remarked.

"Would you go after them?" asked the girl curiously.

"It would ease my mind a whole lot," said he.

"How would you find out the truth about her?" asked Brick, after considering the last remark for a time.

"I'll go up to the house and make myself at home, as usual."

"They'll know that Hampton has talked to you. He's a square-shooter. He'll have sent word to them."

"Hasn't been time," said the young man. "I've come straight down here. I came on foot, but I ran all the way, till I got sight of Valencia."

She glanced over his dusty clothes, and nodded.

"You're an Indian, except the complexion," said she.

"Hampton will send a messenger," he reflected. "I could lie out on the trail and catch him, and find out what the message is. That would give me a few cards up my sleeve. Tell me, Brick, honestly, do you think that Inez would be a snake in the grass?"

"She's too beautiful for me to think about her," said the girl soberly. "She makes me a bit dizzy. But, King, if you walk into the old Ramirez place at a time when they want you out of the way—realize how many knives and guns there are in that house? And how many nice little graves could be dug in the cellar?"

He turned. The mere crest of the hill of Valencia could be seen, and the thick, lofty grove of trees that surrounded the house of Ramirez.

"I've been thinking about that all the way down on the trail," he answered. "Come up on that hill with me, and we'll sit under the tree in the shade. It's hot out here. And besides, up there I can keep a watch on the northern trail, in case a rider comes along, burning up the way."

"I've got to finish patching this fence. It's groggy in the knees and gone in the wind," answered the girl.

He put his arm through hers.

"Come along," he commanded. "I want to talk about you now. We've chattered enough about me."

CHAPTER V

TALK ABOUT BRICK

IT WAS a twisted, battered old tree, bent by the wind, with the limbs streaming out toward the southeast, still fleeing from the thousand storms that had struck it. Under it they sat down, and the young man leaned back with his head resting against the projecting knuckle of a root. He looked up through the interweaving of the branches and then to the side, at the girl.

She was cross-legged, like an Indian, with her chin on one fist.

"How long since you've had a snooze, King?" said she.

"Oh, just a while," said he.

"A week or ten days?" she asked.

"Just a little while," said he.

"Quite a big while," she answered. "Your mamma wouldn't know your eyes, to-day, *Little Boy Blue.*"

"Oh, shut up, Brick, will you?" said he.

"You sleep, and I'll keep an eye peeled," said she.

"No, I want to talk about you," he insisted.

"There's nothing to tell," she replied.

"Oh, there's always something to tell. Go on and bust it loose. There's the family. What a family *you've* got, Brick!"

"None of 'em outlawed yet," she answered very sharply.

"What are they doing?"

"Mother's still in the kitchen finding new ways to cook beans. Father's getting as far as he can around the place on one leg, and John's still polishing his law shingle in Valencia and waiting for his first real chance."

"What a John that one is," murmured the King Bird.

"He's four times the man you are, baby face," said Helena Blair.

"Oh, I know. He's an earnest worker. And he'll be a prominent citizen, too, one of these days when somebody dies and leaves him two or three thousand dollars. Before he's in his grave, he'll rise to be town dog catcher, or something big."

"It's the way you talk that makes me like you so much," said Brick. "It's because your big, kind heart shows through. Oh, wouldn't I like to hand you one, if you weren't down. *I* have to live with that family; you don't."

"It's being up against a wall like that, that's shortened your nose," said he. "But go on and talk about yourself. I mean, besides building fences, and riding herd, and taking care of the horses, and repairing the roofs, and milking the cows, and skimming the milk, and making butter, and collecting the eggs, and getting the groceries, and collecting the mail, and making your clothes, and all the rest of it—what have you been doing, Brick?"

"Nothing much," said she. "I don't have such a dog's life as you think."

"You're a tough little mug," said the King Bird. "What a wife you'll make somebody!"

"Why not you?" said she.

He laughed a little.

"The way you love me, Brick, is a wonderful thing," said he.

"It's your pretty little face that gets to my heart," said she.

"You know the only reason I've ever broken the law?" he asked her.

"You tell me, and make it good," said she.

"It's because you drive me so wild. Your line of talk would make a tame old gray cat go out and punch a mountain lion in the eye. Will you stop calling me baby face, and things like that? I can't help the way I look. If I were a surgeon, I'd operate on my face and change the plan of it."

32

"Well, I'll quit," said she.

"Go on and tell me about yourself," he urged. "What about you and the boys? Anybody getting serious about you, Brick?"

"I get along with the boys, all right," said she. "It's the females that I can't stand. Great Scott, King, how I hate women! The sneaking, smirking, silly rattle-heads, the vain, self-satisfied four-flushers! There isn't one good fellow in ten million of 'em."

"No," said he. "You're the one, though. But why don't you pick out one of the rich young ranchers, around here, and lead him into holy matrimony?"

"Matrimony makes me sick," she told him. "Besides, I'm not soft enough to please any of the young fellows around here."

"They're a pretty husky lot," said the King Bird. "Why should they want girly-girls?"

"The harder the man, the harder he falls for the soft ones," said the girl. "You take a big six-foot lumberjack, and what he wants is something in pink chiffon with a pair of melting eyes, and a still look, like a sick dog, or a dead fish."

"Is that so?" said the King Bird. He yawned.

"That's so," she declared. "The things that I see make me sick. But I get along with the boys, all right. They're friendly, and that's the way I prefer to have 'em. Would one of 'em try to hold my hand? Not while he's sober. Not while he's in his right mind. You know something, King?"

She received no answer, and looking down, she saw that he was asleep.

"Poor kid!" said she, and knocked out of the air a leaf that was dropping toward him.

She turned to give one murderous glance toward the distant house of Ramirez. Then she resumed her scanning of the long, pale trail. For a long time, she sat in that manner beside the sleeper, until out of the distance the small figure of a horseman began to bob up on the rising ground and down in the hollows like a boat on a choppy sea.

CHAPTER VI

THE MESSENGER

SHE STARED for only a moment at that form. The distance was still so great that it took expert judgment to make sure that the rider was coming as fast as his horse could peg along.

She shook the sleeper by the shoulder.

"Wake up, King!" said she.

He was like a rag, soggy with slumber. It could not be knocked out of him.

"No wonder Inez gets tired of you," she said. "The sleeping sickness is wide awake, compared to you, you tramp."

He sat up, suddenly and fully awake.

"What's that?" he asked her.

"There comes somebody out of the great north," said the girl. "He rides as though his coat were on fire. He might be the very messenger that you're looking for, partner."

He jumped to his feet, and then nodded his head.

"I'll have to talk to him," he said. "He's got an election report, or something like that. Wait till I get Molly."

He sent a whistle down the wind, and Molly was beside him instantly.

"I'm going to climb this tree and watch," said she. "If you do any gun work in this case, I'll never speak to you again."

"What am I to do?" said the young man. "Stop him with a smile?"

"I don't care what you do, so long as it's done," answered the girl.

She ran up the tree like a squirrel.

"All right," said the young man, as he leaped into the

34

saddle. "I'll hypnotize him like a snake charmer. So long, Brick."

"So long, King, said she. "He looks biggish. I hope he doesn't hurt you!"

He paused long enough to send her one savage glance of reproach. Then, with an imperceptible gesture, he loosed the black mare down the hollow. It was as though she had obeyed his wish, not his action. And as a swallow dips off the peak of the barn, swoops through the middle air, and lands with hardly more than one wing stroke on the eaves of the house, so the King Bird and the black mare flashed down the hollow and disappeared in a thicket of low-growing saplings.

Helena Blair, alias Brick, stood like a circus performer on a branch of the tree and clearly saw the approaching horseman rise over the last hill and come on the gallop down the slope beside the grove.

He reached the bottom; his horse began the upgrade at a sharp trot when the black mare and her rider flashed from the covert beside the other.

Brick could see, clearly, the glint of the first man's revolver, as he drew it and whirled in the saddle. But no shot was fired. The King Bird had closed on the other, and in a moment the man from the north was prone on the ground.

Was it a knife thrust that had spilled him, inert, from the saddle?

No; he rose now, staggering, and faced the King Bird, in whose hand the revolver was now drooping. The riderless horse ran on a little distance, and then dropped its head to graze.

Yonder in the hollow, the King Bird was saying: "How are things, old-timer?"

"My head's bigger than the rest of me," said the dismounted man, still uneasy on his feet. "What did you hit me with? Butt of a gun?"

"No," said the King Bird. "Nothing but a fist that I found handy. It happened to press the button, and that's what put the lights out. What's your name?"

"Pete Logan."

"You know me?"

"Never saw you before."

"Where you from, Logan?"

"From the Gutterson ranch. Old Man Gutterson sent me in hell-bent to Valencia, to do an errand for him. If it's money you want out of me, you won't get much."

"You haven't been seeing Marshal Jim Hampton lately, have you?" asked the King Bird.

"The marshal? No. Why?"

"You weren't riding a big roan with a pink nose with the rest of Hampton's men, were you?" said the King Bird pleasantly.

Pete Logan had one of those red complexions which never tan properly, merely peeling in spots, while others remain white. Now all of the red spots disappeared and left him a uniform gray.

"Me? With Hampton's men? Where?" he asked.

"You haven't heard that Hampton was out with a whole gang?" asked the King Bird, more gently than before.

Pete Logan hesitated.

"Why, I guess I *have* heard that," he admitted.

"But you weren't with 'em, you big liar?" asked the King Bird.

Logan fairly groaned.

"King," he said, "I know you, and I was up there with Hampton. I guess you seen me."

"I saw you up in the front rank, the other day," said the King Bird, "and you were pumping lead at the tail of my horse as fast as you could pull the trigger. But that's all right. Let it go. You didn't hit me then, and I don't want to hit you now—with lead. I'm only asking some questions."

"That's fair enough," said Logan. He went on to explain: "I'll tell you, King, I was up there with the rest of 'em, after you, just because——"

"I know," said the King Bird. "I don't blame you. I don't blame anybody who starts out on my trail. I've been going long enough and far enough to make people want to put on the brakes for me. But just tell me what brings you this far south."

36

"The fact is," said Logan, "that I was due to meet young Gutterson in Valencia to-day, and——"

"Wait a minute," said the King Bird. "Come back to the start again, and try all over. What brings you this far south?"

Logan threw up his hands in a gesture of surrender. The gun jumped in the hand of the King Bird in response.

"Don't do that!" he exclaimed. "Talk without your hands, if you can. Makes this gun of yours nervous, when you use two hands at once."

Logan grinned. "All right," he said. "I can't lie to you, King. And you've got me cold. Here's the deal: The marshal wanted to rush word down to Valencia. Something got into him the morning after you paid us that call in the old fort. So he gave me a letter, and told me to saddle up. It was about noon. I hit the trail, and came this far before my horse stumbled and threw me on my head. That's all."

"Mind letting me have that letter?"

Logan groaned again.

"I hate doing that," he said.

"I hate to ask you," said the King Bird. "But you see how it is?"

"I know," said the other. "I understand how it is, all right." Then he held out an envelope.

"It goes to you—rather, it goes to your gun," said he.

"It's *your* gun, after all," said the King Bird. He smiled a little as he said it. Then he added: "I might be around this neck of the woods for a while. I wonder if I could make a bargain with you?"

"It looks as though you could—almost any kind of a bargain," answered Pete Logan.

"I'd like it a lot if you climbed your horse and rode north, instead of south."

"Well?" said Logan, frowning with earnest attention.

"Because if I should happen to run into you in Valencia, or thereabouts, it would be a shock to me," said the King Bird.

"Might it start your gun hand moving?" asked the other.

"It might. I don't know," said the King Bird. "Here's your gun, partner."

He tossed it into the air, and while it was still arching high, a weapon of his own appeared in his hand, and he knocked the spinning Colt far away with a bullet.

"Sorry to spoil your gun, Pete," said he. "But there's your alibi. You wouldn't want to show the boys a small red spot on the side of your chin and say that that's how you happened to lose the letter. Now you can tell the marshal that you met me, and pulled your gun, but I had the drop, and shot the gun out of your hand—with a slug that was meant for your heart, eh?"

Pete Logan picked up the revolver.

"All right, King," he said. "This is dog-gone white of you. Makes me sorry that I ever was on the other side of the fence. Maybe the next time we meet up, you'll find *me* playing the white man, too!"

"Thanks a lot," answered the King Bird. "So long, Pete!"

He held out his hand, which Logan took with a hard grip, and then the two parted, the King Bird returning slowly toward the trees where the girl was perched, and Logan catching his horse, which he rode briskly away toward the north.

The King Bird had the envelope open when he reached Brick and found her standing under the deformed tree.

"What did you do to that fellow?" she demanded.

"Just managed to tap the button," he told her.

"Suppose you'd missed, how far would his bullets have knocked you, King?"

"Farther than tongue can tell," he answered carelessly.

"Great Scott, King!" she exclaimed. "You take a lot of chances with yourself—but of course there's not much of you. That's why you're so careless, I suppose?"

He looked grimly at her, then handed across the envelope.

"Look at this!" said he.

She read aloud:

"MY DEAR RAMIREZ: This is to let you know that the King Bird understands how the trap was baited for him down there in Valencia. I suppose that Inez is safe from him. He's chivalrous enough. But you're still young enough to serve as a target for his guns. And you have a son, also. I'm sorry that I missed the King Bird. Don't disregard this warning!

"Yours faithfully,

"JAMES HAMPTON."

She looked up at the King Bird.

"It's true then," she said, "and Hampton meant what he told you. Inez *did* double-cross you?"

"It looks that way."

"Does it make you sick, old boy?" said the girl. "Climb down from the saddle and lean on me, then."

He took back the note, folded it, replaced it in the envelope.

"It makes me a little sick," said he. "But I'm getting ideas all the time. If I put this in a fresh envelope, I may be able to use it again. Brick, I could drink blood!" he broke out savagely.

"But you won't," said the girl. "It's the first time in the world that you've been made to look foolish, but maybe it won't be the last. Watch your step, King. And if I were you, I'd keep clear of the Ramirez house."

"Thanks," said he bitterly. "But I can't help going. The sneaking murderers! I want to see how they'll face me—the mother, and old Ramirez, and the rest of 'em. They were so fond of me. I was just one of the sons of the house, you understand?"

She watched his face with a maternal air, both sympathizing with him and half smiling at the same time, as though his troubles were near her heart, and at the same time as though she knew they were childish things.

"I'll give you the key to the whole mystery, if you want it," said she.

"Go on then," he said. "You always have half a deck palmed and up your sleeve."

"The answer is a tall gentleman by the name of Esteban Something-or-other-and-so-forth Cuyas. Real Castilian what-not, is Don Esteban. And what you won't believe about a Spaniard, he has loads of money. And what's more to the point than all the rest, he's staying up there in Ramirez's house."

The young man gritted his teeth.

"Was he there the evening that Inez sent me that fake news about her brother Ramon?" he demanded.

"King, I'm sorry to say that he was," said the girl. "If you'd come to see *me* as soon as you dropped into town, I could have told you a lot of little bits of news. Wait a minute! Don't go and throw yourself over a cliff! Hold on, King! Oh, well, so long, then!"

For he had flashed away from her, and the black mare carried him swiftly through the hollow and over the rise, and out of sight.

CHAPTER VII

THE PARENTS OF INEZ

The entire town of Valencia had followed the chase of the King Bird with the most consummate interest. The news that last came of the hunt was brought, in the evening of this day, by one who had ridden from the nearest railroad town, that enjoyed the advantages that go with a telegraph office.

His message he carried in person up the hill to the house of Ramirez, and was admitted to see that dignified gentleman.

"Ramirez," he said, "I gotta give you some bad news. They got the King Bird cornered. They got him jammed right agin' a wall, and there's thirty men and horses and guns, all workin' to put him down and under. I guess it'll be hard on Inez. We all know she was pretty fond of him.

You can break the word to the womenfolks as easy as you please."

The dignity of Ramirez vanished. He forgot hospitality and did not so much as offer the messenger a drink, but hurried to find his wife. She was a thin little woman, whose roses had turned sallow in her cheeks. Time had withered her sadly, and, as usual, the withering was worst about the eyes.

She was sewing, when her big husband came striding into the room where she sat, using the last of the evening light.

"Maria," said he, "the last word has come!"

She asked calmly: "Is he dead?"

"Not dead, but almost."

"Wounded?" she snapped.

"No, not wounded, but cornered, driven to the wall—desperate—surrounded by thirty armed men. Heaven forgive me for my share in the horrible business!"

"Not dead, not wounded," said his wife. "Don't talk like a fool, Pedro. If he's neither dead nor wounded, he's liable to light in the midst of us any time."

"Maria, your heart is stone," said he.

He began to stride up and down the room.

"When I think of the hours he has spent in the house, and his charm, and his cheerfulness, and that generous young hand of his that has given us all many a gift, Maria——"

She raised her bony hand, and it silenced him like the motion of an ivory scepter.

"A man cannot be of two minds at the same time unless he's a weakling. Are you a weakling, Pedro?"

"I hope not," he muttered. "But the poor boy——"

"Either you wish the prosperity and happiness of your daughter, or you do not!" she snapped.

"I wish everything for her," said Don Pedro. "But the poor lad who will——"

"Do you prefer him to Don Esteban?"

"Do I prefer the moon to the sun?" he asked.

"Well, then, could Inez marry Don Esteban, with the King Bird still alive, all beak and spur? Wouldn't he murder

Señor Cuyas instantly? Isn't the young brute made for murder, and for nothing else?"

Her husband was silent, for the harsh impact of these ideas addled his wits not a little. He looked vaguely about the big, empty room. He looked out the window to where the sunset fingered the river with gold, and the hills with purple.

"I suppose that you're right," he said. "I suppose that we've done the only thing. But the treachery of it makes my heart ache!"

"Don Esteban is going to propose for the hand of Inez to-night, if his purpose holds," she said.

"Eh?" grunted the father of the family.

"Of course he has already spoken to you. He's too honorable a gentleman not to have done that. He left this room five minutes ago, and told me that he would speak out before you and me at the table to-night, to bring the thing to a final understanding."

"It's come to the end, then?" he asked, flushed with pleasure.

"It has!" she announced triumphantly. "Due to my constant use of brains and patience. Pressure, pressure, pressure has done the thing. It's hard for Don Esteban to make up his mind. Between you and me, I've assisted him a little in the process."

She put down her sewing, for in the failing light she had pricked her finger.

She gave no sign of that, however, for her nerves were of iron, or of even harder stuff.

"The family of Ramirez is about to be reëstablished in the eyes of the world," she announced. "And I think that I may fairly say that the accomplishment is due to me. I've had to convince you, and check Inez. It was not till I talked to the little fool seriously this afternoon that she finally made up her mind that she would even accept the proposals of Don Esteban! She has too much of your nature in her; too little of mine. But I'll launch her in the proper waters in spite of herself!" Her teeth clicked as she ended.

42

And she instantly added: "She, too, has been pitying the gunman, the man-killer, the murderer who has actually made free with our house!"

Her husband was stung to answer: "I've seen the time, and many a time, too, Maria, when you were as kind to him as though he were your foster son."

"I'm not fool enough to throw away anything that is useful," said she. "There was a time when he served a certain purpose. The 'loans' that he made you were all that kept us going through the past year, I suppose. Was I to throw that away?"

"He'll rise into my dreams," said the other solemnly. "He'll rise and reproach me."

"I never heard such stuff and nonsense in my life," said Doña Maria.

She went on in a higher key: "I've endured this life in this naked house all these years. I've seen poverty gathering around us. I've fought against it, and then I've patiently submitted. I've bided my time, hoping against hope. At last Don Esteban crossed my path. I knew that whatever his name was in the eyes of the world, to me he was Opportunity! And I've made the best use of him.

"To-night, Pedro, we make that opportunity ours! For once he has formally made his offer, and it has been accepted by the entire family, I think that we can find ways to keep him from dodging the contract—little ways—among all of us—little ways that will keep him to it."

Her laughter was low and soft, but it sounded like that of a man, her heart had swelled so savagely in her breast!

"Where is Inez?" asked the father. "I have to tell her about the poor lad who——"

"Not one word to her about him!" snapped his wife. "Her mind is enough troubled and at sea. She actually had the effrontery to weep in my presence this afternoon. She actually hinted that I have *dragged* her into this affair with Don Esteban! Pedro, say nothing, do nothing, but leave everything to me. *I* shall make all right in the end!"

CHAPTER VIII

THE KING BIRD'S TOAST

THE DINING ROOM was by far the best room in the house, and therefore Doña Maria was more at ease when her guest was in it. It had a great spaciousness that made it doubly pleasant in cool weather; it was made cheerful by the inset of single tiles, or cheerful little patterns of them along the walls and in the side panels of the deep-set windows. Overhead were massive wooden beams, their under surfaces painted in fading colors, and the table and chairs were massively made and of a good old dark wood. As for the brick floor, she kept a sheen of wax on it, during the stay of Don Esteban, and the back of every servant in the house ached on that account.

On this night of nights, everything had gone off well. The finest dish the kitchen could offer had been placed before Don Esteban—chickens boiled in butter—and the señora was congratulating herself. For now, as dinner came to a close, she could see the glance of Cuyas drift toward the girl of the house, and then toward the rest of the family more briefly, and it was plain that the slow mind of Don Esteban was gathering toward speech. That speech, it was plain, would be the proposal for the hand of Inez before them all; and now as dinner drew to a close with nuts and raisins and red wine on the table, the moment could not be very long postponed.

She was content, but even now, at the moment of victory, her vigilance did not relax. Furthermore, she was annoyed, because she saw that the glance of her daughter continually dwelt on the narrow and receding forehead of Esteban Cuyas.

As a matter of fact, Don Esteban was a distinguished rather than a handsome man. He had wide and heavy shoulders, a small head, and a disproportionately long face. His nose was long, his mouth was not wide, but the lower lip was very full, and since his eyes were small, and not very widely open, he had as a rule a half-gloomy and half-disdainful look. His lips were always bright, as though they had just been moistened.

However, he was an extremely affable, manly, and gentle fellow; his manners were a trifle stiff, but he was generous, straightforward, and kind. The slowness of his mind made him speak little, but his words were well-chosen, and never stupid.

To-night there was an unwonted vigor about him, and a flash in his eyes, for opposite him at the table sat Inez Ramirez looking more lovely than even she had ever been before.

If the face of Don Esteban was not all that a woman could wish, his birth and his fortune were almost kingly. Inez was pleased with the future, in most ways. Besides, she felt that she was saving and rehabilitating her fallen family.

She had thrown herself with all her heart into her rôle, and was endeavoring to fascinate Don Esteban a little more by pretending that it was hard for her either to avoid or meet his glance. Her eyes were always touching on his, and then fleeing off to the side. She smiled, as though embarrassed, and spoke seldom. She hoped that this silence, contrasted with her usual gayety, would have its effect, and in fact, Cuyas was enchanted. Now he could swear that she took him seriously; that he had touched her heart with something more than name and money!

The father of the family and his handsome son, Ramon, took small part in the picture, but it was their talk that kept things going, as it were, and covered over the pauses that were always occurring between the main actors.

And now the great moment came.

Doña Maria knew it the instant that Don Esteban leaned

a little forward in his chair, looking earnestly down at the table, and then suddenly threw up his head.

He said: "May I speak to you all for a moment, seriously?"

A charmed silence instantly spread around the table. And it was at this very moment that a slight noise caught their attention, and into one of the deep casements that opened upon the patio of the house, stepped the slender form of the King Bird.

He stood there for a moment and looked over their astonished faces with a happy laugh, and waved his hand to them.

Doña Maria said to her savage heart: "He has been waiting; he knows everything; he wants to ruin everything; that's how he happened to enter so pat!"

She sat still as a stone, staring, but her lips moved.

She said softly: "José, that is the worst enemy of our house. He must die!"

The gray-haired, scar-faced servant, whose favorite place was behind her chair, turned without a word and left the room.

Ramirez himself had started up, as he saw the newcomer, and cried out in a stifled voice. His son actually ran a few steps toward the King Bird, holding out a hand, as though in protest; and Inez, twisting in her chair, looked fixedly over her bare shoulder, and then rose.

Don Esteban stood up at the same moment. He made a lofty and detached figure.

The King Bird was crying out: "Back once more! Back home! Safely back home! The house never looked to me as it does now!"

He kissed the pale face of Inez; with his arm still around her, he grasped the limp hand of Don Ramon. By both hands he caught Ramirez himself. He kissed the bony, cold hand of Señora Ramirez.

A red blur was before her eyes. She could barely distinguish forms, and not faces at all. Speech was impossible to her. The world, it seemed, was crashing about her.

There was only José, and the order she had murmured to him. If only he would come swiftly, with some of those fierce old servants, fighting men, men blindly devoted to the Ramirez house!

And now the King Bird stood before Don Esteban, bowing.

Ramirez managed to gasp: "Señor Cuyas—the King Bird— so he is called——"

The King Bird took the hand of the big Spaniard, who looked a little dazed, and stared at Inez for an explanation.

"I thought," cried Don Ramon, "that they'd cornered you, King. I thought that you were lost. I thought——"

"Tut, tut, never mind your thinking," said the young man. "They gave me a close chase, but they couldn't match me. They couldn't catch me and the black mare. Do you know what I used instead of spurs on Molly?"

He laughed, as though rejoicing in the memory, and then he said, "Inez!"

She started violently.

She was whiter than ever, and that made her eyes look larger. No life was in them. She kept hold on the back of a chair to steady herself, and the knuckles of her hand stood out in thin, small ridges from the force of her grasp.

"Inez!" went on the King Bird. "That was what I called to the mare, when they were pressing me hard. Inez! And the little black beauty understood, and stretched her stride a little longer, and ran as true as a string, and as straight. 'Inez!'—that was the spur that urged her on. Why, they never could have caught me."

He still laughed.

"Sit down, every one," he commanded. "Sit down, Señor Cuyas. Sit down, Inez. You never looked so beautiful to me. Who in the world except me knows what happiness is? But *I* know!"

Still he laughed!

"My friends, who drinks with me? I am the dead returned to life. I have walked through the fire. And still I am here among you! Drink! Every glass full. And let's look at each other through the good red wine!"

He was filling the glasses as he spoke, and lifting his own.

"Inez!" he called. "Are you dreaming?"

47

Her hand went out automatically and clasped the slender stem of the glass, and raised it.

"Señor Ramirez! Señora! Ramon! Señor Cuyas! To the health, the wealth, the God-given, glorious happiness of all true men, all faithful and beautiful women, all honest souls and brave hearts over the entire world, in every nation, every blood and color! Drink, my friends!"

They looked at one another.

Only Señor Cuyas, making a slight movement, as though to include the others in the respects that he was drinking, raised the glass at once to his lips, which were still crimson, and looked as though they had been freshly painted on a face of stone.

The others, staring rather wildly, finally got their glasses to their mouths, and tasted, or seemed to taste, a few drops. Only Doña Maria left the glass untouched before her.

The King Bird drained his, and hurled the glass into the fireplace, where it shattered on the stones with a loud crash.

Don Esteban found his voice.

"Señor," he said, "still I don't quite understand. You are an old friend of the family, a cousin, a blood relation?"

"I'm a friend, but not an old one," said the King Bird. "But we've been tied closely together—oh, very closely, and we're to be tied still closer. Inez, isn't it right to let Señor Cuyas know that, one day, you and I are to be married?"

Still he was laughing, and the flash of his eyes could have passed well enough for merriment.

Don Esteban managed to get a good grip on the back of his chair. His face grew stonier still. But his eyes, also, were beginning to flash. With a singular meaning, his glance found the eyes of Doña Maria, and then turned with a terrible grimness back toward Inez.

"Young man," said Doña Maria, "how do you dare to talk about the companionship of a boy and girl as if—as though a serious thought ever entered——"

He interrupted her in the gayest of voices.

"Of course I must first have a little money laid aside," said the King Bird, "and then I must make my peace with the law. Both of those things are not hard to do. I've known

48

that in your heart, Doña Maria, you approved, ever since you stood with us at that window, there, and held our hands together, and asked Heaven to bless the future for us. Do you remember that?"

Doña Maria glanced to the side toward the darkness of the open doorway, praying for the sudden coming of those armed men who must be her salvation.

They were not there—neither was there any possible shadowing of them in the open windows, against the stars.

To think of the scores of men who would have been glad to rush into this room, and try to drive bullets into the body of this hunted outlaw—and yet there was not one present. There was only her husband, and her son, both standing as though entranced!

Terrible rage worked in her frenzied heart.

Don Esteban, in a dull and heavy voice, was saying: "It seems to me that I've been misinformed."

He looked straight at the girl, but she, slowly turning her head, regarded the King Bird, and the pallor began to leave her face, and an incredibly faint smile touched the corners of her mouth.

The King Bird was very near her. He alone could hear her whisper:

"I see the devil is in you again!"

"You've not been misinformed," said Ramirez, with streams of perspiration running down his face. "This wretched business—I have to say——"

"Ah, Ramirez," said the young man. "There's another thing. I have a letter for you. It's a letter that will interest everybody. It may even interest you, Señor Cuyas. It was written by the Federal marshal who was hunting me—James Hampton, a man catcher, and other things. He writes in this manner to Ramirez, my dear old friend, who has made me like a son in his house. Here, Ramirez. Read it aloud!"

Doña Maria looked again toward the windows, and now in the midst of her despair, came a savage gleam of hope, for she could see the heads and shoulders of men who were gathering outside of one of the embrasures.

49

In the meantime, into the hand of Ramirez was thrust a paper.

"Read it, Ramirez. Let every one hear, my old friend!" cried the King Bird cheerfully.

But under his breath he had whispered:

"Or I'll cut out your heart, you treacherous cur! I have the knife in my hand!"

The voice and the whisper were both in the ears of Ramirez. In a trance he read loudly, with a heavy, mechanical voice:

"MY DEAR RAMIREZ: This is to let you know that the King Bird understands how the trap was baited for him down there in Valencia. I suppose that Inez is safe from him. He's chivalrous enough. But you're still young enough to serve as a target for his guns. And you have a son, also. I'm sorry that I missed the King Bird. Don't disregard this warning!

"Yours faithfully,

"JAMES HAMPTON."

CHAPTER IX

INEZ'S EXPLANATION

THE MIND of Don Esteban worked very slowly indeed, but one of the words in this letter struck so deeply into his consciousness that he exclaimed: "Trapped? Do you mean that he was—betrayed by you, Señor Ramirez?"

"No, no, no!" screamed Doña Maria.

She was out of her chair, with her two bony fists brandished above her head.

"It's all a lie—all treason. Oh, the scoundrels! Attempting to ruin the Ramirez—the honorable Ramirez! Scoundrels, villains, wretches!"

Don Ramon actually drew a gun, though he did not seem to know what to do with it, and his sister, reaching forward, easily tore it from his nerveless fingers.

Señor Ramirez himself was exclaiming in a heavy voice of doom: "Ah, that ever this should have happened to us!"

Just then, with the screeching of Doña Maria to give them courage and unity, five armed men rushed in through the very same casement by which the King Bird had entered.

This was the sort of thing that Don Esteban understood perfectly. There was no fine hidden point here, over which he needed to deliberate, but instantly he threw himself in front of the King Bird.

By so doing, he certainly saved the life of that grim-faced José who was about to take a bullet between the eyes, from one of the two guns that glimmered in the hands of the King Bird. In fact, Don Esteban almost got the same bullet through his own body, but the young man was in time to lower the raised hammer which his thumb had flicked back— gently he lowered the sharp point, so that it rested harmlessly upon the cap.

José, seeing the tall Spaniard before him, with arms outflung to the sides—as though such a gesture could stop bullets!—stopped short, bewildered, and his companions were checked with him.

Doña Maria was screaming out something about destroying the villain, but Don Esteban raised a voice of harsh thunder.

"What is it? Treachery? Murder? Back to the door behind you, my friend! Ramon—Señor Ramirez—are you traitors?"

A very odd thing happened then, for Inez stepped to Don Esteban, and gave him the gun she had secured from her brother.

"Take that," she said. "You may have to use it."

She turned on the five confused servants, who were looking vaguely at the people standing there about them, totally bewildered by these happenings.

51

"Leave the room—put up your guns," she commanded. "It is all a joke. You fools, you've gone too far."

"That's it," exclaimed Ramirez, half dead with the conflict of this emotions. "Only a joke, Don Esteban—a joke!"

But Cuyas and the King Bird had reached the farther door of the room, which opened upon the grove of trees in the front of the house, and as they stepped through it, Inez hurried suddenly after them.

Doña Maria was no longer crying out. Great as her ecstasy of rage had been, she controlled herself suddenly. She saw that perhaps the game was not entirely lost, though the cards were certainly not such as she could play. So she cried out in a voice that was not loud, but charged with despair and hope and grief and anger:

"Inez!"

Her daughter paid her no heed. She had gone straight on with the two men, and as they came out under the trees, she was the first to speak, saying:

"I'm sure that the devil has stopped working in the house for a minute or two, King. You don't need to be afraid to stop here for thirty seconds while I say something to you."

He answered crisply: "Don't waste time on me, Inez. Don Esteban, here, is the one for you to concentrate on!"

She replied surprisingly: "Yes, he has enough money and enough name to be worth a lot of concentration. But I've been working so hard on him all these days that I need a rest. Esteban, forgive me!"

Señor Cuyas answered, in his deep, grave voice: "I forgive you perfectly and forever, Inez. I begin to see many things. Doors are opening before me. To me, the truth is always a welcome guest, even if I have to sit up till midnight for it!"

"Inez," said the King Bird, "I didn't know that you had this in you—this straight way of going about things. I thought that you were all blossom; and then, to-day, I suspected that you were all thorn—with poison on it; and now I see that you're sort of an honest girl, along with it."

"You don't know me, because I don't know myself," said she. "I wanted to tell you one thing—that when I sent you up the road, supposedly to meet Ramon, I knew I was sending you into trouble, but I never dreamed that they would try to murder you. It was to be a matter of lariats, thrown at you suddenly from both sides of the road. You were to be jumped into jail, and out of our way. That was the idea. Treacherous enough, too."

"And in the jail?" said the King Bird.

"I didn't think much farther than that. Your life would be safe. They want you for a good many things, but not for murder. As a matter of fact, I didn't think beyond the point where the door of the jail closed on you."

"But you wanted to get rid of him, Inez, and why?" asked Cuyas sadly, curiously.

"Because I was tired of acting a part for him," said she. "Just as I've been tired of acting the sweet, dumb idiot for you, Esteban. I was playing another part for him, a sweet part, too—always gay, always the little light-foot. Bah! I used to be so sick of that part, King, that I came to hate the very sight of your face."

"Why weren't you yourself?" asked the King Bird quietly. "Ever try that, Inez?"

"Never," she said. "I've always had to be one thing to my father, and another thing to my poor mother, and another to Ramon. I've never been myself. I'll tell you why."

She paused. Neither of the men spoke. Then she framed her face with both hands, and looked up to them in the starlight.

"Because God happened to give me a beautiful face, everybody has always expected something extraordinary from me; and my family did the greatest part of the expecting, of course. D'you think I'm a vain little fool to talk about my beauty? I'll tell you, I've almost hated that face, too, until I didn't want to look at it in the mirror. But I've known— every girl knows—why the men came trooping around me. D'you know what person in the world I've envied with all my heart?"

"Tell me that, Inez," said Cuyas, quickly and eagerly.

"A brown-faced cowgirl, with a snub nose, and her hair pulled into a knot behind her head, and a ragged old sombrero on, and a man's overalls. She's real. She's honest. I

53

wanted to step into those overalls, and forget my family, and take her horse, and just go riding over the rim of the world to find new things. You know who the girl is, King. She's Helena Blair."

"Do you know," said Don Esteban, "that I begin to feel——"

"Don't change your mind about me," she answered hastily "There's a bad streak in my family. It must be in me, too. And if you went on caring about me, I never could go on caring about you, any more than I could for the King Bird!"

"While you're being honest," said the King Bird, his vanity strangely unhurt by this confession, "tell me what it was about me that bored you the most."

"Why," she said, "you seemed to me a bubble, just floating on the surface of life. Your horse, your gun, and your saddle, meant about as much to you as things could mean. You've just been riding—the direction hasn't mattered. Just going has been the trick, for you, not the getting there. I wanted to find a man with a destination in view. That's what I've looked for."

"That's clear enough, and simple enough to understand," said the young man.

"And for me?" asked Cuyas, his voice rather hard and small.

"For you?" said the girl. "As long as I'm talking poison for myself and everybody else, I'll tell you what was wrong, Esteban. You were always stumbling on small things, it seemed to me. You never knew whether to sit in the sun or the shade, so to speak. You couldn't make up your mind about the horse you'd ride. If you spoke, you had to wait so long before finding the first word, that I forgot what I'd asked you before you answered me."

"Clearer and clearer," said Cuyas. "I'm beginning to learn more about myself in these few moments than I've known in a long life."

"Why do you trust my opinion?" asked the girl, rather bitterly. "It's only mine, and therefore it's probably wrong. King, you'd better go now. I can't tell. There may be trouble creeping toward you on the ground, for all I know. Listen!"

She raised her hand, a pale gesture in the starlight, and they heard from the house voices raised angrily.

"Good-bye," said the King Bird.

"Are you shaking hands with me?" she asked.

"If you will," said he.

"Does that mean you're forgiving me?"

"With all my heart," said he. He chuckled a little, and added: "Does that make me seem shallower and lighter than ever?"

"I suppose it does, in a way," said she. "But it makes me thank God there are people like you in the world. What a good fellow you are, King—what a wonderfully kind, gentle, honest, good fellow you are—masquerading like a little boy as a great, bad outlaw!"

She laughed faintly.

"You'll be leaving us, Esteban," she said to the other. "But will you go back with me now?"

"Will it help you if I go back?" he asked.

"Not a bit," she answered. "I'd rather be alone with my housework."

"Then I won't go back," said he. "It would be painful for everyone. My things can be sent down to the hotel in the town. And I want to walk on a little with the King Bird."

"I understand," said the girl. "Good-bye, then, Esteban."

"Good-bye, then," said the big Spaniard.

He raised her hand to his lips.

"Whatever you have been at other times, to-night you are very brave, very strong, and very wise!"

CHAPTER X

BAD NEWS

THE TWO men walked down the hill together toward the town. They came close to the sheen of the lights, and then the King Bird said: "Sorry—I'll have to leave you here."

"Leave me?" said Esteban Cuyas, surprised. "I was about to hope that we could talk a little together."

"Lights are hard on me," said the King Bird, chuckling. "They're hard on my eyes. I don't think that I'd better get any closer to the lights in that town!"

The Spaniard nodded his small head and his long face in the darkness.

"I suppose that I must understand," said he. "You are a man, señor, who must live outside of the law? Is that not so?"

"That's so," said the King Bird.

"And yet," said the other, "I can't imagine why."

"Why, it's this way," said the young man. "Inez was right. I have to keep on changing the scene. It doesn't matter where I am, if I'm not going to stay there very long."

"Your fault is the reverse of mine," said Don Esteban. "My trouble is that I can never decide to move. But why is the law against you?"

"Because I live outside it, that's all."

"Outside it?"

"I don't work for a living," said the young man. "I take what I need, and go on with it."

"You mean—that you—er——" The Spaniard paused.

"I mean that I'm a robber," said the young man. "Is that clear?"

"Perfectly," said Don Esteban gently. "I beg your pardon for pressing the point."

"There's another side to it," said the King Bird. "I take from the fellows who have already helped themselves. I mean to say, that's the game for me."

"You rob the robbers?"

"That's the general idea."

"Then the law officers ought to be your friends."

"Law officers are a queer lot. Robbery is robbery, to them."

"And a Federal marshal on your trail?"

"That was because a friend of mine was caught for a little job of running Chinamen across the frontier. I don't know why Chinamen should be shut out of the country. They're quiet fellows. They work like the devil, and they hurt nobody. They keep in their place, too. But at any rate, there's a law against bringing them in. And a friend of mine kept on doing it.

"This Marshal Jim Hampton is a great man on the border. He caught my friend and slammed him in jail. I managed to get him out, and Hampton chased the pair of us, till we managed to get away. But later on, he caught my friend again, and I had the luck to get him out a second time. There was another chase after that; and a third one wound up the other day that was started by Hampton just on general principles, and an old grudge. You see how I always manage to stay outside the law?"

The Spaniard whistled softly.

"But, señor," said he, "a bullet out of the dark might kill you at any time!"

"Bullets will kill, all right, if they hit the right spots," said the King Bird.

"But what is your end? What is your goal?"

"Inez told you that—just to keep on moving. Somewhere beyond the next town is the town that I'm aiming at."

"And in the end?"

"I don't know. The end will take care of itself."

Don Esteban sighed.

"Señor," he said, "I envy you. You are both brave and happy!"

"Señor," said the King Bird, "you were brave enough to step between me and a flock of fast-flying lead, to-night, and you did it for a stranger. Some day I hope I'll be able to do something in return. As for envying me, you might as well envy a wild duck because it flies north and then flies south."

He whistled. Through the darkness, from a near-by thicket, loomed the form of the black mare, Molly.

"All things are with you as by magic," said Don Esteban. "Perhaps we shall meet again. In the meantime, happiness and fortune to you."

They shook hands.

"Suppose that I wanted one day to ride with you, it doesn't matter where?" asked Don Esteban.

"In that case," answered the King Bird, "go to the house of the Blair family. They live just out of town. They always know where I'm to be found, or they have a pretty good idea. I'll leave word with them that they're to tell you anything they know. And no matter what trail I'm riding, high or low, I'd be glad to have you with me."

They parted there, where the thin spears of light from the town lamps came splintering through the foliage of the trees. Don Esteban went on down the hill to Valencia. The King Bird took Molly across country to the little ranch house of John Blair.

He put the mare up in the barn, found the oat bin in the darkness, with the measuring can lying on top of the sweet-smelling grain, and poured two good measures into the feed box of Molly's stall. Then he went into the house through the kitchen door.

Mrs. Blair, as usual, was hovering between the stove and the sink, when he stepped into the room. She was a tired little woman with a smile that made her young, and whose vanishing left her older and more tired than ever.

She was carrying a pot of boiled potatoes to the sink, and she cried out a greeting to him, and smiled over her shoulder as she poured the water into the sink.

"Helena told us that she'd seen you!" she said. "Will you stay for a bite? She'll be back in a minute or two. She just went to town for some bacon. We're clean out. I don't know how that happened, either. Seems to me only the other day that there was half a side, pretty nearly."

To dry the potatoes, she began to toss them a little into the air. Great round puffs of steam went up from them, like smoke signals from a blanketed fire, and those balls of white mist flattened against the ceiling, and left a dark, glistening spot there.

"John's in the front room," she said. "Go in and talk to him, King. He's always glad to see you. You do him a lot of good!"

He went into the living-dining room, and found that John Blair was studying his newspaper, with his wooden leg, as usual, stretched out on another chair, to rest his hip muscles.

He exclaimed at the sight of the young man, and started to get up, the newspaper falling one way, and his tobacco pouch another. The removing of the wooden leg from the chair took time, also, but now he was standing in front of the King Bird, smiling, and shaking hands. He was a good-sized man and once had stood inches taller than at present, but labor had bowed his shoulders and bent his back. He had had prosperity enough, in the old days, when he owned a ranch of thousands of acres, but bad times came, he lost one leg through wounds received in a murderous gun fight, and ever since that time, the course of the family fortunes had been down-hill.

But he kept his courage, and his smile; and he, at least, had never allowed the King Bird to make loans, big or small, to help him in times of need.

He gripped the hand of the young man and held it for a long moment.

"You're all right, King?" said he. "I'm glad of that. Helena told me. But it seemed to me that you must be scratched up a bit by all the bullets that have been flying around you. Sort of sunburned by all the powder that they've shot off at you, son. Sit down here, and I'll set on another

59

place. Helena'll be back in a moment. She went down to town to get some bacon, or something like that."

He started for the kitchen, but the young man headed him off.

"I know where the dishes are," said he. "Go back and read your paper, and read it aloud. I haven't had any news of the world for half a month."

He went into the kitchen, to find Mrs. Blair smiling at him, as she freshened the fire in the stove.

"This'll make a party for my dear girl," said she. "Helena's never so happy as when she has you around to annoy, King."

"She's a pest," said the King Bird. "She's faster with her talk than a wasp on the wing."

He carried back plate, cup, saucer, knife, fork, and spoon from the kitchen china closet, and arranged them for a place at the table.

"Here's news, and mighty bad news," said Blair. "You know Kinney, the millionaire?"

There was a sudden crash on the floor. The plate had fallen and splintered to a thousand pieces.

"Hey!" exclaimed Blair. "What's the matter?"

The young man was on his knees, sweeping up the scattered fragments.

"Plate slipped out of my fingers," he said briefly. "Sorry."

"That's a funny thing," said Blair.

He took off his glasses and squinted his long-distance eyes at the wreckage, and the rapid fingers of the young man that were gathering it up.

"That's the first time I ever saw or ever heard of you making a mistake with your hands, King," said he.

"Just a slip," said the young man. "I'm sorry. But go ahead!"

"With what?"

"With the Kinney business!" exclaimed the young man impatiently. "What's happened?"

"The Kinney business?" said the old rancher. "Oh, that's bad stuff, bad stuff. The poor devil!"

The King Bird cleared his throat.

"Is he dead?" he asked.

"Kinney?"

"Yes, yes," exclaimed the young man eagerly. "Is he dead?"

"No," said the other. "Not dead. Not as bad as that. But I guess some ways he wishes that he *were* dead."

The young man stood up with a start. He had the splinters of porcelain in his hands.

"What *did* happen?" he exclaimed.

"Funny thing," said the other, shaking his head. "There's a man with two sons—and now he's not got a sign of either of 'em under his roof. That's what I call bad luck. That's what I call *real* bad luck."

"*What's* happened?" exclaimed the young man.

"You know about the first one?" asked Blair, beginning to load his pipe.

The King Bird, with an impatient muttering, turned on his heel and went into the kitchen, where he crashed the débris of the plate into the scrap can.

"Sorry!" he said to Mrs. Blair.

"That's all right," she answered. "We've got some plates left, anyway. And that'll be good for the chickens. You know chickens can hardly get enough gritty stuff for their crops. It helps them to digest."

He took another plate and carried it back into the dining room.

"What's the matter, King?" asked Blair. "Are you cross, or something?"

"Cross? Of course not! I was trying to get at what had happened to the Kinney outfit."

"Well, to start at the beginning, son," said Blair.

The young man frowned, then shrugged his shoulders and sat down, making a cigarette with a twist of those marvelously dexterous fingers.

"This fellow Kinney, that has about all the cattle in the world, this James Kinney, with a couple of gold mines here, and forests there, and a river or two thrown in for luck—this James Kinney had a son by his own front name. But after his first wife died, he married again, and the saying is that the boy never could stand the thought of living in the

61

house with a stepmother, and four years ago, he slipped out, and left a letter and no more, behind him. And in that letter he swore that he'd never set foot in his father's house again, and that he'd never claim the name as long as he lived.

"Kinney raised Ned all over the range; and there's still a big outstanding reward. But that boy disappeared. Bullet tagged him in some saloon, maybe. Anyway, there's the end of son No. 1. And now comes the exit of son No. 2."

"Exit? Dead?" asked the young man.

"Kidnaped," said Blair.

"Kidnaped? The poor little cross-eyed devil!" exclaimed the King Bird.

"Hold on," said Blair, amazed. "How d'you know that the lad's cross-eyed?"

"I don't," said the King Bird hastily. "That was just a manner of speaking about a youngster that's out of luck."

"Was it?" said Blair. He shook his head. "Sort of a funny coincidence, though," said he. "Because as a matter of fact, that boy Robert Kinney *is* cross-eyed a little bit. He's described here. Half a column to describe him in every detail, right down to the eyelashes!"

"How did it happen?" asked the King Bird, sitting forward on the edge of his chair.

"Nobody knows exactly. But two or three days ago, he went out with his pony and his .22 rifle, to shoot squirrels, or something like that. And he didn't come home. They thought that he might have had a shooting accident, and they combed the range for a whole day or so. But there was no trace of him. And then somebody happened to pick up the trail in the Ginger Pass. Miles and miles away from where he should have been. The trail left by the mustang pony's shoes.

"They followed that trail up, and got to the dead mustang, where it had been shot through the head and tumbled down a ravine. That was all. They couldn't find a sign of the boy, and when the searchers got back, there was a demand for a cool hundred thousand at the Kinney house. The boy'd been kidnaped!"

The King Bird leaped to his feet.

"They ought to hang kidnapers!" he exclaimed. "No, they ought to hang 'em in chains over a slow fire, and roast 'em to death!"

Blair stared.

"They ought to, and that's a fact. But you surprise me a good deal, King."

"Why?"

"Didn't know that you were that much interested in kids."

"I'm not. I don't give a rap. Only—it's the idea of the thing. A little youngster like that."

"And here the kidnapers say, in their letter, that if they don't get the money, the boy'll never be seen again! Think of that mother, with an only child gone—think of poor Kinney, with a second son lost! That's what I always say—once bad luck finds you, it never forgets the way."

"Will Kinney pay the ransom?" asked the young man suddenly.

"No, sir, he won't. And that's a funny thing, too. You'd take it that a man with millions, mind you, wouldn't mind so much paying a hundred thousand. Suppose anything had happened to Helena, in the days when I had a little property —I would have given up the whole thing, aye, and mortgaged my soul, too."

"But Kinney won't." The young man sneered. "He thinks too much of the law, doesn't he?"

"How'd you guess that?" asked Blair, surprised again.

The young man snapped his fingers.

"I just guessed," said he. "I've heard something about that fellow Kinney. Law! The devil with the law, I say!"

"And that's what the law says right back to you," answered Blair, smiling. "But I'm sorry for Kinney. I'm real sorry for him."

He consulted the paper again. Then he went on:

"Kinney says that he'll never encourage that sort of a crime by paying money to the criminals. He'll let the law take its course. He won't pay a penny down."

"That sounds just like him," said the young man, talking through his teeth.

"You ever talk to him?" asked Blair, surprised again.

"I know people who have," snapped the King Bird.

"Why son," said the rancher, "I never saw you so upset before about anything."

"Millions! Millions!" exclaimed the King Bird. "But he won't pay a fraction of the whole estate to get his son back. What good is his money to him? Will he eat it."

Blair shook his head.

"You take a man with a conscience," said he, "and you never can tell how it will work. A conscience is like stomach trouble. It always shows in the face, and it never leaves a man happy. Hello, there's Helena now."

"That's not the pinto," answered the King Bird instantly. "It's a horse with a longer stride."

"No, maybe you're right. What an ear you have!" said the other. "I remember a fellow in the old days who claimed that he could tell the difference between——"

He stopped, for the beating of the hoofs had swung up close to the front door. A shadowy form swept past, and through the open doorway flashed a bit of white paper that fluttered, and slapped down on the boards.

The King Bird caught up the envelope almost before it fell.

He leaped to the door, but the rider was a dwindling form in the night, already.

The King Bird came back into the room, looking at the writing on the paper.

"For mother and dad," he read aloud.

He laid the paper in the lap of Blair. Then he stepped to the kitchen door and closed it.

He kept his hand on the knob, while he muttered, over his shoulder:

"What's up? Quick! What's up?"

He saw the head of Blair slump against the back of the chair, saw the face of the rancher whiten. Like a flash the King Bird had the contents of the envelope in his hand—two fifty-dollar bills, and a rapid scrawl on a sheet of paper.

He read:

DEAR MOTHER AND DAD: Good luck came my way this evening. I've got a job, and a fine one. Just for the moment it has to be a secret. But very soon I can let you in on it.

The worst part is that I have to take it at once. I can't even go back home to tell you what it is, or where I'm going; I can just send you this note.

You can only know that I'm safe and sound, and happy. And one of the happiest parts is that I got some advance salary, which I'm sending back to you by messenger.

Be sure to remember that we owe the grocery store thirty-one dollars and fifty cents. Mr. Gresham was pretty cross about the bill, the other day.

There's the general-merchandise store, too. You'd better pay them twenty-five dollars on account, and, mother, you use the rest to get a dress. You need one. *And* some nice bright shoes, poor dear.

There'll be more money. Depend on that.

Terribly sorry to leave without seeing you. Don't make too much of a mystery of it, and believe me, I'll be back soon, and let you know all that's happened.

> Your loving daughter,
>
> HELENA.

The King Bird found that he was reading and rereading the letter, when a thin, work-reddened hand moved out beside him, and took the paper.

It was Mrs. Blair, who had come softly into the room.

The King Bird watched her with anxious eyes, prepared for a terrible cry. But nothing came.

She merely folded the letter carefully, and put it in the bosom of her calico dress. The money she laid on the knee of Blair.

He sat low in the chair, his chin drooped against his breast.

"Take the money away. Put it in the stove. I never want to lay eyes on it," he muttered.

He struck both hands against his face.

"It's my fault," he said. "I've raised her like a poor waif. I've given her a dog's life. I've favored John, and let her drudge like a dog! Oh, God forgive me!"

His wife kneeled beside the chair.

"You remember this, John," she said softly. "There never was a better girl than Helena. There never was one like her, that couldn't do wrong."

Blair brushed her away and staggered to his feet.

"King!" he cried, holding out a hand to him.

The King Bird gripped the hand hard.

"I'm in it," he said. "I'm in it to the wind-up."

"God Almighty bless you," said Blair. He added slowly: "I thought I knew what misery was, before. I didn't know anything about it. King, tell me——"

"What?" said the young man.

"Are you going to have luck? Are you going to find her?"

"If I have to ride to hell and back!" said the King Bird.

CHAPTER XI

THE WONDER HORSE

THE FULL round of a golden moon was up in the east, when the King Bird stepped from the house, and looked toward the black hills. In that direction the rider who brought the letter had vanished. There was only one immediate hope of finding Helena Blair, and that was, it seemed, by tracking the bearer of the word from her.

Even daytime tracking could be hard enough in that wide country; moonlight tracking might be an impossible thing! But there was one thing to help him, and this he noticed at once; dew was gathering on the grass, wet and cold, and the dust was darkening with it.

But a myriad tracks of horses led up to the house and away from it. How could he pick out the mount of that rider?

He closed his eyes to remember. It had been a pale color —he could safely say that. It might be a light bay or chestnut, perhaps, or a cream color, or a gray. It was a big horse, and by the speed at which it was going, and the rhythm of its hoofbeat, it was a long-striding animal.

That was something to go on.

Furthermore, at great speed it had come close up to the door of the house, and therefore would swing wide in cutting back onto the road.

He hurried to the side of the road and there, quite apart from all other sign, he saw the imprint of hoofs—heels that had been driven down deep and hard, in a direction pointing straight at the low bank that rose, and the gleaming barbed-wire fence above it.

It was as though the rider had put his horse at a wire fence, but considering the bad light, that seemed impossible. The King Bird vaulted the fence and just beyond it he saw that the dangerous feat had actually been done. For there were the tracks of the horse in landing!

A mighty space it had cleared, from the edge of the road over the fence and into the field, and yet there was no slipping, no sign that it had floundered, for the tracks went straight on. By the size and the stretch of them, the horse must be a giant, and it seemed to have taken the jump in its stride, so to speak!

The King Bird was on the mare in a moment.

Molly, too, could be trusted to take even a wire fence by night, if there were as much as a clear gleam of starlight striking along the top wire.

And the King Bird, moved with curiosity and a certain eager lifting of the heart, took her back fifty yards down the road and sent her at full speed at the fence.

He could see the slight turn of her head, as she asked if he really meant to try such a thing, and then as his voice called softly to her, she straightened out at the jump and took it valiantly.

He knew that she had taken off closer to the fence; and as she winged faultlessly across it, he saw her land shorter than the previous horse had done.

Something pinched the heart of the young man with a sudden fear and envy. She had always been matchless—

always, and at everything. If it were a race at a rodeo, or a run across country, she was always the winner, always the easy winner; and at jumping she had no mate.

But here was a horse that seemed to have cleared a stretch beyond her!

He checked her, and dropping to the ground, he sighted across the grass. Then he found the trail where the dew had been taken off the grass, a long, shadowy streak that curved gradually off to the right across the field. The gathering brilliance of the moon helped to set it out more distinctly, by the contrast.

He was in the saddle again at once, and calling to Molly, he sent her at her flowing, easy gait rapidly away on the hunt.

It was a quarter-section field, neatly squared. The trail led straight across it to a point where the fugitive had jumped the corresponding fence into a narrow little lane. He had not gone on into the next field but had turned to the side.

And again the force of going had swerved the rider from the beaten center of the way into the short grass at the side of the lane.

There the young man found the sign again. He had the peculiarities stamped in his mind. There was the size of the hoofs, for one thing, and the beautifully perfect roundness of them. In addition, there was a slight pinching in on the outside of the near foreshoe. More than all, was the great length of the stride.

He followed to the left down the lane, which twisted among the fenced fields, and so came out into the open range.

No fences, now, but at this point the rider had brought his mount down to an easy canter, to judge by the space between the hoofmarks. Even that shortened stride would have been a long span for most horses to stretch!

The young man began to take into his mind a picture of a great horse, winged with speed. A thirteen-hundred-pound giant that might stand seventeen hands! With less weight, the imprints of the hoofs could hardly be so deep. With

68

less height the weight could hardly be carried forward at this splendid sweeping speed!

Thirteen hundred pounds, more or less—and the black mare was under a thousand!

Again the wonder and the cold envy slid through his heart and took his breath.

But he would not believe. Big horses may make jumpers and sprinters, but what about a fine ten-mile run across open country?

That was an entirely different matter.

The sign was still easy to follow, and at a smart gallop, because as the moonlight brightened, it set the dew gleaming on the grass, and showed yet more clearly the dark spots and streaks where the other had gone.

It seemed that he did not know the country, for he had headed straight toward the edge of a little steep-sided draw.

Yes, at a point where the rider must have seen the shadowy gulf of the depression, he actually sent his mount along at full speed again, charging it!

Was he drunk, or mad?

The young man reined the mare on the edge of the draw, half expecting to see, in the bottom of the great ditch, the crumpled, lifeless forms of horse and rider.

He could see where the big creature had taken off, driving its hoofs deep into the soil on the verge of the bank. But there was no sign of an accident.

Had he cleared it?

With a gasp, the King Bird measured the distance with a careful eye, and knew that Molly never could clear it—never! It would have been an impossibility.

He turned her to the side, found the easy way down the bank, where it sloped out gradually, and so up at a corresponding place on the farther bank.

He found the trail again.

Yes, the flying monster actually had cleared the gulf with more than a good yard to spare, and had gone sweeping on.

One thing was certain—that if the mare were to catch this winged giant, she would have to do it on smooth ground. She could not match him and his kangaroo tactics over the rough ditches and hedges and fences!

The King Bird was glad when that canter of the fugitive turned into a trot, then into a walk.

He was drawing near now, very near, and it was time to scan closely every thicket before them, and every rock, for this fellow might turn and strike from covert, like a wounded beast.

But as he went forward, the young man scanned the imprints left by the walking horse, for more is to be learned from the way a horse walks than by the way it gallops, some men hold.

One thing was instantly clear. The action of the horse was low. It was wasting no effort. Most of your heavy mounts will bring up the foot higher, and carry it down again with a stamp, but this fellow was a true grass cutter, and skimmed the dew from the heads of the grass from beginning to end of his step.

Only here and there was a break in the dark lines, and that was where there was a rock projecting a little from the grass, or perhaps just lost to view within it.

It was a horse familiar with mountain going, then, and sure-footed as a goat—a horse with eyes in its hoofs, as the saying goes!

With every good quality that the King Bird could attribute to that unseen rival of Molly, his heart was pinched smaller and smaller with cold.

He looked down at her with fear and with pity. She looked suddenly narrow to him across the withers, and he had to reach down and work his fingers along the smooth and delicate flow of muscle in her shoulder, before he was heartened again.

She was flawless, but was she now matched against one just as flawless, and a bigger machine, withal?

They were traveling now in a wide, easy circle that cut around behind the town of Valencia, and headed for the hills.

The fugitive was trotting. Up hill and down dale he went on, taking in a splendid span at each stride, and not until they came out on the easy level of the upper plateau that stretched on for miles and miles with only little low ripples of ground to break the distance, did the big fellow in the lead come back to a walk again.

Was he tired? Had he been ridden far, that day?

It seemed so. For the rider was now saving him over ground that was perfect for galloping.

On the other hand, the mare was not in the absolute pink of condition. She, also, had covered a good many miles since the morning, though most of them had been made without a rider in the saddle.

Still the trail led on clearly before the King Bird. He took the mare out of her canter, and brought her down to that easy trot at which she could go from morning to sunset, unfaltering, and he knew how to sit that pace without moving in the saddle. There could hardly have been a more effortless action in horseflesh, no matter where one hunted for it, not even in the ambling mules of the Near East.

There would be sight of the stranger now, before many minutes, as soon as they had broken through the skirting of little groves of trees that fringed the highland, unless, indeed, the man had taken refuge in one of the thickets, and intended to spend the night there.

And now, beyond one of those groves, a whinny loud as the blast of a horn, or a chorus of horns, rang on the night air. As the King Bird put the mare to a full gallop, and rounded the edge of the woods, he saw his quarry before him, stretching away for the distant hills.

CHAPTER XII

DEFEAT

IT WAS the mare herself who took hold and broke away at full speed, as though she instantly knew that this was a race. Her rider sat bolt erect in the saddle, aiding her not at all, for he was stunned.

That creature before him, over whose back a rider was bent low, was not like an earthly form, but something molded of pure moonlight, and descended to frolic across the mountains for the night. It was either white or silver-gray. It seemed to be running to the knees in water or black shadow, and by that, the pursuer knew that it finished with dark points.

The mane fluttered from its arched neck, as it ran with raised head, turned a little to watch the enemy, and the long tail was swept out in a straight line by the speed of the going.

The mare seemed extended to the full—still, with raised head, turned a trifle, the big creature easily held off her challenge. It was a stallion. Nothing else could have that magnificent neck, that fierce and beautiful head! And it was running well inside its strength, it appeared, to hold Molly even.

Yes, suddenly it seemed to the amazed heart of the King Bird that he was mounted on a common little range pony, vainly striving to keep up with the stride of a thoroughbred!

But the speed of a sprinter is one thing, and the race is not always to the fast starter.

Over the neck of the mare he leaned, to cut the wind with head and shoulders only. Shifting his weight forward, so that he would not compress the running muscles that arch up into the back and under the saddle, he took a pull on the head of Molly, in order to steady her as she stretched to the full of her speed.

Out she went, link by link, seeming to settle a little toward the ground as every ounce of her energy went into the effort. The earth was a gleaming blur beneath them. The hard wind of the gallop fanned back the brim of the King Bird's sombrero, and stung his eyes until he had to squint them almost shut.

Through that wind, he looked forward and laughed to himself as he saw that the stallion was no longer galloping at ease.

It, also, was stretched out straight as a string, and working at its best, it appeared, while the rider, in perfect jockey's position, steadied the animal in its mighty stride. And what a stride it was!

There seemed to be an invisible support that sustained the great body in air for a brief instant every time it flung forward from the ground.

Seventeen hands—at least that—and yet made with the delicacy of a carefully modeled statue! A winged, a glorious creature that seemed to disdain the very earth it ran upon!

And yet there was something to Molly.

He could feel her own confidence in herself as, after reaching full speed, she made effort on effort to increase her pace, and bring this huge animal back to her.

But no, the silver giant had increased the gap between them.

"He's a sprinter," said the young man, through his teeth. "Only a big worthless hulk of a sprinter—a trick horse. We'll catch him in the long run. The wind is what counts, and the heart!"

But his heart was bitter, for he knew that at last she had encountered a rival which could fairly beat her over a good mile of measured ground, a rival with a stride far greater, with a great jumping margin over her, with a beauty, also, far greater than hers!

73

She was as lovely as a deer, but this great beast that fled before them had something of the falcon about him; he was like a king of the upper air.

With voice and hand, the young man brought Molly down to three-quarter speed. She would hold that pace a desperately long time. It was that which had held off challenge after challenge from the grim posse of the marshal. That three-quarter speed was enough to distance the ordinary range mustang in short order.

Yet it dropped her rapidly behind the stallion!

The young man groaned.

He remembered now, savagely, what the marshal had said to him—that his earthly paradise was that of a fool, in effect. That he had built his glory on the beauty of the girl he loved, on the splendor of the horse he rode, on the matchless joy of the freedom that was his.

The marshal had vowed that his freedom was that of a hunted fox; and the girl was untrue, and the mare would be surpassed by the gray stallion of Dick Macey.

Had he not said gray?

Yes, and yonder it was. There could not be two of the same kind. A gray stallion that was matchless. Even little Brick had known about it.

Then a sudden hope rushed up in him.

For the distance was no longer increasing. The stallion galloped on before him, but not an inch did it gain! Held to a fair level, the two swept across the rolling plain, while the foothills swelled larger and blacker before them toward the northwest, and the moon and stars poured their shadows over the bright grass.

Never had Molly run better. Night was a time she knew as well as day, and there was never a doubt of her footing, never a stumble or a falter in her going. Never had the King Bird ridden with such painstaking care, or thrown himself more faultlessly into the swinging rhythm of that gallop which he knew so well.

Another mile, and another, and another, and still the silver giant was there before him.

74

They seemed to be running on a treadmill; nothing could be gained and nothing could be lost—the earth was simply spinning back behind them, and beneath.

Would the big fellow never come back?

Would his head never be thrown up, and begin to bob?

Anxiously the young man watched for these signs of a failing horse. Eagerly he stared to see the movement either of spurred heel into the flank of the stallion, or the swing of a quirt to get more out of it. But as far as he could see, the rider ahead of him was making not the slightest effort, beyond perfect riding, to urge the silver horse to a sharper gait.

As for Molly, he did not need to touch her, either with hand or with heel. A word would be enough. Not even a word was needed, but only the passing of that that electric current which flowed ceaselessly down the reins, out of his tingling hands. Somewhere in the depths of his soul it originated; somewhere in the depths of her soul it was received. Straight and true she ran, and never a falter, though he could feel the increased labor of her sides, as her breathing grew deeper.

There was a scant two miles now, before the long level of the plateau was lost in the tangled ways of the foothills. Once among them, it would not be hard for the fugitive to turn to one side or to the other, and lose his pursuer, at least for a few vital moments.

Now, or never, was the mare to catch the other.

And the message flowed surely down the bridle reins, and the mare again raised herself to a great effort.

It was coming out of her heart. Mere strength of body was not in it, but strength of nerve and spirit, and all the loyalty of that great heart of hers.

And they gained! Surely and steadily they gained, until he heard clearly the heavy beat of the hoofs of the giant before him.

A rioting joy came up in the heart of the King Bird. An excess of love for the mare flowed out from him. He was half blinded by delight, as he saw the other rider turn his head and look quickly back—sure signs of a beaten man in a race!

Then a strange thing happened, more wounding than bullets to the young man—for the hand of the other rose and fell, and the gray stallion started as though freshly at the beginning of the race.

Away it went. Stretched out low and true, the great horse cleft wind, and with every stride it made, the mare seemed to be jerked away to the rear.

Was the stallion at full speed? No, for swifter and swifter it went!

There was a scant mile left to those foothills. They would never catch the gray now.

Catch it? As well strive to catch a hawk in the sky!

Stunned with grief, the King Bird saw the distance grow.

And then, before him, he saw the head of the mare waver, just a trifle.

She was beginning to labor in her stride, at the very end of her strength—he had ridden her out—and yet the silver giant was fleeing away from her as smoothly as water flowing down a flume!

He could not believe it, but the fact was before his eyes.

He could understand the entire thing now. There never had been a moment when she was capable of holding pace with the other, but the rider had merely played with him, holding back the stallion to the gait of the mare—until in the end he decided to draw away!

He snatched the rifle from its scabbard, and called to the mare.

She made a sudden stop, and he pitched the butt of the gun into the hollow of his shoulder.

It was an easy target—that man and horse together, bobbing in the sights.

Only, suppose that the bullet struck the horse, and not the rider?

He jerked down the rifle suddenly.

Molly was outmatched, but that was no reason for murdering her rival. In a sort of agony of admiration, the King Bird watched the other draw swiftly away. The moonlight seemed a mist that was gathering between them. And now, in the black mouth of a ravine that split through the foothills, the King Bird saw the silver giant disappear.

For his own part, he dismounted heavily.

The mare was standing with her head low, her breathing labored, her knees trembling.

She was quite run out. The veriest range nag could run her to the ground now!

So he loosed the girths, and pulled the saddle from her back. Then he gathered a quantity of the grass, twisted it hard, and began to rub Molly down vigorously.

But half his mind was wandering away from his work.

The marshal had been right about two things. Perhaps about the third he was right, also.

Grimly the young man worked on.

Poor little Helena Blair was as far as ever from his help. Still farther, perhaps, since he had played his hand, given warning of his coming, and spread the alarm to the ranks of the enemy, whoever they might be.

Defeat bowed the young man's spirit more than labor had ever stooped his shoulders!

CHAPTER XIII

THE RAVINE

HE COULD have gone on after a few moments, for the mare recuperated quickly, as usual. But instead, he remained for an entire hour, working hard over her. At the end of that time, she was grazing again, and the King Bird dropped where he stood, gave his body a roll in a warmly lined slicker, and was instantly asleep.

He slept only while the moon was climbing for thirty or forty minutes through the sky, then he roused himself, and seemed perfectly refreshed.

He saddled Molly again, and caressed her with an extra gentleness, for we love our friends most when their weaknesses are revealed to us. She had fallen in his eyes an illimitable distance; she had been first, and now that she was second, she might almost as well have been hundredth. For that very reason, his hand and voice were kinder to her than ever.

Even now he did not mount. He pulled off his riding boots and hung them on his saddle. On his feet he drew moccasins, and struck out at a brisk gait for the shadowy mouth of that same canyon which had swallowed up the gray horse.

Many things might happen. The fugitive might have hidden himself in covert to surprise his follower, and in that case he probably had decided that the King Bird, being distanced, had given up the chase. Or he might have camped securely somewhere along the trail, or again, he might have plodded on steadily, letting the stallion walk, for the big horse would feel some effects from that severe run, great as its reserve of strength might be.

Three or four miles an hour is a walking pace. And a man on foot with the wiry endurance of an Indian runner will overtake that rate surprisingly.

He pushed himself relentlessly straight through the black throat of the canyon, and came out to find that the trail was lost where the moonlight fell again! Nevertheless he did not turn back, but turned up to the left, and after a steep climb, reached the next higher level. There, as he had hoped, he picked up the trail once more.

He dropped on one knee beside the first clear impression of the big hoofs, and watched the grasses. They trembled a little as the mountain wind stirred them, but they were not unbending and rising perceptibly but slowly, as the strong grass will do when it has just been beaten down by an imprint.

Therefore the horse must have passed an hour and a half or two hours in the lead.

78

Now the ground rose gradually before the King Bird, and as he followed the trail, it seemed clear to him that the fugitive was making for a cleft in the mountains, where the big range divided deeply, and the peaks fell back on either hand. Once that goal occurred to him, he stopped looking for the dim, moonlit sign. The dew had fallen only slightly in these uplands, and it was better to take chances, no matter how long.

So he struck straight for the point of his expectation, and though it was an up grade, never once did he let his run fall away to a walking gait. Remorselessly he drove himself up the incline. And the mare jogged easily beside him.

Her tough mustang constitution had already completely recovered from the strain that it had endured. She seemed as fresh as she had been at the beginning of that losing run. As she moved, her head was high, and turning this way and that to study the sounds and the signs of the night, and, above all, to read the scents that carried to her nostrils hardly less meaning than they would have done to the nose of a wolf. Above all, mountain lion, wolf, coyote, she recognized, to right and to left. But things from which she would have fled did not matter now, except to make her press a little closer to her master.

Three more long hours they struggled, until at last they were in the opening of the pass. Now, as the way sloped gradually down, with few rises, the King Bird climbed into the saddle. He was nearly spent, but the clean breath of the mountain wind would soon let his lungs cease laboring, and in the meantime the mare had labored very little for hours and hours, compared with what the heavy stallion had done, bearing its own weight and that of a rider up the slopes.

A fierce hope suddenly boiled up in the heart of the young man. For as he came to a patch of soft ground, that filled the center of the pass, he scanned the grass closely. There was not a trace of dew here, and the moonlight seemed dimmer as the gray of the morning began, but even so he was able to find what he wanted—the great round imprints left by the gray horse!

And he could see the down-crushed blades of grass slowly, bit by bit, unfolding and reraising themselves.

It was not long ago that the fugitive had gone by, and suppose that the stallion were sighted, could it stand against another challenge?

It was tired, very tired. For even where the ground sloped down, the rider had not asked it for a canter.

The rider himself was badly spent. For here the trail led clearly under a tree whose branches were low—hardly more than saddle-high. Only just under the sweep of them did the sign of the stallion veer to the side, as though its master were sleeping in the saddle, and had roused at the last moment, as the branches loomed before him.

A tired rider and a tired horse!

If that were Dick Macey in the saddle, how much wiser he would have been to rest and then go on, rather than kill both himself and his mount with such plodding labor!

Rapidly the walls of the pass moved by. The sky was brightening, and the snows of the upper peaks began to gleam with a golden sheen of the morning. The fresh day was coming upon them, and it seemed to the young man that the defeat of Molly had been a dream of the night, that could not be repeated in the daytime.

That was his last thought as he came out of the pass, and saw before him a fine, rolling country, a great wild hinterland, covered with big groves of trees, here and there, and far-spreading thickets, and cut across and across by sharp-sided ravines.

It was a hole-in-the-wall country. He could not very well hope to follow his quarry except by the aid of clear sign, in a region like this. And there was not likely to be clear sign in most places, for often gravel covered up the valley floor, and sometimes the bare surface of the rock showed through, acres at a time. It would be an endless task, when the trail disappeared, and it was necessary to explore the ravines on either hand.

Then, more gloriously welcome to his eyes than ever the rising sun to men lost in a wilderness, he saw before him the great gray horse, and in the saddle on its back, a bowed form, that gripped the pommel of the saddle with both hands, and sagged wearily to the side!

He wanted to shout out a blood-curdling screech of joy, but he checked that, for there was the possibility that he might be able to steal closer to the enemy before he was discovered. In fact, he might have done so, but the stallion itself, half turning on the side of a hillock, looked back, and stopped, and whinnied loudly.

The rider wakened with a start that knocked the hat off his head. Then, looking back, he saw the King Bird, and the speeding mare! He stooped from the saddle, scooped up his fallen hat, and shaking his fist at the pursuer, let the stallion out at full gallop. His fury was so great at being overtaken again, that he was shouting in a blind rage, and the words trailed back to the young man.

The King Bird laughed as he rode, and steadied Molly for her second effort.

And she?

The heart might have been taken from him by the first defeat, but not from her. With pricking ears she responded. It seemed clear that she recognized an old antagonist, and was eager to close with him.

And down the long, gradual incline of the valley they shot together.

Hope mounted like a hawk in the heart of the young man. No big horse like that should be at home in the mountains. Weight is too much against it. And the rider was a heavy fellow, too. In every way the mare had been saved, and better handled, and surely she could overtake the big horse now!

But the gray held off her challenge, at the first. It was no laughing matter now, though. With heel and hand, Dick Macey, if that were he, was calling on the gray for everything that was in it, and that which remained to the weary stallion was just enough to keep the mare at her distance.

For three terrible, heart-breaking miles they ran, and then, as before, the gray began to draw gradually ahead! It was not a rapid gain, and the stallion was running all out to make it.

It seemed to the King Bird that he was bound to close with the enemy. He had a sense of some great event in the offing, as he stormed down the valley, as the echoes flew from rock to rock like the clangor of giant hammers on giant anvils, and the great faces of the cliffs blazed with the fire of the rising sun about him.

It was a wild and an eerie feeling. He was half frightened, and half rejoiced—when suddenly the stallion no longer raced before him, and the long slope of the valley swept empty before his eye!

Then, on the left, he saw the reason.

A defile opened with a narrow mouth, drenched with shadows, and secret as the maw of a snake. Yet he twisted the mare to the side and shot through into the little canyon. Before him, he could see nothing, for all was a tangle of brush and of stones, but he could hear the noise of the fugitive, driving the big horse on.

The heart of the King Bird laughed wildly and savagely in him. He would have that fellow, before he had reached the end of that ravine. He would have him out of his saddle!

Why had the fool gone into such a trap as this?

Then before him, out of the thickets, he heard the thin, piercing thrill of a whistle.

He broke into clear ground, with the gray a scant hundred yards before him. As he did so, he saw three men rise from behind rocks with leveled rifles!

No man could have dodged that danger more swiftly than the mare. She knew a rifle quite as well as her master, and doubling about like the agile-footed cat that she was, she drove back into the tangles of the thicket that they had just left.

Rifle bullets whined and crackled through the shrubs, as the King Bird made the mare lie flat behind a rock, and himself dropped on one knee beside her.

CHAPTER XIV

THREE GUNMEN

HE OFFERED an interesting study, the King Bird, as he waited there on one knee, one hand on the ground, and a revolver in the other. For his head was canted to one side, and in the dappling of slant shadows that fell from the brush across him, he was smiling.

He had the happy air of a creature that is born to the wilderness. If wild cats could smile, he would have resembled one, every nerve strung taut with the danger that was around him, and yet every nerve delighting in it, also.

One thing was certain, presently—the riflemen were not advancing toward the thicket, and that made him lift his head with a renewed interest. They were only there to check a rashly intruding stranger. They were protecting something, therefore?

He was on his feet as he thought of this, and at once he began to move forward through the thicket, cutting off to the left. He only paused once, to look back regretfully toward the mare. Any stranger who chanced along might lay hand on her bridle now, and make her his, for she would remain there as securely as a young antelope, left in the grass by its mother, until the voice of the whistle of the master reached her ears.

She returned his look with interest, lifting up her lovely head, and canting it a trifle to the side, her big eyes, like the eyes of a deer, turning toward him, as she struggled to understand why he who never deserted her was leaving her now in a moment of trouble!

The young man smiled back at her, and then turned with silent feet into the thicket.

He skirted far to the left, and came out from the brush among rocks, interspersed with random shrubs. They made good cover for him as he cut in behind the boulders and made for the position of the three.

He found them almost at once, grouped behind a natural rampart of rocks, smoking and talking together.

The King Bird, with snakelike caution, wormed his way within easy earshot of them.

And the first word that he heard was:

"And why should Dick Macey be running away from one man, I'd like to know?"

Said another: "It was only a kid, too, by the size of him, and the cut of him."

"It ain't age and poundage that makes a gent good with a gun," said the third.

"There you go with your smart cracks," remarked the first man. "Would you lay off of them wise sayings of yours, once in a while, Garry?"

"For you, brother," said Garry sardonically.

He was a long man, so thin that he would have had to be multiplied by two to make him of normal proportions. Of his features, only his forehead was of ordinary size, and this at the expense of his chin, which did not exist at all.

"Wisecracks make me sick," said the other harshly. He looked ready to make trouble at once.

Tall Garry answered: "If you want a fight, son, you go right there into the brush, and look up that kid that seemed so easy to you."

"Any snake is mean company, in a hole in the ground," said the other. "Only, about Dick Macey runnin' away—that's what I don't make out. You'd think that the gent behind him was Jud Hobey, or the King Bird, or something."

"Yeah, you'd think that," said the first speaker. "Macey was a fool to bring that gent right in here to the valley, too. He not only run, but he run to cover. Suppose that this starts a search around here?"

84

"It won't do 'em any good to search," said Garry. "You know that. We got everything all cached away so's it can never be found."

"Not unless it speaks for itself," said the other. "I wonder just what the kid's doing, over there in the brush?"

"Sneakin' away," said the third man, "and every time he or the hoss steps on a twig, he thinks that we're after him, and gets heart failure."

"He ain't feeling any too happy, for one thing," said Garry. "I sure tagged him with a slug just as he got into the brush. Under the right arm, I guess."

"Why don't you go into the bush and get him out, then?" asked the aggressive member of the trio.

"Why not let him bleed a while?" answered Garry.

"Dry meat's no good," was the answer.

The speaker rose.

"I'm going off to the side, there, and cut in to the mouth of the ravine, and beat back, and see what I scare up. Nick, you take the other side. We can't let that gent lie out there. I don't think that Garry hit him, but I sure plastered him, and low, too. Just over the cantle of the saddle, I'd say. Just as he was dippin' into the brush, I got a dead bead on him. Garry, you stay here. We'll drive the kid right up into your arms."

They rose, and one walked toward the far side of the ravine, while the other moved straight at the King Bird's place of concealment.

The young man lay still, gathering himself slowly, ready for a spring up, and a gun play. But the other turned suddenly to the left of the rocks that hid the young man, and went on.

Garry, as his friend disappeared, squinted cautiously through a cleft in the stones just before him at the thicket into which the King Bird had disappeared with the mare.

Then he sat down, and was in the midst of the making of a cigarette when the King Bird himself arose and stepped forward, a gun dangling idly in his hand.

"Hello, partner," said the King Bird.

Garry twisted his head around like a bird on a perch, stared at the newcomer, and turned white. A flutter of yellow dust from the tips of his fingers told that the cigarette had been torn to atoms. But he only muttered: "So there you are, eh?"

"Here I am," said the young man. "You might unbuckle that gun belt and slide away from those guns."

It was done instantly, as though with pleasure.

"Now we can chat a while," said the King Bird. "How's things, anyway, Garry?"

"Tell me, did you work underground, or drop out of the sky?" asked Garry.

"I came crawling, that's all," was the answer. "How about a little talk?"

"That's fine with me. What about?"

"Everything you know."

"I ain't an author," said Garry.

He grinned, his face twisting to one side, and the lower lip pulling away from the upper. It was plain that he was terribly frightened.

"Where's the cache?" asked the King Bird.

"The cache? What cache?"

"The cache that nobody can find," said the King Bird.

"You've been listening in for quite a spell, have you?" asked Garry.

"Quite a time."

"I'll tell you what," said Garry. "I'd like to get in on the joke that you played on Macey. What made him run so fast and so far?"

"He just started running, and then he was afraid to turn back," said the King Bird.

"Who are you, brother?" said Garry.

"Why, my name really doesn't matter. Some people call me the King Bird."

Garry stared, then he laughed.

"That's good!" said he. "That's a fine bluff, kid."

"Is it?" said the King Bird.

"Sure. I've *seen* the King Bird. I've seen him fly!"

"Where?"

"Why, in a saloon, where there was a lot of action started. And all the rest of the gang was goin' one way, and he started the other. And the gang stopped; and he went on; and the difference was left on the floor. He salted three or four gents, that time."

"That's pretty rough," said the King Bird, suddenly remembering the same occasion out of his brilliant past.

"Yeah, he's rough. You got the same color hair and eyes all right. But don't go saying that you're the King Bird, boy. You might get yourself hurt, when you ain't got the drop on somebody."

"And that's fair enough, too," said the King Bird. "I don't mind that at all. Now suppose you answer my questions."

"What questions?"

"About the cache?"

"What cache, son?" demanded Garry calmly. For he was regaining his assurance.

"The cache that Dick Macey has gone to."

"I don't know anything about that."

"That's too bad then," said the young man. "I thought you might be useful enough to make something more than a meal for some old buzzard with only half a stomach."

He raised the gun.

"What's that?" asked Garry.

"It'll soon be over. Turn your back, if it'll be easier for you to take it that way."

"Boy, you ain't aiming to murder me, are you?"

"Murder? You shot at me—three of you. Murder? Oh, no, it's just scavenger work that I'm going to do."

"Why, what's the matter, kid? You—what you want to know, anyway?"

"About the cache," said the young man.

"I—er—look here," said Garry, and came to a pause again, gaping.

"Well, what?" asked the King Bird briskly.

Suddenly he stepped closer, and laid the muzzle of the revolver against the stomach of the tall fellow.

"Either way," he said. "It makes no difference to me.

You talk, or I drop you, and get one of the other two. It's all one to me, brother!"

Garry groaned.

"Suppose I tell you," said he, "it would do you no good!"

"I'll take a chance on that," said the King Bird. "The best way is for me to be shown to the spot. Wait till I get my horse, and I'll come along with you."

"I'll wait right here for you, on my honor," said Garry, with a dull gleam of hope.

"Sure you will," said the young man, and sent the long, soft whistle down the wind toward the mare.

CHAPTER XV

UNDERGROUND

MOLLY came to them, with the empty stirrup irons tossing at her sides, and Garry regarded her with a rather awed interest.

"How long'd you take to teach her what she knows?" he asked.

"About three years—a lesson every day, and a long one," said the King Bird.

Garry stood entranced.

"She looks like the King Bird's mare," he declared, "only she ain't big enough. I see what it is, brother. You've started out and made yourself a copy of him, have you? But you got a long ways to go before you're a King Bird!"

He even chuckled a little as he said this, and the King Bird urged him to hurry on as guide.

"Your pair of friends down the valley may find out that I've disappeared and come looking for you," he explained. "Hustle along, Garry."

"You're goin' to do it, are you?" asked Garry.

"I am."

"All right," said Garry. "You got a gun on me. I'll take you where you wanta go, but it's goin' to mean the finish of both of us. Come on!"

And he strode rapidly up the valley.

A pace behind him, the King Bird followed, and he ventured to ask:

"How long has the girl been up here?"

"What girl?" asked Garry.

"Helena Blair," said the young man.

"That's her name—and you know her?" exclaimed Garry. "Dog-gone me, but maybe that's why you came!"

"Maybe it is," agreed the King Bird.

"Go back again, then, brother," urged Garry. "She oughta be all right. Nothing oughta happen to her if things go right. And she's doin' good—real good."

"Walk right on, Garry," directed the young man.

"We're almost there now," said Garry. "Now, lookit!"

He stole forward through the brush carefully, and while a screen of greenery still remained between them and the sunlit world, he pointed toward the ragged side of a mountain that rose by the ravine.

"You see?" asked Garry.

"I see the mountain," said the young man.

"See that old dump on the side of it?"

"I see that."

"It's inside there, in the shaft that was sunk, I dunno when."

"That's hard to get at," agreed the young man. "No other way in?"

"There's a side feeder that sneaks in over yonder. But both the two of them shafts is guarded night and day, brother. How'd you manage to get in there?"

"Where are the guards?" asked the King Bird.

"Right at the mouth of the main shaft, and down where the small tunnel busts in on the big one."

"We'll try the small shaft, then," said the young man.

89

"Hold on, brother!" muttered Garry. "You ain't meaning it, are you?"

"I've got to mean it."

"I'll tell you another thing. There's likely to be five gents in there, and they're all heeled, and they all know how to use what they're heeled with."

"We're two," remarked the King Bird. "Two to five is not so bad."

"You goin' to make me go in there with you?" asked Garry, his face green with fear.

"That's my idea," said the King Bird.

"That'll make one more agin' you when the pinch comes, you fool!" said Garry savagely.

The King Bird smiled. "If you go in with me, they won't think that you're a friend, Garry," said he. "Your back will be against the wall as much as mine."

"Of all the sneaks," groaned Garry. "Of all the murderin' sneaks——"

"Why, murder's in the air here," said the young man. "It's a regular Murder Valley, as I found out down yonder when the three of you started pelting me with lead. Don't whine, Garry."

The latter took a breath, and then shrugged his shoulders.

"If I'm goin' to die to-day, I'll die to-day," said he. "And that's all there is to it. If I'm to help you in yonder, I get a gun, don't I?"

"Of course you do," said the young man. "You get a gun and you go first. If anything goes wrong, I'll be close behind you, partner, with another gun."

His smile caressed the big fellow, and Garry snarled like a fighting cat. He took the proffered gun, and for an instant a grim resolution seemed to be rising in him; but it was the very negligence of the King Bird that seemed to convince him that the quiet way must be the best way, after all.

He led the way for a distance through the thicket, and again, from the verge of the green gloom of the leaves, he pointed up the mountainside.

"You see that snake hole up yonder?" he said.

"I see it," answered the young man.

"Well," said Garry, "it's big enough for a man to crawl into, but we gotta climb to it up those naked rocks. And suppose that we're seen?"

"We have to take the chance," said the young man.

"Chance? It ain't a chance; it's murder!"

"We'll go on," said the King Bird.

He spoke to the mare, and she sank to the ground like an obedient dog on the edge of the thicket. She would stay there until he called for her—or until she was found by enemy searchers. That thought chilled the heart of the King Bird almost more than the danger which he was to face in person.

"You ain't goin' to use common sense? You're goin' to go on up those rocks?" insisted Garry.

"With you in front," said the King Bird.

A frightful stream of oaths answered him. Then, groaning, Garry stepped out into the open, gave one wild glance around him, and fled like a deer up the steep slopes and the boulders that gleamed in the morning sun.

He had put up his gun, needing both hands and feet for his climbing; but though the King Bird kept his Colt in hand, he managed to keep on the very heels of his agile guide.

So they crouched, at last, just outside what had seemed from below, no more than a snake hole.

Below, the disturbed rubble and débris that had been taken from the shaft, tumbled down the sharp slope of the mountain.

"Here we are," said Garry. "I'll play the game straight with you and tell you that there ain't a chance of doin' nothin' inside. There's gents in there that can hit a dime when you chuck it in the air!"

"Then we won't waste any dimes on them," said the King Bird. "Go in, Garry. There may be some hawks in the air watching us now."

The tall fellow cast another wild look about him, and high into the air overhead. Then he ducked into the darkness of the tunnel, and the King Bird followed.

The shaft was not so small as he had feared that it might be. The actual mouth was smaller than the inside dimensions,

91

and the drift seemed to have been a long rise that had been sunk from the main shaft, perhaps following some thin vein until the miners actually reached the open air and the light of day to repay their efforts.

The darkness was not perfect, for there was hardly a bend or a sway in the little shaft, and the eye of the daylight followed the two dimly down the length of the passage.

They must have gone fifty yards when Garry paused.

His whisper came back to the young man: "Now's the time! There's a guard here, not far in front. Slow—slower than a snake, and softer, kid!"

He wormed his way forward, and the King Bird came close behind him.

A strong smell of cheap pipe tobacco greeted them. Then a glimmer of lantern light appeared before their eyes.

Garry, issuing from the narrow shaft into a room, raised himself slowly on his long arms, and then stood up with the King Bird behind him.

"He ain't here," said Garry. "Dog-gone me, but that's a funny thing, because there's always a guard here!"

They could see where the man had been posted. There was a half-tattered magazine on the floor, sprawling face down. There was a sack folded by way of a cushion on the rock which had served the sentinel as a chair, and the rank odor of his pipe lingered in the air. But he was not there!

It was a place where the miners either had found a great pocket of pay dirt, or else they had followed the traces of color in all directions for a considerable distance, for there was a very considerable room, rounded off on one side, and squared as though on purpose on another.

From one end of it, and turning at a sharp angle, the main shaft ascended gradually.

"I dunno that I like it," muttered Garry. "He might come back, though. We'd better wait a minute and grab him when he comes."

"We'll go on," insisted the young man. "If there's trouble ahead of us, the faster we get to it, the better for us"

Garry threw up his long arms until they touched the ceiling of that excavation.

92

"There ain't any other fool!" he groaned. "You're the only one, the biggest one in the world."

"Look," said the King Bird. "We're in luck. This is the lucky day, Garry, for the two of us, and nothing is going to happen to us. Go ahead. I'm right at your elbow if the trouble starts!"

"If you're as good with a gun as you are with your gab," said Garry, "maybe we *will* have some sort of luck."

And he led out up the main shaft.

It was an incline at only fifteen or twenty degrees, and it had been hewed out to such dimensions that they could walk easily through it side by side. There were timberings only here and there; the quality of the rock, in most places, was such that timberings were not needed to hold the tunnel.

It seemed to the young man, just as they started, that he could hear voices out of the pitchy blackness far ahead of him. But after that there was no sound except a distant music of trickling water.

So, through the total dark, they stepped on, the left hand of the King Bird constantly touching the gun arm of Garry —for very good reasons!

And then he heard the whisper of Garry before him: "Now we're there. We're goin' to step into the center of fireworks!"

CHAPTER XVI

BLOCKED IN

As Garry spoke, he was fumbling forward, and presently the slightest of creaking noises and a draft of fresh air announced that he had opened a door.

He whispered over his shoulder so softly that the King

Bird could hardly hear him: "There oughta be a lantern here—this is the place! There's *gotta* be a lantern here!"

He dropped on his hands and knees and went cautiously forward. Straight across a considerable expanse of rocky floor crept Garry, and then stood up with an exclamation.

"They're gone!" he gasped at the ear of the young man.

"Out of the mine?" murmured the King Bird.

"Yeah, it looks that way."

"Garry, if you're tricking me," said the King Bird, "I'll make you sweat for it!"

"There ain't a soul here. *He's* gone, too; and where would they be taking him, I wonder? Wait a minute. I know where a lantern oughta be!"

He found it against the wall, fumbled for an instant, and then scratched a match. It showed to the young man the eyes of Garry staring with pupils dilated by the darkness in which they had been straining. Then, as the flame ran across the wick and the lantern chimney was lowered, the King Bird saw by a steadier light the place where they were standing.

It was simply a crossing in the mine, the main shaft branching out in two side shafts, both big cuts, and this accidentally formed room had been enlarged here and there by picking out some softer sections of the rock. These fragments were piled in the cross drifts, and what remained was a chamber roughly rounded.

It was covered with litter. There were three or four roughly improvised stools, all but one overturned. A pair of blankets was tumbled on the floor. Near them was a pair of very small riding boots. A battered sombrero hung from a bit of rock that jagged out from the wall. A scattering of cards in a circle seemed to indicate an interrupted game at which several hands had been dealt. And in the very center of the floor lay a newspaper which rattled softly in the blowing of the draft.

The eye of the King Bird picked out a black-type headline which declared that the entire countryside was rising because of the kidnaping of the Kinney boy.

No doubt this was a living room for several people. Piles of cut pine boughs were scattered about the place, and on these the men must have slept.

"They've just moved out," said the King Bird. "We'd better move after 'em."

"Out the main mouth of the shaft?" exclaimed Garry. "I should say not! If they moved out this quick, it's because they guessed that you were comin'. And they'll be waitin' to salt us away. We might try the little side shaft, though, and if——"

The rest of that sentence was never uttered, for a heavy blast of air struck them in the face, the roar of an explosion almost deafened their ears, and all about them bits of loosened rock crashed down from the top of the shaft.

The King Bird was staggered; Garry fell flat, and the lantern in his hands cast one last flicker and then went out.

In that moment of darkness another blast sounded more distantly, far down in the interior of the mine. More rock fell, but far away from them.

The young man lighted a match and touched it to the wick of the lantern again.

He saw Garry groveling on the floor, his hands to his throat, his face convulsed.

"They've blocked us in! We're goin' to strangle to death in here! They've blowed the mouths of the two shafts, and we're goners!" screeched Garry. "I'm chokin' now—I'm done for! Oh, you've done for the two of us!"

"We may be done for," said the young man. "I suppose we are. But we'll work away till we're sure of it."

"Work at what?" cried Garry. "What's there to work at?"

The King Bird held up the lantern and shook it.

"What are you doin'? Are you crazy?" howled Garry.

"This lantern's nearly full," said the King Bird.

He turned down the wick until the light was only a glimmer.

"If we keep it low like this," he explained, "it will last us for a day, I suppose. Don't worry about the air. There's plenty of air to last us in here. We'll die of thirst before we choke. Garry, get up off your knees, and we'll tackle this job. I don't suppose that we can do much, but we *might* be able to pick a way out of this den."

Garry broke into a laughter more maniacal than his howling had been.

"Look!" he commanded. "You fool, take a look, and then tell us that we got a chance!"

He pointed to a mass of rock eight feet in height that filled almost the entire shaft immediately in front of the crossing where they stood.

"The whole mountain's dropped on us," cried Garry. "The whole mountain's between us and the light. Oh, if ever I get out, I'm goin' to do nothin' but work hard and live straight. I don't need no money for it. All I want is water to drink and bread to eat, and the feel of the sun!"

The King Bird considered him carefully.

"I never heard of an old mining shaft that didn't have a few shovels and picks lying around in it," he observed. "Know of any around here, Garry?"

"There's some in that drift there at the left," said Garry. "What good is picks and shovels?"

"Get 'em, will you?" asked the King Bird shortly.

They lay at the very mouth of the drift, and the tall man came shambling back with them at once to find that the King Bird was carefully turning in his hands that battered sombrero which had been hanging against the wall, and which the explosion had knocked to the floor at his feet.

"Goin' to find a way out in that hat?" asked Garry, half groaning and half sneering.

"This belongs to Helena Blair," said the young man. "Did you see her here?"

"I'm sick of you and all your questions!" yelled Garry, his face contorting in fury. "You got the drop, and you can shoot me. I don't care. We're goin' to die here, anyway. I don't care what happens to me. You got us in here. Now you can murder me before I'll answer your questions!"

He screamed out the words, and as he ended, the echo down one of the shafts repeated them.

Garry gasped. "What's that?" he whispered.

"Nothing," said the young man.

"I *heard* something," said Garry.

He leaped to the side of the King Bird, his face contorted with dread, his eyes green with frenzy.

"What if they were comin' for us?" he whined. "Oh, what if they was to come for us in here—and knock the light out as they came—and in the dark come reachin' for us?"

He gripped the young man with his other hand.

"You fool," said the King Bird, "it was the echo of your own voice down that shaft."

"You lie!" whispered Garry. "I heard something. I—— You lie! You wouldn't dare go down there!"

"Certainly I'll go," said the young man.

He picked up the lantern and entered the mouth of the shaft, but Garry was at him instantly.

"Come back!" he breathed. "Don't leave me, kid. Don't leave me alone in the dark. I'm goin' to go crazy! There's hands on my throat—I can't breathe!"

He tore open the neck of his shirt as he spoke. He was shuddering with every breath that he drew.

"You'll forget all this when you start working along with me," said the young man. "We're going to laugh at this when we get out of the mine, Garry. We're going to laugh at the way the fools thought that they'd trapped us. The small shaft down there is no good. One blast will choke that like a bullet lodged in the throat of a gun. But this one's different. They've cut it big enough for a team to drive through, and I'll bet my money that we'll work a way out. Come on. Come on, Garry, and stop the whining."

"You think there's a chance?" whispered Garry.

"Think? There's better than a chance!"

Garry looked up savagely.

"If ever I get out," said he, "I'll hound 'em one by one till I have their blood. One by one, I'm goin' to run 'em to the ground. I'll burn 'em alive, is what I'll do."

"Maybe you will," said the young man. Come along and we'll look things over."

He led the way, and they found that the great stone which had fallen in the shaft by no means completely blocked it. There was an ample passage to the side, and beyond this they passed up the incline, stepping over or around the rocks that had dropped from the top or the sides of the shaft, until at last they came to a great shelving mass of boulders, small rocks, rubble, and powdered stone almost as fine as sand that blocked the mouth of the tunnel securely.

"Ah," murmured Garry. "Just when I was hopin', you lead me into this here!"

"Here's where we start to work," said the young man. "That's all. You're not afraid of work, are you? Like this!"

He had his shirt off as he spoke, and, tying the sleeves across the neck of it, he formed a capacious sack which he instantly filled with rocks, shouldered, and started back down the shaft. Garry followed that example.

He fetched the two shovels and the pick that he had found, and with the shovels they filled in the fine stone, or scooped it back to a distance down the shaft.

They stopped talking. They merely worked, not in a rapid frenzy, but with a steady earnestness. Speed would not help them, really, but only a long and constant effort.

It was discouraging business. For they had to relay the débris down the shaft to give room for what was coming, and in doing that labor they were constantly hampered by the apparently inexhaustible downpouring of the sand and finer rubble. Long hours went by for them, and their backs were aching when, with the loose stuff finally cleared, their headway was stopped by an enormous mass of rock that fairly and completely filled the shaft from side to side.

When the full face of that disaster was known, Garry flung himself down on the ground and sobbed.

CHAPTER XVII

IN THE DARKNESS

THE KING BIRD stood with his arms folded, his feet spread a little apart, and his chin high. He stared at the enormous bulging face of the rock as though at the face of a human enemy that must not be given precedence.

Only after a long moment he looked down to the lantern, with whose light he had been scanning the huge stone, and noticed that the flame was sagging a trifle to the side.

Was it going out? That would be the final signal for their death.

They had been laboring for a full twelve hours, and the oil might well be consumed.

He picked up the lantern and moved it enough to hear the oil swish inside the tin. It was still nearly half full!

Why had the flame sagged?

He turned up the wick for an instant and replaced the lantern on the ground. Now unquestionably the flame from the wick flared up and sagged a little bit to the side. He put down his hand, and a faint but perceptible draft of air blew upon it!

With that he sprang to Garry and shook him by the shoulders.

"D'you hear? Garry, Garry! There's the air from the outside blowing around the rock. It's night out there, or we'd be seeing daylight through the cracks. There's nothing between us and the outside but this one stone!"

Garry, staggering to his feet, for a moment was lighted with hope; he was dark enough the next instant.

99

"One stone," he groaned. "Only one mountain, and one jump to take it in! Look for yourself! It's hard as granite. We couldn't cut through it in a week, even with dynamite. And if we can't drag it in or push it out, what *can* we do? We're corked in here! This here is the bottle that we're goin' to die in, I tell you!"

There was no doubt that everything he said was true.

There was no way of budging the stone. There was no way of cutting through it. The only possible way was around it.

The King Bird took up the pick and struck tentatively against the wall of the shaft at the right of the boulder, and the pick jumped back from the hard surface as though from adamant, and made the haft tingle in his hand with the sharp vibration.

There was no hope there.

He crossed with a step to the other side, and struck even more lightly. To his amazement, the point of the pick lodged.

He jerked it out, swung hard, and buried the point three or four inches in the solid stone. A great chunk broke out and fell at his feet.

He heard the gasp of the tall man. At his feet crouched Garry, snatching up the fragments as they fell, and hurling them back down the shaft.

Then Garry himself seized the pick, as the King Bird grew tired, and flung himself at the task with a maniacal energy.

At his third stroke the pick glanced down and tore a gash in the side of the lantern, rolling it over and over.

The King Bird snatched it up. Every drop of oil had run out of it, and they were left in deep darkness.

Then, what he knew would follow, burst on his ears— the long, hideous scream of Garry as the blackness, like the darkness of death, covered them. He tried to find the big fellow and give him some comfort; a driving blow in the dark sent him away and half stunned him.

The raving continued. He crouched in a corner, heartsick, until the voice fell away to a hoarse whining and whimpering. Moaning followed. It was like death indeed to be enclosed with such sounds.

But to do nothing was a worse way of dying than while making some effort, so the King Bird found the pick, took it up, and fumbling until he had located the proper place, he began picking at the rock with short, rapid strokes. Few strokes were random even in that confused work. The débris began to rattle about his feet. An hour he continued, and as his arms grew numb he carefully felt before him and measured the work that they had accomplished. It was half the reach of his arm.

He heard a snoring sound—it was the craven Garry, who had moaned himself to sleep! Dropping down on the rock floor, the King Bird lay with arms wide, trembling with weariness.

He waited until his muscles were steady. Then he rose and commenced picking at the rock again. His sense of touch had to be his light. But he began to know the dimensions of the cut from constant touching of it.

So he worked on through the long remainder of that night, and every moment of that time Garry slept peacefully, though many a rock chip must have rattled about him as he lay!

Then the dawn came. There seemed no relief from the darkness, at first, but as the sun brightened, thin fingers of light stole in about the rock and broke up the blackness. It was by no means equal to the radiance that the lantern had cast. But now, peering through a dull and murky twilight, he could make out the actual face of the cut at which he had been laboring. It was deep now. It meant squeezing the body into a narrow cleft a foot and a half wide and picking with short strokes at the face of the side wall of the shaft.

He gripped the shoulder of Garry with his hand.

"Wake up!" he commanded.

Garry sprang to his feet with a gasp.

"There's light enough for you to work by," said the young man. "Get in there and start with the pick again. We'll be out of this by noon!"

Garry, with an exclamation, advanced into the cut.

101

"*You* done all this?" he asked.

"I've done that," said the young man. "I'm resting now. Hammer away!"

He lay flat and listened to the chinking of the pick against the stone. It was slow going now, for the work had dulled the pick, which seemed out of temper when they began with it. But still the blows were causing the stone chips to fall with a rattle to the ground. And that sense of progress lulled the young man to sleep.

He could not tell how long he was asleep before a loud yell filled his ears.

It was Garry again, screeching: "The pick's gone through. We're out—we're as good as out! Come look at it!"

They were not out, but the pick had actually gone through the rock, and where it made the rent, a blinding eye of light looked back at them.

Garry, laughing, raving, seized the pick again and attacked the wall before him in a frenzy. Great chunks fell with a solid thudding, and the eye of light widened to a hand, to a great white moon, to a space through which Garry himself dragged his long body and stood capering and throwing up his arms, while the King Bird slipped out after him and surveyed the greenery with eyes that could not drink it in enough.

He could not avoid saying: "I suppose they're somewhere in the woods yonder, drawing a bead on you, Garry?"

The tall man doubled up and leaped sidewise, as though dodging a bullet.

Then he gasped: "None of your jokes, kid. You oughta be grateful to me. It was me that got through to daylight. It was my luck that done the trick, not yours!"

The King Bird looked up at him with a faint smile, and then up toward the sun, which was drawing halfway down the sky from the zenith. All that he saw was beautiful to him, even the ragged march of the pines up the mountainside to the timber line, and the bare gleam of the rocks above that sharply drawn line.

"Garry," said the King Bird, "we've been through something together. Will you do something for me?"

102

"Yeah? And what's that?" asked the other, his voice instantly sharp with suspicion.

"Tell me where you think they may have gone, and tell me why the girl's with 'em, will you?"

Garry squinted at him with evil eyes.

"You come and jump me when I ain't lookin', you drag me up here and put me out with my pals, you put me through a day and a half of hell—a year and a half is more what it feels like!—and then you want me to do favors to you, eh? Not a chance!"

The young man regarded him calmly, without wonder, for he knew so much about this man now that nothing he heard could surprise him greatly.

"Besides," said Garry, "I dunno where they'd be. They got brains behind 'em. They got the finest brains in the world behind that outfit. They might jump to any place. I dunno where they'd go!"

"I suppose that you're finished with 'em?" asked the young man. "You'll never dare to show 'em your face again?"

"Yeah, I'm cooked," growled Garry. "That's the luck that you brung *me!*" He glowered at the young man.

"You were going to have their blood, all of 'em," said the King Bird. "I seem to remember you saying something about that back in the shaft?"

"Yeah? Maybe I said it, and maybe I mean it," muttered Garry. "But I know where my bread's buttered, and you took it away from me! I'll be even with you one day, kid! I'll tell you that—I'll be even with you!"

"Perhaps you will," said the King Bird. "I'm sorry, in a way, that you're not back with 'em. You belong to that sort of an outfit, Garry. Take you by and large, you're the worst excuse for a man that I ever found in my life, the most sneaking cur that I've ever rubbed shoulders with."

"You forget that I've got a gun now, you fool!" said the other, half crouching, the evil in his nature working in his face.

"I don't forget," said the young man. "I'm half hoping that you'll draw it, Garry."

He waited. Garry stood straight.

"You can't help talkin' that way, kid," he said. "It's just that you're young and you don't understand. Anything more for you in this trail?"

"Why, I've lost the trail," said the young man. "That's pretty clear. I'm not through with it, but I'll have to find a new start. So long, Garry."

The latter, by way of adieu, shrugged his narrow shoulders, and with still hungry but frightened eyes, he watched the King Bird walk down the slope, his head still turned over his shoulder to keep on guard, and so disappear into the shadow of the trees.

Then Garry shook his fist heartily in the direction of the young man who had disappeared, and facing toward the head of the valley, strode down the mountain slope with great steps.

CHAPTER XVIII

STALKING

THE KING BIRD, from the shadows of the trees, paused long enough to mark the direction in which the other moved. Then he turned and ran straight down the ravine to the place where he had left the mare.

She was still there on the thicket, lying prone, her head high, and her eyes bright as the sound of his approach drew nearer. A gesture from him brought her to her feet, and there she staggered for a moment, cramped and numb from the unnatural length of time that she had been down. She would have trumpeted her joy, but another sign from him silenced her.

He gave himself one moment of luxury, stroking her,

then he turned up the valley again, with the mare walking at a stumble, then trotting behind him.

He found where the trickle of water that, in flood time had carved this valley, was spread into a narrow pool. There he drank, throwing himself flat. The mare drank also, plunging her muzzle in almost to the eye, then throwing up her head suddenly with a showering of water drops when she needed a new breath. And again she drank, and again.

He watched her with an eye of love. She was not the gray stallion, to be sure, but she was herself, and with his aid he would match her again against Dick Macey and the monstrous gray. Not for a single run, not for a single day even, but over some great sweep of mountain and desert where the brain of the rider could tell as well as the speed and stamina of the horse.

When she was sufficed he went on again up the valley.

It was the tall, gaunt form of Garry that he wished to follow, hoping against hope that it would lead him to some goal near Helena Blair. He had taken one prize with him from the mine, and that was her battered old sombrero.

She grew upon his mind as he ran. He was tired, and he would have been half sick with fatigue if he had not ruled this weakness sternly from his mind. She had been a friendly tomboy in his thoughts before this. Now she was something more—just what, he could hardly say, but he was only sure that he did not regret any of the effort that he had made for her so far.

As for Garry, to that man the ways of the gang were so dear that he was almost certain to seek for it in some of its haunts. He would risk their rage because he had been taken by the enemy. He would attempt his explanation of being forced on the trail with the King Bird, and no doubt that explanation would be honest enough to have weight.

At any rate, Garry was the one means that the King Bird had of getting in touch with his quarry, and therefore he struck out after the fellow.

There was no use trying to pick up either his trail or that of the other men who had been in the valley. For much of the surface was merely sheer rock that would not take the impression of the shod hoof of a horse, to say nothing of the footfall of a man. But Garry had headed toward the upper end of the ravine, and the moccasined feet of the young man sped steadily in that direction.

He gathered his strength, and found more and more of it ready to be drawn out.

The mare had enough to take care of herself in this head-long scramble through thickets and over steep rocks. But when they came to the valley's head, where the trickle of water disappeared and there was merely a broad sweep of rolling country studded with monstrous rocks, and shadowed here and there with low-growing jungles of trees, he mounted Molly and galloped straight on.

He was guessing again. Garry might have turned to one side or to the other, but the presumption was that he had struck out in a straight line for some goal when he turned up the valley toward its head.

Now he crossed the sign of horses, and, diverging a little, he followed them. Those hoofmarks had been made not very long before, and almost certainly they were from the horses of Garry's associates.

Carefully the young man scanned the ground, and found, at last, what he had half expected—the big, truly rounded marks of the shoes of the gray stallion.

Dick Macey was among the rest, then. And Brick would be with them, too.

For what earthly purpose could she have come to them? How had they persuaded her? Why, above all, was she worth so much money to them?

These questions roused him to a cold frenzy.

Finally he found his quarry striding before him over the hills—a narrow form that loomed against the sky and then disappeared, half a foot at a time, as it stepped down the farther side of a slope.

That was Garry, moving with the surety of one who has before him a very definite goal.

The King Bird laughed, and his laughter made no noise.

Mischief was in him, and more mischief than one man would be able to digest. It was not his custom and his rule to be thwarted as he had been on this trail, and a hot vengeance was gathering in him and burning against the moment when he could expend it.

He dismounted and waved Molly back.

Two or three times he turned to check her, until at last she knew her distance and followed on cautiously behind him.

It was not the first time that she had played that game, and she knew and loved it almost as well as her master. She could spot the moving form that he was stalking. There is no animal in the world that cannot understand stalking, and well she knew that she and her master were expected to keep out of sight of the tall, gaunt form of Garry as he stepped boldly forward, with rarely a look behind him!

So she trotted confidently down the hollows, but when she came to a hilltop she went slowly, and looked over the top of it as any wild Indian might have done when, on a dangerous trail, in the near presence of an enemy.

And there was always the master before her; he whose mere gesture could carry a whole volume of pre-digested meaning.

To Molly it was a game that had been played before, and therefore it was known, and she played her part in it to the letter!

They were coming down now into what had once been rather closely inhabited range country. Twice the King Bird saw the relics of old ranch houses perched on hillsides, or in hollows sheltered from the force of the cold north winds.

Now it was apparent that Garry was not at all sure of himself. He went with a certain hesitation, and looked with a good deal of care on either side now and again, though fortunately he hardly ever gave a glance to his rear.

So it was that the King Bird was fairly close up when a man rode straight out before Garry and pointed a rifle at his head.

Garry flung up his long arms with a startled exclamation, and the King Bird, sinking behind a rock, looked back and saw the head of the mare rising from a hollow.

He made her the sign to lie down. Twice he made it, rapidly, and she melted instantly from sight.

Then he could give his attention to what was happening before him, and it was worth hearing. The voices were raised loudly enough for him to hear nearly every word that was spoken.

The man on horseback with the leveled rifle had now, as the King Bird could spy from around the corner of his boulder, dropped the gun to the ready, though he still kept the muzzle of it directed at Garry.

He was one of those lean and withered men that one meets on the range, this rider, and he wore the old fashion of saber-shaped mustache, sweeping down in sad and formidable lines on either side of his mouth.

He was saying, in a deep, booming voice: "What sort of a crooked game are you playin' now, Garry? What's your aim to come spyin' up the line after us, you low hound?"

"I ain't a low hound," said Garry earnestly. "Lookit, Jake! What could I do when he took me by surprise and pulled down on me? He'd 'a' killed me. He ain't got no more sense."

"I ain't got no more sense than to kill you now," said Jake, "and I'm goin' to do it. There ain't nothin' I hate like a traitor."

There was a yell from Garry.

"Lookit, Jake," he howled. "I been through hell—I been as good as dead. You fellers went and buried me alive with him. What had I done, I'd like to know?"

"You showed him the place where we was hid away," said Jake grimly.

"I had to. What else was I goin' to do?"

"There ain't anything else for me to do than put a bullet through your rotten brain, brother!" said Jake. "And that's what I'm goin' to do. All the boys feel the same way."

He actually raised the butt of the rifle to his shoulder as he spoke.

Garry fell on his knees.

"Jake," he yelled, "Jake, old friend, listen to me—lemme have a chance to tell the boys. I didn't mean them no harm.

He made me walk ahead of him with a gun in the small of my back. I didn't show him nothing about the old mine. He guessed about that. He drove me ahead of him with a gun. Don't kill me, partner. Lemme tell the boys. Lemme talk to them. If they wanta kill me after they know what's what, I won't say a word. I'll just stand up and take it."

"I kind of wanta kill you, and I kind of oughta, too," said Jake. "Dog-gone me, I oughta kill you just to stop your yappin'. What you comin' this way for? To show the King Bird the way to us?"

Garry leaped from his knees to his feet, and bounded into the air as though a bullet had driven through him.

"King Bird?" he yelled. "Is that runt the King Bird?"

"Hey, didn't you know that?" asked Jake.

"He told me!" cried Garry. "Dog-gone me, if he didn't tell me. But that didn't make me believe him. I thought that the King Bird was a lot bigger."

"Didn't you see the mare, you fool?" demanded Jake, scowling more blackly than ever.

"I seen the mare, too," said the tall man, "but the fact is that I didn't think the King Bird could be so small, or ride such a small hoss, neither. The mare looked mighty small to me."

"Too bad about you," snarled Jake. "Why, I never seen such a fool as you! I dunno but what I'll let you go back and face the rest of 'em, and let you tell 'em what you've been and done. They'll be a pile interested. How'd you get out of the mine, anyway?"

"I dug a way out," said the tall man. "The King Bird, he was so scared that he wasn't much use, but I took and dug a way out of the mine. I was pretty near wore out when I cut around the boulder that fell in the mouth of the shaft, and at last I slammed that pick through into the thin air. It was a fine feelin' to see the sun, Jake!"

Jake nodded.

"The King Bird showed up yella in the dark, did he?" he asked, grinning with brutal gratification at the thought.

"Yeah, he done that," said the tall fellow. "Plain yella.

109

Just a dirty dog, after the blasts went off and we were choked in there."

"You go on along and march ahead of me. I'm goin' to let the boys pass on you. Where's the King Bird? Where'd he go?"

"He had enough of the game," said Garry. "He cut straight down for the mouth of the ravine, him and his mare."

CHAPTER XIX

THE GUARDED HOUSE

THE KING BIRD watched them move down the valley, Garry in the lead, and turning his head now and then to talk with many gestures to Jake, who followed with his rifle ready for action. From a distance the King Bird followed, and he was content, as a wolf is content when it has followed the trail for days and at last sees the elk staggering and bogged down in deep snow.

So the young man, as he watched, laughed to himself.

They led him straight toward a house not two miles down the valley, an old, broken-backed building with the wreckage of a large barn behind it. The King Bird, from the comfortable shelter of a thicket up the hill, lay prone, his chin in his hands, and through the fringes of the grass, and through the outer branches of the brush, he surveyed the place with lazy contentment.

Behind him he could hear the mare grazing, tearing the grass off short with a sound like the ripping of tough cloth. She was very contented there. So was the young man to have her near. But ahead in the corral was a sight that troubled his heart. It was the gray horse, standing near the bars and

110

looking straight toward the thicket in which Molly was sheltered.

Garry and Jake had entered the house; there was nothing to take the attention of the King Bird except the big horse, and he studied it like a book. There was not a line of the gray without meaning. Even its expression and carriage were necessary to the picture, for otherwise it would have seemed too heavy. Heavy the animal was, but all was perfect harmony about it.

Again and again the young man swept the stallion with a critical glance, and found nothing to complain of. A little whirlpool of dust and leaves came toward the horse, and out of sheer excess of spirits it chose to take alarm. One bound placed the gray on the farther side of the corral, with tail arched out and silver mane fluttering, while it pricked its ears at the dissolving little cyclone. If ever dumb beast had laughed, the stallion was laughing at that moment. And the young man who watched it laughed also.

It might be—might it not—that Dick Macey would not own that horse forever.

And with such a pair as Molly and the gray he could fly among the hawks, above this silly little world, turning mountains into mole-hills.

That was in the mind of the King Bird as he stared down at the corral and the horse in it.

He heard a faint babbling of voices in the house. Then out the side door, toward him, came five men.

The first was Dick Macey—the King Bird knew him well, and would ever know him, for he had studied the lines of the half-breed's head and shoulders too thoroughly during the long pursuit by moonlight. That was not the same as seeing the face, however, with the sun directly upon it. It was a flat mask of a face. Although he was half Indian, the skin was a deadly, leprous white. The man seemed to have no nose. It was simply mouth and eyes in a flat, white imitation of a face.

With Macey came Jake and Garry, and the two whom the King Bird had seen with Garry in the valley.

It was plain that Garry had made his peace with the rest

111

of them. He was laughing and talking and gesticulating vigorously; and now it was plain that he was indicating how he had hammered with the pick at the wall of stone. The others whooped with pleasure, and while they laughed, Garry stepped inside the house and came out again, carrying bread in one hand and a great chunk of cold meat in the other.

The eyes of the young man who had watched grew dim with hunger. For many hours he had not broken bread, and hunger was a torment in him. He had to pull up his belt and set his teeth in order to endure the pain of that sight.

He hated Garry with a childish intensity and blindness of hatred as he watched the man feeding with great, wolfish bites. He, the King Bird, could devour whole roasted oxen, and a dozen ovens could hardly furnish forth enough brown-crusted loaves of bread to satiate his appetite.

He licked his lips and sighed as he continued to stare. Then he forgot his hunger, for through the doorway ran Helena Blair, carrying a bucket. She stepped along with her usual swing to the pump near the side porch, and filled the bucket rapidly. He could hear distinctly the sound of the pump as she drove the handle up and down. Macey offered to help her, but she dismissed him with a sway of her head that plainly told him to go about his business.

This pleased the young man greatly, and he could hardly have said why.

What had induced her to join this gang, and to stay with it?

It seemed to him that he would willingly give a year of life to have five minutes of explanation from her.

Now back she went to the house, holding the heavy bucket of water steadily, balancing herself by keeping her left arm straight out from the shoulder. He saw the sun's intolerably bright image drop into the bucket and float on the surface like a bit of oil; and as she went up the steps, lightly enough, a bit of the water splashed out and left dark spots on the wood.

Jake followed her to the door and leaned against the jamb of it, his arms folded and his boots crossed. His long mustache could be seen quivering with speech.

It seemed to the watcher that all of these fellows, except Garry, were a likely lot of villains. Garry was villainous enough to attempt anything; he simply lacked the essential force to put his evil desires into effect. But the rest appeared a hardy crew. They had the look of murder about them; the indefinable taint of savagery was as clearly visible from the distance as if the young man had stood shoulder to shoulder with them.

And yet with these scoundrels Helena Blair was associated! She must have gone willingly. At least, that had been the tone of her letter home. And still she could remain here among the hills, working for them. Was she their cook? No, they would never saddle themselves with the incubus of a woman for the sake of her cookery. Besides, Brick was a better cowhand than a cook.

The King Bird shook his head as he considered these things, and at last he cast the problem away from him. There was nothing that he could do to solve it so long as the sun was shining. There was nothing he could do to fill his starving body, either. So he retreated deeper into the grass, closed his eyes, and instantly was sound asleep.

He did not need a friend to waken him at the right time, for the cool of the night wind sent a shudder through his body, and he roused himself to find that the sun was down, the sunset flare ending, and from the house below him one light was shining in the side room.

More than that, the smell of cookery drifted up to him on the gently moving wind, and he groaned softly.

The black mare stole nearer and sniffed at his cheek when she heard this sound of complaint, and in amusement and affection he put his arm around her neck.

Then he stood up and stretched himself. It was nearly the time to go to work, but not quite. For in front of the house, and, again, to the rear of it, men were walking up and down, up and down!

He understood that his problem was increased in difficulty a thousandfold by their presence. And he was a little surprised by these precautions. It was not usual for such outlaws to work with such deliberate care. More was trusted to chance, as a rule, but this group believed in throwing away no chances.

The form of the guns the sentinels carried interested him no less. For they were equipped with sawed-off shotguns; big, double-barreled riot guns that were ideal for the night work that lay ahead of them.

The King Bird began to shake his head.

For the problem, on the whole, seemed absurd. Even if he got into the house, how would he be able to persuade the girl to come away with him? And if he persuaded her, how could he possibly managed to escape with her?

Yet he was not unhappy. Neither weariness, nor hunger, nor the depressing chill of the approaching evening could subdue his spirits. For down there in the hollow was the adventure waiting. He sat on his heels, and, staring out through the brush, he smiled, and even chuckled softly, considering what was to be done.

The last light of the sunset ended. The wind of the night increased. And the stars became bright, and then were made dimmer by the rising of the moon, before he determined on what he was to do.

Then he stood up, paused a moment to pat the head of the mare, where she lay warm in the grass, and went on rapidly down the back of the hill.

CHAPTER XX

TRAPPED

THE MOON was well up as he came through the brush, and, at the edge of it, dropped to one knee and considered the house before him. It was a broad, yellow moon, knocked a good bit out of shape, for the time was past the full, and it sent a dim and smoky light over the tops of the trees and upon the ruined ranch house. It made the form of the sentinel who paced nearest to him seem larger than human, and sent a huge shadow sprawling and crawling after him.

Another man stepped from the front door of the house. It was Garry, who yawned and stretched his lengthy arms above his head.

"Hullo, Jake," said he.

"You're late, you tramp," said Jake. "Why can't you wake up on time, eh?"

"I was back diggin' in the mine in my dreams," said the tall man. "What a rotten night I had. Gimme the gun. There ain't any sense in standin' watch like this, anyway. Nobody could find the place up here."

"You keep the wool out of your brain," advised Jake. "You take a business like this and nobody's ever safe, so far as I can make it out. Not with a King Bird hangin' on the trail."

"He's quit," said Garry. "I tell you, he's got enough."

"He was makin' a fool of you when he said that," answered Jake. "He just wanted you to move on, and him behind you! That's all. Likely he's out there in the brush, waitin' for a chance to jump you and run a knife through you."

Garry grabbed the riot gun and shook it with a strong grasp.

"Here's a friend that'll stand watch with me," said Garry.

"Sure, it's a friend," said Jake. "But the King Bird, he'd rise out of the ground at your feet and slam you for keeps. You keep your eyes open and your finger on the trigger."

He went into the house, and big Garry, for a time, stared helplessly about him. Then, holding the gun carefully, he began to stalk up and down with the air of one who expects tigers to spring on him at any moment.

The King Bird waited for that overtense anxiety to diminish somewhat. And presently Garry had paused to roll a cigarette, holding the riot gun in the loose crook of his arm.

It would have been a simple matter to jump him at that instant, but the King Bird, instead, chose to slide past the

115

sentinel's line of march and then crouch again close to the window of the front room of the house.

He could not manage the door—that was too fully in the view of Garry. And when he tried the window with his hand, it resisted strongly his upward pressure. But at the second or third attempt he forced it up a trifle. He had to keep rising and dropping down again in his efforts, as the sentinel walked back and forth with a measured tread. And finally he had the window open and was ready to attempt the entrance.

By this time he had peered through the window into the interior long enough to see that there was no one sleeping in the room. It was a small place, the front door of the house opening upon it, and also this single window; no other. Another door communicated with the inner part of the house.

In fact, he could not have asked for a better point of vantage at which to make his entrance.

He waited now until the tall form of Garry and the stalking shadow beside him had moved back out of view as Garry made his next round. Then into the window went the King Bird, and was halfway across the sill when there was a faint creaking above him, a whirring sound, and the window slammed down on him, catching him across the small of the back.

He could not have been in a more ridiculous, or dangerous, or helpless position. The window, which had been loose enough to drop, had jammed to the side in falling, and resisted his efforts to raise it.

A voice said abruptly in the next room: "Hey, who's there? That you, Garry?"

He did not answer this.

He began to sweat, and not with the heat of the night. But finally he managed to work up the window bit by bit. In his haste, he allowed it to creak again.

"Is that you, Garry, you fool?" demanded the voice from the next room. "If I gotta get up and find you sneakin' around, you ain't goin' to never forget it."

Then the blaring voice of Garry himself, raised to a screech with fear and excitement, shouted out: "Who's there? Who's there?"

The King Bird jerked himself violently over the window sill, regardless of the noise he made. At the same time, Garry was shrieking:

"Look out, inside! Look out! He's climbin' through, and——"

One barrel of the riot gun roared out, and a charge of heavy buckshot smashed the window glass to bits, and filled the air about the young man with hurtling death.

Before him, on the inner threshold, another form loomed, cried out at the sight of him, and slammed the door.

He heard the bolt as it went home, and he turned with a spring for the outer door.

It was locked, also. Locked from the outside, and the key, perhaps, left there.

Fortune and bad luck had trapped him thoroughly and unexpectedly. There remained the window through which he had climbed for a sudden exit, but that was fairly hopeless. No man can make a fast exit through a narrow window, and while he was clambering through he would be blown to bits by the guns of the others.

He looked desperately about him. The inner door *must* give him a chance at escape, so he sprang to it, and the instant his hand fell on the knob and shook it, a bullet drilled through the door panel beside his head.

He stepped to the side as another shot came hurling through.

Some one took a shot at the front door just for luck, and the bullet, cutting through, nicked the side of his leg.

He dropped to the floor and tried to think.

The whole house was filled with bustle. Outside and inside, voices were calling out, and footfalls were sounding.

He had not dreamed that so many people were here. And in the meantime, he would have to be lucky enough to get out of the place before he should have the privilege of fighting his way through the enemy.

The ceiling he could not reach. He tore up a board from the floor and stepped through upon the hard ground just beneath.

He was totally at a loss now. Stealing to the window, he looked out and spied nothing at all. They were out there, but they had disappeared from view. Other voices grew up about the house; he heard the hoofbeats of horses—and he was sure that they were retreating. Perhaps every man of the lot had trekked away from the house by this time, and yet he could not believe that they would go off so readily and leave him unharmed after he had hounded them so far.

His answer came instantly, and pat upon his thought.

A voice spoke from the next room, saying: "King, look out the window."

CHAPTER XXI

THE CELLAR

HE OBEYED, and with the sheen of the moonlight working upon her like the gleam of watered silk, he saw Molly standing at the edge of the brush, secured on a long lead.

A groan broke from the lips of the King Bird, and the man in the next room heard it.

He answered with laughter.

"You see how you're cornered, King?" he asked.

The King Bird could not help answering: "It looks as though my back's against the wall, partner."

"I'm no partner of yours," said the voice of the stranger. "Know me?"

"No. I don't recognize your voice," said the young man.

"It's too bad, then," said the man in the next room, "that

118

you'll never have a chance to see me. Unless you take the offer that I make to you."

"What's the offer?" asked the King Bird.

"That you unstrap your guns and come out the front door of the shack backward, with your arms up over your head."

"I don't think I'll do that."

"I don't want you to, very much," said the other. "It's not pleasant thinking, even—what we'd do once we got our hands on you! But I'm making the offer, and making it for the last time. Understand?"

"I understand."

"Only, boy," said the voice beyond the door, lowering, "while you're dying, as you'll be pretty soon, I want you to know another thing."

"Fire away," said the King Bird. "Whatever else happens, your *talk* won't be the death of me."

"Why," said the man behind the door, "I'm one who knows all about you. Everything!"

"Do you?"

"Yes."

"I doubt that, stranger."

"Shall I name your father?"

"Never mind that!" exclaimed the King Bird.

"I can show you that I know," said the man behind the door. "And just to sweeten up the end for you, I can tell you that you're wrong about your father. He's not the sort of a devil that you think. He's a hard man, but he's fair and straight. He'd be glad to see you back with him. He'd give you a new sort of break in life."

"*Now* he might." The King Bird sneered.

"Aye, he'll have no chance," said the stranger. "I'm the one that gets the chance at you."

There was controlled laughter behind the door.

"And the best of it is," said the voice, "that you don't know who I am, and that if you met me on the street, you couldn't blame me at all."

The laughter sounded again.

Then: "Good-bye, King. This is the finish for you."

And finally: "Sorry to be rough!"

Then came the shout, at a distance: "Ready! Let it go!"

What were they to let go?

The King Bird knew in another moment, when he smelled the faint odor of wood smoke and heard, after an instant, a light and busy crackling sound which was, he knew, the noise which the wind makes among dead leaves, or flame in dry wood!

The instant he heard the fire, he felt certain that he was indeed gone, and then a flood of hysteria came sweeping over him. He wanted to scream out something—that he would accept the offer to surrender, that he wanted a chance to say good-by—to Molly, the mare! Then there were messages which he could beg to send—last statements—speeches—anything to put off, for an instant, the blast of red fire that would be the end of him.

And yet he mastered himself, because he knew that to cry out and implore, now, would be merely to win their laughter! Bitterly he understood it, and dropping again to one knee, he cast wildly about in his mind.

Whatever hope there might be, there was none for him in this room.

He went to the inner door and shattered the lock with a bullet. He pushed the door open, hearing a shout many times repeated that answered his gunshot outside the house.

The next room was a long affair with the wreck of a big table in the center. It had been the dining room in the habitable days of that house. Now it was faintly lighted by a shaft of moonlight that sank into it from two windows on the side, and by a red gleam and dance of flame from the room beyond.

He stood in that doorway. It was the kitchen, and the fire had been started in two corners of it.

At one side, the flames were already tapping their fingers against the ceiling. On the other side, they had chosen to spread out, and were eating a good-sized hole through the boards of the wall. Once through, and the wind giving a draft to help, the whole house would soon be afire!

There was no way to go from this kitchen except down

into the cellar, whose door opened at the side of the kitchen floor.

He jerked back the narrow panel and looked down.

It was a shallow, small place. There was sufficient fire to show its utmost limits to him. Across the top of it ran the beams that supported the floor of the house; the bottom and the walls were simply earth, and parts of the side walls had fallen in. There was no sign of what it had been used for, except as a tool shed, perhaps. For there was the head of a sledge hammer, and a broken pitchfork, and a shovel with part of the handle adhering to it.

The sight of the shovel gave him an idea which contained some hope.

He was up the stone steps of the cellar in a flash, and wrenched the cellar door and kitchen door off their hinges. These he carried down, and leaning them against the cellar wall, they formed a narrow lean-to that would afford shelter to one human body.

On these doors, placed side by side, he began frantically shoveling the loose earth that lay on the floor of the cellar. Feverishly he worked and heaped the moist soil completely over one of the open ends, and well up on the side, until it reached the top. And still he shoveled frantically.

Earth will not burn, at least, and unless the heat was great enough to stifle him, he might be able to endure the bitter moment until the flimsy house had burned over his head, and the red coals were at last cooling.

As he plied the shovel, he heard the fire roaring like a storm above him, and a fiercer and a redder light fell upon him.

With a great groaning, the kitchen roof parted. Half of it fell, and a shower of burning wood dropped into the cellar. That was what drove him, finally, into his place of last resort, even before he was really ready to get into it. Inside it, he worked on with the shovel, eagerly, but with small strokes, heaping up the earth which he had previously shoveled opposite the open end. He had to work with the shovel inside to dig out more soil, until he finally managed to heap up the wall to the top.

121

Now he lay flat, and waited.

The waiting was the worst of all.

Fresh uproar began, and then continued steadily, and as the big timbers of the building fell, he knew that the climax was coming for him.

The heat was not great, at first, as he lay on the moist ground, with the protection above him, but when the fire had thoroughly baked the ground that was heaped on top of the doors, then the rank smell of the heated wood choked him, and the heat above him was so great that he seemed to be breathing fire.

He reached up and found the doors hot, and growing hotter.

He had to lie flat on his face, and part his lips, and hold them close to the ground, which alone remained cool.

Every moment he told himself that the end had come and that he would not be able to endure another moment for the lack of fresh oxygen.

Hysteria almost mastered him a dozen times, and it was then that he remembered having heard of the Hindu fakirs who permit themselves to be buried alive, and remain in the ground for more than a day. They, to be sure, were able to manage with little or no air admitted. He thought of them, and of the iron resolution which enables them to endure the test, without going mad.

So would he endure, and not allow imagination to add to his trouble.

And that trouble was great, and growing greater. He heard the fall of the timbers. Certainly if a considerable portion of them fell into the cellar and burned there, they would turn it into an oven, and he could endure only a few moments. But luck was favoring him in that respect, at least. Then he heard more distant sounds than the crackling of the breaking rafters.

They were firing off guns. He could swear that he heard the bullets strike among the flaming ruins of the place. And, more than this, he could hear the loud yelling, the repeated cheers.

What manner of men were they, when they cheered the burning of a man alive?

Or did they imagine that the gunshot which shattered the lock of a door had been through his own brain, forestalling the death by fire?

That yelling continued, and while it lasted, he found that he hardly felt the terrible torment of the heat.

But afterward, it began again, until the end of a falling timber butted straight through his flimsy partition, and a cloud of smoke and the red blast of the furnace were let in against his face!

He kicked out the last wall that he had filled in. Before him and above him was only the remnant of the bonfire; the majority of the damage had been done, and there was the narrow flight of the cellar steps.

He was up them, running like a scorched cat, with the flames leaping at him, and biting him like red snakes.

Out he darted into the open, before one of those terrible, impalpable heads could wholly fasten upon him. The pain forced him to throw himself on the ground, where he rolled, waiting for the barking of the guns that would kill him more mercifully.

But no guns sounded!

They were waiting for him to rise, so that they might howl with laughter for an instant at his antics, and then load him with bullets!

No, when he leaped to his feet, not a rifle or revolver sounded. He reached the line of the brush, and there, dropping to his knee, gasping, wondering when the fire would leave his burning lungs, he made sure that the enemy had actually passed on!

That was what the discharge of guns and the yellings had meant, no doubt. They simply had waited until the flames raked the house fore and aft, and then they had cheered, and departed.

What was the girl thinking, he wondered, while these things went on? What were her reactions to the burning of an old friend alive?

123

He pondered this grimly, and then stood up. They were not very far away, and now they had on their trail one who might do more to them than they had hoped the flames would do to him!

In the vastness of his anger, his mind grew calm and cool, and with clear-eyed reflection he considered them all—considered the girl, even, and took the sombrero which he had carried twisted like a rag around his belt, and shook it out before his eyes, and laughed a little.

It had been something like a flag—and something of a joke, too—that battered old sombrero. He looked at it now, threw it on the ground, and kicked it from him.

But when he started walking, he picked it up again, and tied it to his belt.

A man could do various things with it—soak it in oil, and light it, and hold it like a torch under the chin of one of those fellows who had tried to cremate him. That was one pleasant possibility that occurred to him.

There were other things that could be done.

But before he attempted much of anything, he must have food.

He had gone too long without a meal. His weakness was not entirely the effect of the great heat that had baked him and the nerve shocks that he had sustained; more than all else, there was the vitiating effect of a three-day fast.

Yet he stuck to the trail at an easy trot. He could not afford to lose time, he could not risk missing their trail.

He ran on for an hour, with an occasional stagger. Their sign was clear before him. They were making no effort at speed, and at the end of the hour, he saw two riders straggling to the rear, and one of these was the long, gaunt form of Garry, foolishly perched on that trim little beauty, Molly!

The King Bird looked with red-stained eyes.

But he would not seek revenge on Garry particularly—they were all due for killing, they were all worthy to die by the fire they had condemned him to. He would not cherish any special hatreds, not even for Garry, whom he had seen through the long peril of the mine. Garry would go down with the rest, when the chosen time came!

He began to breathe more easily. He forgot his weakness, and the hunger pains that were beginning to work in his stomach.

So he followed that trail patiently all the rest of the night, sometimes working on with his head down, half sick, half giddy, but always persisting steadily.

He saw the sun rise. It seemed to push suddenly up above the horizon and stare at him, angrily. Then, through the woods, he saw that the gang was heading in an easy detour around a small village.

CHAPTER XXII

THE DEPUTY

THE KING BIRD surrendered to the demands of that weaker creature, his inner man. He left the trail of the party, and went straight into the town.

It was one of those wretched little mountain places which grow for a time, and then sink back into despair, as it were, and sometimes revive, and, sometimes fall into nothingness.

A single street curved in a crooked arc around the base of a mountain. Down that mountainside tumbled a creek that cut straight across the town, and was spanned by a narrow bridge that was once strong enough to hold up a whole freighting outfit, but that now shook and groaned treacherously under a single horseman.

Two thirds of the houses were broken-down and vacant, and the others had an air of approaching ruin. Yet the little place had had an ambition, one day, and still there was a stone arch across the road with a legend on the face of it which read:

"Watch us grow. Elmira, the queen of the Rockies!"

"Elmira, the queen of the Rockies," had not grown very long. And yet there was no reason why it should not. There was plenty of cultivable soil in the valley, and there might have been twenty times as many ranch houses as ever had been stretched down the length of it. But a whim of fancy or a freak of bad times is enough to discourage an entire community. The calamities of a banking crisis may all be attributed by a farming community to the bad condition of the land.

Some such unlucky state of mind had come over the people of the Elmira Valley. They had pulled up stakes and left good grass, good water, and plenty of fertile ground. Another wave of settlers would one day find it, a branch railroad line would be built to it, and it would become a permanently established member of the group of mountain towns.

It was not hard for the King Bird to envisage all of these changes, but in the meantime, he would have been glad if it had been even a tenth of its present size, so long as he was able to find a place to buy cooked food.

He found it in what was left of the Elmira Hotel. One wing of that building had fallen in, and had mostly been used as firewood. The other wing was resting on uncertain knees, and to the dining room one approached over a veranda whose boards sagged with sad noises underfoot.

There was no waiter. There was only, at this time of day, the cook. And the cook was now sitting on the veranda, peeling potatoes. Elmira breakfasted at an early hour, and the cook did not propose to get up and hobble about on his wooden leg to prepare a meal for a single guest.

He said, in answer to the inquiry: "Sure, this is the hotel, and this here is the dinin' room. You're late for breakfast, and you're mighty early for lunch, if you was to ask me! Whatcha wanta eat?"

The King Bird considered.

"An old rind of a yellow cheese would be a fine thing for me," he said. "And a couple of crusts of moldy bread would be about the best thing I ever saw, and then a fine glass of sour milk would finish off a good meal for me."

The cook laughed.

"That's what you *would* eat, eh?" said he.

"Yes. That's what I'd eat. I hope you're not all out of those things?"

"I asked you what you *wanta* eat?" said the cook.

He rolled himself in his chair a little, and poised his peeling knife in a fat hand.

The King Bird was willing to gratify this expectancy.

"Why," he said, "I wouldn't mind starting with the ribs of a steer, barbecued brown—and they wouldn't have to be so barbecued, either, as a matter of fact."

"Just the ribs of *one* steer?" The cook grinned.

"Yes. And a few loin steaks left on the ribs for a decoration. Then I could follow on with a dozen eggs."

"Nice fresh eggs, eh?"

"They don't have to be so fresh, either," said the young man. "I wouldn't quarrel with any sort of an egg, myself!"

The cook laughed again.

"What else?" he asked.

"You could follow up the eggs," said the King Bird, "with forty or fifty nice thick flapjacks, the kind that mother used to make, and a couple of quarts of maple sirup to trim them up. And after that, I'd take on just one turkey. Just one nice, big, fat turkey. Just one forty-pound turkey, with the stuffing and the cranberry sauce, and all that. And I'd need no more than a gallon or two of coffee, and perhaps along toward the finish I might ease off on three or four deep-dish apple pies. Or pumpkin pies, for that matter. I'm not particular."

"You're kind of holler, kid, are you?" asked the cook.

"Hollow?" said the King Bird. "If you dropped a stone into my mouth, you'd have to listen for thirty seconds before it hit bottom."

The cook rose, grinning.

"All right, son," said he. "You come back into the dining room, and I'll warm up that stove and see what it can do for you."

"I'll go as far as I can pay," said the King Bird.

"Pay?" said the cook. "It ain't a question of payin' when there's a hungry man around. Thank Heaven, we're far enough West for that! You come back and lay into a chair, and I'll do some cookin'. It's a long time since I cooked any for a gent that really needed food!"

He led the way, stumping with his wooden leg over the doorsill, and back through the shadows of the long, dreary dining room. Thin, stale odors of old cookery hung in the air, and to the King Bird seemed delightful fragrances.

"Two eggs and five strips of bacon and a chunk of bread will be about my measure, partner, and a couple of cups of coffee," he said.

The cook whirled around on his wooden stump, a turn so rapid that he almost lost his balance.

"Hey, are you a false alarm?" he demanded.

"Look," said the young man. "I haven't eaten much for two or three days."

The other whistled.

"Then you've got to go slow. You don't look weak, though."

"I haven't had time to ask myself whether I'm weak or not," answered the King Bird.

He sat at a table, and presently he heard the hissing of the bacon in the frying pan, and the odor of coffee stole out from the kitchen to enchant him. A drowsy contentment came over him.

Somewhere in the world there was a place where men did nothing but sleep and eat, and that was the place that he wished to find!

A man came into the doorway, a fellow of somewhat less than average size, with blond hair that had a golden gleam to it, and a thin, handsome face.

He paused mid-stride, with his hand still on the edge of the door, then turned swiftly about and left the place. He went with his head a trifle down, taking great steps.

"Does he know me?" asked the King Bird of himself.

He hardly cared. He could forget now that he was the King Bird, with a price on his head. There was nothing this side of eternity that mattered very much to him except the scent of the food that was being cooked in the kitchen.

The cook called out: "Hey, come and get it, kid!"

He went in to find a great tray heaped with food. There was more than the original order. There was a big dish of stewed fruit, and a vast wedge of gingerbread, and other delicacies.

"There ain't much trimmings left in the pantry now," said the cook, "but you go in and start on this!"

The young man returned with his cargo to the dining room, and ate, not hurriedly, but slowly, with small bites, masticating everything thoroughly, though it seemed to him that there was no pleasure left, except that of bolting everything whole.

He knew what grim effects that sort of a procedure might have, however. Leisurely he worked at the eggs and bacon and the bread, and sipped the strong coffee, and vast comfort, and strength, and the need of sleep invaded him.

The screen door was pushed open, and closed with a jangle, and the clank and rattle of spurs came back toward him.

A big man with his right sleeve rolled up over a brawny forearm laid a fist on the table, and in the fist was a .45-caliber Colt, with a shop-made and a home-worn look about it.

"Stick your hands up, King Bird," said he. "You're mine!"

"Wait'll I finish this chuck," said the King Bird. "Then I'll throw my hands up."

"You fool," said the other. "I'm a deputy sheriff. And I've got you. I mean business. Hoist your hands!"

"Go chase yourself," said the King Bird. "I'm hungry."

"Are you crazy?" asked the other.

"Wait'll I finish breakfast," said the young man, "and you can take me to jail, fast enough, but what makes you drunk enough to think that I'm the King Bird?"

CHAPTER XXIII

OUTWITTED LAWMAN

THE GUN quivered in the powerful hand of the deputy sheriff. "I like to hear you talk, boy," said he. "But if you don't hoist your hands——"

"Oh, quit it," said the King Bird with irritation. "If I'm the King Bird, go ahead and take the flock of guns off me, while I finish eating. You can't spoil my appetite."

"I can with one slug out of this gun, kid, and you're sure goin' to get it!"

"I'd as soon die as be so hungry," said the young man. "What's the matter with you, anyway? Didn't you ever see the King Bird?"

"I'm seeing him now!"

"Not half of him." The outlaw chuckled. "Would the King Bird let any mug of a sheriff walk up on him like this? Say, what's the brand of redeye that they serve out around here? Sit down, brother, and tell me all about it, but don't make a fool of yourself and talk about the King Bird!"

"It's a good bluff," said the other. "I don't mind saying that. I'm going to count to three and then——"

"Hold on," said the young man. "Now I *see!* Oh, the low hound. Now I see the whole thing."

He put back his head and chuckled, then laughed outright.

"You see what?" asked the deputy sheriff.

"I see where you picked up the good news about the King Bird being in town!"

"Go on with your little song and dance for a minute," said the other. "But I'm watchin' your hands all the while, kid!"

"Go ahead and watch 'em!" remarked the King Bird. "I'll tell you who gave you the good news. Fellow with yellow hair, sort of sleek and shining, and a thin face—rather handsome, eh?"

"What of it?" asked the deputy sheriff.

The King Bird made a sandwich, using the last of the crisped bacon. Slowly he munched the first large mouthful until he was able to speak.

"Think of that bird crooking me like *that!*" said he. "Is he still around town?"

"I dunno. I suppose so."

"No, he's gone on through," said the young man, "and all that he does is to leave word with you that you're to look out for the King Bird, and then he describes me. Is that it?"

"He told me that you're in here, and he's right. I don't need no description of the King Bird. I been readin' them for four years!"

"Descriptions that said I was his size?" asked the King Bird, frowning.

"Yeah, just about."

"Why, I've seen him," said the young man. "He's three inches taller."

"Yeah?"

"About that. Heavier, too. Why, how could I be the King Bird, I'd like to know?"

"I dunno, but you are. You're cool, too. You're cool enough to be the King Bird."

"I'd be the King Bird to that sneak of a low-down hound," said the young man. "I've been following him clear across the mountains, till my broncho broke down, up the valley."

He added: "Wait a minute!"

"I'm waiting, and I'm watching, too, son," said the deputy sheriff.

"Keep on waiting and watching, then, but tell me this: Doesn't the King Bird always travel with his black mare, Molly?"

The deputy blinked. It was plain that this detail hit him hard.

"Well, maybe he does," said he. "But the mare might be cached outside of the town, somewhere."

"You mean that me—as the King Bird—me—I'd walk into a town like this, and sit down in broad daylight, and order up a meal, and sit right here, and eat it?" asked the young man.

"The King Bird has all the nerve in the world. He might do that," declared the deputy sheriff.

The King Bird laughed. "That's pretty good," said he. "That's rich, in fact. I never heard anything richer. Why, the whole country's looking for him, since he dodged the marshal! Would he be fool enough to act like this?"

"Any man that can beat Jim Hampton three times is bright enough to do all kinds of things," argued the deputy, rather vaguely.

"All right," said the King Bird suddenly. "I'm the King Bird, am I?"

"You sure are!"

"Then search me!" said the young man.

He threw out his hands.

"Come along and search me, and find the guns," he demanded. "Go on and do it! If I'm the King Bird, I'm traveling heeled, I suppose? Now, you come and find the guns!"

The deputy drew in a breath.

"Ain't you got any guns on you, kid?" he asked.

"I did have," said the young man. "You'll find a broken Colt back there under a bluff. That used to be a good gun. I was going to use that, pumping lead into that sneak with the blond hair and the thin face—the one that told you about the King Bird being in here!"

He laughed again.

"I wouldn't mind a rest in jail for a few days," he said. "I can't catch him while I'm on foot, and I haven't enough money to buy a decent horse, here in town."

"What's his name?" asked the deputy, giving up most of his hope.

"I don't know."

"You don't know?"

"No. Blondy is all I know for him. And he's a blond beauty when it comes to dealing poker hands that are framed. He trimmed me. I had a roll that was worth handling, before I met that crook."

"Did you?"

"He cleaned me out. I've got chicken feed left, and not much else. But I'll get him, some day. I've got him scared already. Think of him telling you that I'm the King Bird! He's scared enough to want to get me off his trail!"

The deputy sheriff nodded.

"He's kind of excited, all right. He was all out of breath when he found me!" He added: "What *is* your name, kid?"

"Why, I'm the King Bird," the young man said, and laughed.

The deputy sheriff laughed in turn, and, putting up his gun, he slid down in his chair a little, and made himself comfortable.

"Well," he said, "I thought for a minute that I was going to be either dead or famous, to-day. That's the luck of it. You don't have no luck, when you're living in a place like this, away off at the end of nowhere."

He shrugged his shoulders.

"For a minute," he said, "I kind of thought that you was the King Bird, all right. But I guess I was crazy. I can see that you ain't his size. You got the color, though—the hair and the eyes."

"What would the King Bird say if he knew I was arrested for him?" The young man chuckled. "But look here, if you want a job, what about going out and picking up that hound of a Blondy?"

"What charge?" asked the deputy, frowning.

"Crooked cards!"

"Crooked cards?" said the deputy. "That don't get you nowhere, brother. The judge and the jury, they always get to laughing. You can't do nothing when you pinch a gambler. I've seen it tried, a lot of times. They're always too slick, and the evidence ain't ever worth nothing. There's only one way to deal with 'em."

"What's that?"

133

"Deal with a gun, when you catch a crook at the table!"

"You mean, start shooting?"

"That's the trick."

"I tried it," said the King Bird, "but he was out the door before I had my gun ready."

The deputy chuckled.

"You're not one of these lightning artists on the draw, eh?" said he.

He rose.

"I'm not lightning. Not quite," said the King Bird.

"Well, good-by," said the deputy. "I wouldn't mind handling that thug for pulling my leg this way, at that! The King Bird! He seemed all heated up. He was panting, I tell you. Dog-gone him, he certainly had me fooled!"

"So long," said the King Bird. "Better luck next time. But I wouldn't wait for the King Bird to throw up his hand, as you did. I'd kill him first, and ask him the questions later on."

"*You'd* 'a' been out of luck if I'd done that," said the deputy sheriff.

"Yes, I'd have been out of luck," said the King Bird. "So long."

He watched the other stride from the place, open the door, hesitate for a moment, and then with a shrug of his big shoulders go slowly down the street to the right.

The King Bird made himself a cigarette, and smoked it as he sipped his second cup of coffee.

He was beginning to feel foolish, between sleepiness and happiness. And as he smoked, he pondered the way before him.

How far off were the men who carried with them the girl—and black Molly?

His mind would not stay on the thought of Brick. She might have protested against the butchery of her old friend. Her voice might have been raised, no matter how vainly. But there had not been a sound from her!

The fellow with the blond hair, he surmised, might be he whose voice had laughed at him through the door; he who had offered him life if he would back out of the house with

134

his arms stretched high above his head. If so, he was the controlling spirit. And he knew a great deal. He had said he could name the father of the King Bird!

All sleep, and all happiness, left the body of the young man. His brain cleared. And now he began to remember, more clearly, what his weary eyes had seen through the trees, when the riders turned, and began their detour around the town. Two of those horses had empty saddles, and bore between them what looked like a litter made with a pair of long saplings, and a blanketed form lay in the center of the litter.

He had been dim-eyed, dim-witted, when he saw the procession, or he would have taken keener heed of the details. Perhaps that litter contained the heart of the entire mystery.

He went into the kitchen.

"What's the bill, doctor?" he asked.

"Fifty cents," said the cook, who was slicing potatoes, and standing at the sink.

He did not turn his head.

"Here's a dollar, and thanks," said the King Bird.

"The fifty cents is all I want," said the cook.

"Give the other fifty cents to the first tramp that comes along. Give it in the same sort of a meal," said the young man, surprised.

"No," said the cook, still without turning. "I don't handle that kind of money."

"Hello!" exclaimed the young man, amazed.

The cook gradually turned. His round, fat face was dark —darker even than its growth of beard warranted.

"What sort of money?" asked the King Bird.

"Crooked money," said the cook.

"Oh, you heard the deputy talking, in there?"

"I heard you make a fool of him," said the cook.

The King Bird was silent, and the other went on:

"I wouldn't break in and tell him what kind of a fool he was. I ain't the sort that would wanta cause the hangin' of any man. But I don't want none of your money. And I don't want none of you, you gun-handlin' crook. Murderer is what

135

you are, and all your kind. Get out of this here kitchen, and stay out. I'd be walkin' on two legs, if it wasn't for one like you!"

"I'm sorry, doctor," said the King Bird slowly. "I'm *mighty* sorry. You won't be shaking hands either, I suppose?"

"No," said the cook. "I'd rather be hanged myself than shake hands with one of your kind. But I'll wish you luck. Dog-gone me, I dunno why, but I'll wish you good luck to keep your worthless neck safe!"

CHAPTER XXIV

AT THE FORD

HE BOUGHT a bay mustang gelding for seventy-five dollars. It was not a pretty horse, and had a lump of a head and a slightly roached back, and the gait of a draft horse. But it had a stretching gallop, and a long, rolling canter, and it had all the signs of a horse that can "stay." That was what he wanted.

He got a cheap saddle, and an old bridle, and rode straightway out of the town.

Off to the left he cut from Elmira, and keeping the mustang to a round pace all the time, he came to the rolling country beyond, the foothills which flowed like green waves across the feet of the mountains.

There he struck sign that seemed to him indubitably that of the party he wanted, and presently, sure enough, he made out the big, rounded imprints that could hardly belong to any horse other than the gray stallion. He kept to the same rate of going, therefore, and pressed on, his eyes sharpened as he glanced into the thickets, or examined the rocks that rose in nests on either hand.

136

They must have halted when the blond fellow with the thin face rode into Elmira, on whatever errand. Naturally they had been in no haste—when they were confident that he had been burned in the old ranch house. And now word must have been brought out to them—and not very long before his coming, at that.

Well, their speed would be that of the slowest member of the party. Perhaps their speed would be that of the horse litter! And in that case, he would surely find them—unless they found him first, with a bullet through the brain!

And if a cold and steady hatred was working in him, he could well imagine the frenzy of astonishment and of rage that must be in the others.

He followed the sign down the side of a steep-banked creek. It was by no means fordable in any place that he came to, and he had an idea that when it was passable, the whole troop might cross to the farther side. A very small rear guard would there hold him back, while the others swept away and established a good lead.

He was prepared for that, and following the clear trail through the grass, when something moved in the grove across the creek, and he covered the spot with a revolver instantly. He had his two guns, still. A lucky thing that the deputy sheriff had not called his bluff and searched him for his weapons.

As he whipped out the gun, the clear voice of Helena Blair cried out:

"Don't shoot, King! It's I!"

She came riding her own pinto pony through the grove, and into the open.

Such a shock of pleasure ran through him that he forgot all about his former fears and doubts of her good faith.

She waved her hand to him and rode down to the edge of the creek bank.

"Hello, Brick," he called to her. "Great Scott, this is good! Where's the ford? I'll be with you in a minute."

"Listen to me, King," called the girl in answer. "If you come over, you're not to try to take me away with you."

"I'm not what?"

"You're not to try to take me. I want to talk to you and explain things. You've got to give me your word you won't force me to go back with you now."

He ground his teeth.

"Brick, are you crazy?" he yelled back at her.

"You promise?" she asked him. "Otherwise, I've got to cut away through the woods, and clear out. Will you promise?"

He groaned.

"I'll promise!" he answered.

"You stay on that side," she said. "I'll come over to you."

She rode down the bank, and he followed her until, fifty yards from the start, the bank suddenly sloped away at an easy angle, and she ran the pinto down the sweep of it, and up the farther side to meet him.

He dropped from his horse and shook hands with her as she came up and swung down to the ground like an agile cow-puncher.

She looked a little thinner. There were distinct shadows about her eyes. But she was not very greatly changed. It seemed to him that a year had passed for him, since he last saw her; but for her, it had been only a few moments.

She glanced back over her shoulder, exclaiming. Let's get to cover, King. You've been riding along in the open so that anybody with half an eye could pick you off. D'you think that they're not ready to kill you any way they can?"

"Not after last night," said he.

He followed her behind a big rock shoulder that heaved above the ground.

And there she caught his hands again and looked eagerly up into his face, and then stepped back, and surveyed him.

"King, you've been through the mill. You look like it!"

He glanced down at himself.

He had been sufficiently ragged to attract wonder and pity even in the town of Elmira. Whether in the mine or in the burning house, his clothes had been torn and singed until they were mere rags, hanging about him.

"I've been through the mill," he admitted.

"And your face, King!" she exclaimed. "You look ten years older. And you're thin."

"*You're* fit enough," he answered her. "Things don't seem to have borne down very hard on you."

She winced.

"We're not to talk about me, much," she said. "It's you, and what you have to do, King."

"What have I to do?"

"Leave this trail."

"Is that all?"

"Yes. Not quite all. The mare will be returned to you. They'll send the mare back, and leave her where you can find her."

"Thanks," said he.

"You see how it is, King?" said she. "They'll do what they can to get you off the trail. They don't want any more trouble with you. You know, they could post men along the way, and nine chances out of ten pick you off."

"They might try that," he said.

"You'll take their offer then?" she pleaded.

"I can't," said he.

"Why can't you?"

"That would be breaking a promise."

"Promise? What promise?"

"That I'd bring you home. I told your father and mother that I would."

She caught her breath.

"Was it terrible for them? Were you there?" she asked.

"Yes, I was there. It was terrible, all right."

"Will you let me explain?" she asked.

"That would be in order," said he.

"I had to come," she answered. "It was a chance to make some money, and we had to have it at home."

"Just turning an honest penny, eh?" said he.

"I didn't know who they were or what they were like, or what the work would be, really," said she. "I only knew that there was a sick person, and that I would have to go in secret. I could guess by that, that it was not exactly inside the law. I didn't know everything."

139

"Didn't you?"

"No. Are you doubting me, King?"

"No, go ahead. What are you? The doctor for that gang?"

"Yes. Not for the gang, for the sick—you know, don't you?"

"Who's sick?"

"Yes. You know who it is, don't you? That's the chief reason that you're following, isn't it?"

He shook his head. "I saw the litter this morning for the first time. I don't know who it is. I'm following because of you," he told her.

She shook her head violently. "That's no good, King," said she. "I'm terribly sorry—I can't go back with you, though. I wouldn't go. It would be deserting him."

"It's a man of course, that's sick? You're pretty devoted to him?" asked the King Bird.

"He's the most wonderful——" she began.

His face pinched, as she stopped short.

"The most wonderful crook in the world, eh?" said he.

"He's not a crook!" exclaimed the girl.

"No? Just *happens* to be traveling with that gang of murderers?"

"Why, he's the most innocent——" she began. Then she stopped again, and exclaimed hurriedly: "But I can't tell you a word more than you know already. I've sworn that I won't. That's the only reason that they would let me come back to you, King! They're a pretty savage lot, and they're going mad because you've stuck to the trail so long."

"I'm sorry about that," said he. "I'd like to see 'em all, and tell 'em how sorry I am about it!"

She sighed, still, as always, studying his face.

"You're killing yourself, King," she told him. "You're simply killing yourself."

"Don't bother about me," said the young man. "If I had a grain of sense and resolution in me, I'd take you now, and tie you to your horse, and drag you all the way back home to Valencia. But I'm fool enough to stick to my word. Only —Brick, what's your excuse for breaking the heart of your mother? Your father's smashed by this, too. But your moth-

140

er's not strong. She's not made to hold up against your little tricks, you know!"

He took a savage pleasure in seeing her wince.

"If I could only explain!" she breathed.

"Yes, if you only could!" He sneered. "The wonderful fellow, the innocent fellow in that litter, I suppose that he's not part of the explanation? How much d'you love him, Brick?"

"I *do* love him," said the girl. "Only——"

"You love him," said the King Bird, and turned white. "I might have guessed anything else, but I didn't think that you'd lose your head about—I mean, not as quickly as that."

"But don't you understand?" she cried. "He's only——"

"Only an innocent, eh?" said the King Bird. "What is it? A bullet wound, or several of 'em?"

"It's a bullet wound, but——"

"Quit it, Brick," said he. "You make me a little sick. I've been thinking a lot about you, on this trail. Now I know why you didn't make any fuss back there when they started to burn me out. It was because you didn't care. You wanted me off the trail and out of the way—even if it was burning alive for me. Was that it?"

At that, she started off from him, and stared. "What do you mean by that, King?" she asked. "What do you mean by burning you out—burning you alive?"

"Just that," he told her. "That's what I mean. Are you saying that you don't know that they had me back there in the old wreck of a ranch house?"

"They had you there long enough for the rest of us to get away again," said the girl. "But burning—what do you mean by that?"

"Look!" said he.

He indicated his singed clothes. Half of an eyebrow was gone and represented by a red blister; his eyelashes were white at the tips, and most of them were gone, also. Some of his hair had shriveled.

"When the house started burning, they held me in it with their guns. I got down into the little hole in the ground that served as a cellar, and heaped earth over a pair of doors,

141

and lay there in the dugout, stifling, while the worst of the fire burned over. It was a narrow thing in the end, for me—after the timbers broke down my shelter. But somehow or another I managed to get out."

He looked narrowly at her.

"You didn't know that they'd burned me out?"

"No," said the girl.

"You didn't see the smoke and the flames?"

"We were deep in the woods. King, what are you thinking about? That I'd stand and watch such a thing without losing my wits?"

"It's all right, Brick," said he. "You don't have to lie to me. I can stand it, I suppose. But I thought that you and I were hand in glove. I thought we were partners. But I can imagine how it is, after you've lost your heart to a man; old friendships disappear then. They don't matter at all!"

"Lost my heart? To what man?"

Suddenly she threw her hands up against her face.

"I'm going mad, King!" she cried. "I could put you right in three words. He's only—— But I can't say it. I've sworn not to say it!"

"He's only a jailbird—an outlaw, perhaps, like me?" said the King Bird. "Well, it doesn't matter. We've had our chat. You can go back to 'em, and I'll give you a half-hour start. That's a fair chance, I guess? And then I'm coming after you. You understand? It won't be a matter of parleying and talking then. I'll take you if I have to tie you like a calf, and I'll carry you back to your father and mother. That's what I promised to do. And after that, you can run away again as fast as you please. I'll wash my hands of the business."

His lips were a little stiff with scorn and disgust, and there was a cold agony in him, too, unlike anything that he ever had known before.

She was shaking her head and looking at him with a mournful despair.

"Everything's all tangled up. There's nothing that I can do to put it straight," said the girl. "You won't even believe me. Not if I swear, and cross my heart to die. But if you

142

keep on the trail, you'll do a terrible wrong! You'll be the cause of a death, King, that'll wring your heart. And if he dies," she broke out, in a higher tone, "I'll never forgive you! Never, never!"

"We'd better say so long," remarked the King Bird grimly.

"I can't," said the girl. "My brain's spinning. I've got to say something to stop you. I can't let you ride on this trail. It's murder. That's what it is! They'll kill him. The poor——"

She beat her hands together.

"King," she screamed, "will you trust me, and believe in me?"

"No," he answered. "Not a word that you'd say to me. I wouldn't trust you because I couldn't. You've fallen in love with your wounded hero. That's all right. You're going to lay down your life for him, if you have to. That's all right, too. I don't mind that. Only I'm going to live up to the job that I've taken. I'm going to take you back home with me, Brick. Now go on back to 'em."

He added savagely: "I couldn't know how much I used to think of you except by the way that I despise you now, Brick. Go on, and get back to 'em. And tell 'em that they haven't been able to bury me alive or burn me out, and the next chance will be *my* chance—and Heaven help 'em!"

He ground his teeth as he spoke, and the girl, turning suddenly away, flung herself into the saddle on the pinto, and rode off slowly. Her head was down. Her shoulders heaved. He could not be sure whether she were laughing to herself, or sobbing.

Laughing seemed the more probable answer.

"Women," said the King Bird to himself. "Women, they're no good. They're no good at all. They're sneaks!"

He saw her cross the creek, and watched her horse fade into the brush, and as she disappeared, a rifle shot rang from the covert, and a bullet touched the tip of his ear with a wasp sting.

A sort of madness came over the King Bird, as he ducked back behind the rock.

Even his old companion, even Brick, could stoop to such a point, and act as a decoy for a gang of crafty murderers,

143

who had no shame in their make-up. There was no honor in her, then—no honesty, no faith!

He was sick at heart; and then all the fury in him burned up. But he had given his word that he would allow her a half-hour start, and to that word he would cling.

CHAPTER XXV

JAMES KINNEY

THAT HALF-HOUR start that he allowed her cost him the loss of the trail. Of course the others had been forging steadily ahead all of the time that she held up his pursuit. And when he followed the sign through the grassy lowlands, through the thickets, he came in a single mile to a barren, rocky region where almost all sign disappeared. Every quarter of a mile, a new ravine opened its mouth among the hills. He took a central point, and for three days he lived on toasted rabbit meat, and cut for sign, widening and widening his circle.

Then he gave it up—not permanently, but because he saw that they might be a hundred miles away from him, by this time. It was better to retire, and then try to make a fresh start, rather than muddle away all summer on the old lines.

So he went back to Elmira, a short distance from the place where he had started riding in circles, day by day. His mustang was worn out. Its shoes were in rags of metal. It limped in three legs; and he had to walk all that journey back. A settled rage was in him; a settled frown was on his forehead. It was the question of the girl that ceaselessly tormented him, and, above all, whether she had been laughing or weeping, when she rode away from him, three days before.

Just out of Elmira, where the creek's currents were stilled in a big pool, he stopped to drink, and the quiet water showed him his face clearly. It was a picture that startled him, for the old King Bird had disappeared, and this was one with a new head, and ragged feathers.

His face was overgrown with a ragged brown beard; his eyes were sunk deeply; the frown resided continually between his brows, and even the masking beard could not hide the sense of lines which were worked into his face.

Yes, he looked older, ten years older. Even the caustic tongue of Brick could no longer call him a "pretty boy."

He was bitterly glad of that, and he walked into Elmira in the evening of that day with a perfect confidence that he would not be known even to an enemy as old and familiar with him as Jim Hampton.

Before he was a block down the street, the deputy sheriff went by on a mustang, leading a pack mule, and halted after two looks at the young man.

"Hey, hullo!" said he.

"Hello," said the King Bird, halting. "How's things?"

"Pretty good," said the deputy. "We got some new men in town, partner. There's one of 'em who'll be glad to see the King Bird!"

He laughed loudly, as he used the name, and he added, at once: "Funny thing that I ever could 'a' taken you to be the King Bird. I *wanted* to think so. That was all."

"That was the way of it," agreed the young man. "Know anybody around here with a couple of good horses to sell?"

"Try Milligan, down at the end of town. He's got some pretty good mustangs. They ain't much to see, but they're real mountain hosses."

"Who's in town that wants to see the King Bird?" asked the young man.

"By name of Kinney," said the deputy.

"Kinney?"

"Yeah. Him that had his son kidnaped. He's got an idea that the crooks are up around here, somewheres."

"Has he?"

"Yeah. I guess he's wrong, but that's his idea. He says

145

that this here is a perfect lay for crooks—a real hole-in-the-wall country, and he's kind of right, at that."

"If he really wants his son back, he can pay the cash," said the young man.

"Sure he can, but he ain't that kind. I think he'd hire the King Bird to go on the trail, though."

"You think he would?"

"Yeah. He likely would. Why else would he be wanting to see him? He's advertised in a coupla papers. Wants to see the King Bird real bad!"

"I might as well go and apply for the job," said the young man. "You took me for the King Bird. Maybe he'll hire me for the same reason?"

The deputy chuckled.

"Yeah, and maybe he wouldn't," said he. "I dunno. He's down at the hotel, I guess. Go try your luck."

Still laughing, he rode on up the street, and the King Bird walked slowly on, leading his tired horse. He himself was not tired. He had performed enough in the past five or six days to exhaust a corporal's squad, but yet even the very surface of his strength had not been rubbed away. He had grown lean and battle-worn, but the great well of nervous energy inside him had not been even tapped as yet.

In the twilight, he paused beside the veranda of the hotel, and saw a man walking slowly up and down, the boards squeaking a little under his feet.

"Is there a Mr. Kinney around here?" he asked.

The other stopped pacing and came to the edge of the veranda.

"I'm Kinney," said he.

He was a formidable-looking man, more than middle size, with a great, leonine head on his broad shoulders.

The King Bird looked him over with an intense interest.

"D'you want me?" snapped Kinney.

"You want *me,* I hear," said the young man.

"Who are you?"

"The 'King Bird,' some people call me."

The other jumped down from the edge of the veranda. As he came close, he said:

146

"You're too small to be the King Bird, my friend."

"I'm the King Bird," said the young man.

"You're too small, and too young, in spite of the hair on your face."

"All right," said the young man. "You don't want me, then?"

"I want some sort of proof," said Kinney. "I can't afford to talk to every Tom, Dick, or Harry, who pretends to be what he isn't."

"What sort of proof do you want?"

"A sight of that famous black mare would be enough."

"She's gone—for the time," said the King Bird.

"I thought she would be," said Kinney dryly. "What other sort of proof can you offer, my young friend?"

"What sort of a proof do you want—outside of the mare?"

"The King Bird has a gun that doesn't miss its mark, very often."

"This is a bad light for shooting."

"Yes, but not impossible."

"No, not impossible. Got a silver coin?"

"Want me to cross your palm?" asked Kinney, more dryly than ever.

"It won't be worth much, after I'm through with it," said the young man. "Chuck it up into the air."

"There it is," said Kinney.

He spun a fifty-cent piece high in the air. The King Bird fired from a gun that dropped out of the air, as it were, and appeared in his hand. The twinkle of the silver coin disappeared at the height of its rise.

"Is that enough?" asked the young man.

Two or three men came to the door of the hotel and looked up and down the street, curious as to the shooting. They saw nothing to catch the eye and turned back again.

"That's not enough," said Kinney.

"What else do you want?"

"I don't know. I wonder if I should take a chance? That was a very pretty shot, after all."

"Wait a minute," said the young man. "I'll give you something else. I'll give you my word that I'm the King Bird."

147

"Ought that go very far with me?" asked Kinney.

"I keep my word clean," said the young man.

"And so does the King Bird?" asked Kinney.

"He's supposed to," answered the other.

"Is he? Yes, and I think that I've heard that, too."

"What do you want of me?" asked the young man.

"Come inside, to my room."

"I'll stay out here. Inside rooms are not good for my health. Not even up here in a mountain town."

"Why not?"

"There's a price on me."

"I forgot that, for the moment."

"What do you want with me?"

"I want a piece of work from you."

"What sort?"

"I suppose you know that my son has been stolen?"

"I've heard that."

"You've heard that the robbers want a hundred thousand dollars from me?"

"Yes, I've heard that, too."

"I would pay a good many thousand to any extraneous agency that could bring the boy back to me. What would your price be for attempting the job?"

"I don't know. Depends on what I had to do."

"What would you want for a down payment?"

"Nothing, because I'd collect after I did the work."

Kinney chuckled. "I begin to think that you're the King Bird, without a bit of doubt," said he. "I believe that he has somewhat this air."

"If I go after the boy," said the King Bird, "I may scare them into doing him harm."

"Something has to be done," said Kinney.

"Why not pay them the money?"

"Pay blackmail?"

"Pay the price on your boy's head."

"Never while I'm in my right mind."

"Why not? You're rich."

"Because I won't gratify the cowardly scoundrels! I won't pay out honest money to thieves."

148

"You'd pay me, and I'm an outlaw."

"What are you trying to do, man?" asked Kinney. "Badger me?"

"I'm trying to find out how your mind works, and that's all, because this is the second son that you've lost. You let the first one go without even lifting a hand to get him back."

"That's not true," said Kinney. "I offered a reward that's still standing."

"You blocked him from home," said the King Bird. "He knew that he couldn't come back without making a dog of himself."

"What?" exclaimed Kinney.

"Without apologizing to you," said the King Bird. "He wouldn't do that!"

"How do you know that?" asked Kinney, starting.

"I knew Jimmy Kinney," said the King Bird. "I knew him well. He's told me everything that passed between you and him."

"The devil he did!" muttered Kinney. "My friend, this is a very strange story. Do you know what became of him?"

"He's alive," said the King Bird. "He's alive and well. And he's farther than ever from coming back to you."

"Alive? Thank Heaven!" murmured Kinney. "Young man, if you could get word to him that the necessity for any apology is gone—if he'll return——"

"That's not the only thing," said the King Bird. "There'd be the same story all over again. You've got to be the tyrant. Everybody in your family has to jump when you snap the whip, and Jimmy won't stand it. You've seen the last of him, I think."

Kinney drew in an angry breath.

Then he said, in a hard voice: "You speak freely. Very well, we drop the question of Jimmy—for the present. We speak about the other boy."

"Does he mean more to you?"

"We've talked enough about me," snapped Kinney. "We'll be strictly businesslike in the rest of this affair. I want to know if you'll undertake the search?"

149

"I have another job on my hands," said the King Bird. "It's a trailing job, too, and I've been beaten at it, so far. When I finish that, I'll take on the other. I'm sorry for the poor little cross-eyed youngster."

"Who told you that—— No, but the descriptions don't say that of him," said Kinney. "That's been remedied by operation. How did you know that his eyes were crossed at one time?"

"Jimmy used to tell me about him."

"He did?" Kinney sighed.

"He did," said the King Bird.

"He was jealous of my second son?" asked Kinney.

"Jealous? No, he thought a lot of the youngster. In fact, he still does."

"I thought——" exclaimed Kinney, and then checked himself.

"You thought that was why he moved out, eh?" asked the King Bird. "You're wrong."

"My friend," said Kinney, "will you tell me what Jimmy is doing now?"

"He's on my side of the fence."

"Outlawed?"

"Yes."

"But under another name?"

"Yes."

Kinney turned away and walked several paces back and forth. The dusk was thickening.

"God be kind to him!" he muttered at last. Then, in a different voice:

"But there has to be one master in every household."

"Why do there have to be any masters at all?" asked the King Bird.

"That's exactly as Jimmy would speak," said Kinney angrily. "Let him go, for the minute. We're speaking of my second boy. You say that you have another trail that you're following. Will you drop that and take up this one?"

"Until I get news of the first trail, I might try my hand."

"Good! I think that you might do something. I don't know why I feel confidence in you."

"Thanks," said the King Bird shortly. "Can you give me anything to work on?"

"I'm reasonably sure that they're near this place," said Kinney. "They sent me orders to come here with the money."

"Did you bring it?"

"Yes."

"The whole thing?"

"Yes, and more."

The King Bird whistled.

"A neat little pile of money to be in Elmira," said he.

"Now, then," said the older man, "I'm reasonably sure, also, that since I've arrived, I'll receive word as to how I'm to pay the money—where I'm to leave it—something like that."

"Perhaps," agreed the King Bird.

"If I get such a word, I could let you know about it, and you might work with me."

"That's true."

"If they attempt to get to my room in the hotel, you might be watching that."

"I could."

"And if I can get my boy back, safe and sound, and bring some of them to justice, I'll spend more than the sum they ask. You understand?"

"Tell me why you brought the coin—when you'd made up your mind not to pay blackmail?"

"I brought it to try my own strength of mind. If I weaken, I have the money ready at hand."

"Good!" said the King Bird. "I like that idea. Chilled steel is as soft as mud, compared with you, Mr. Kinney. I'll take your job!"

CHAPTER XXVI

THE KIDNAPER

MR. KINNEY, when he left the King Bird, went straight into the hotel and had his supper, which consisted of boiled mutton, with boiled carrots and nondescript greens, which he ate with vinegar. He drank two sips out of the big mug of steaming coffee, and went up to his room.

There he prepared for bed, and when he was in pajamas, he took out a good-sized leather book that contained a "fill" of fine linen paper—his diary for that year. He was a man who never had had a confidant in his life—neither his first nor his second wife, nor either of his sons ever having stepped past the lock-steel gates of his privacy. He preferred to put his intimate thoughts on paper, with ink, and now he spent a full hour, writing rapidly, in a fine, somewhat cramped hand.

It was not a pleasant task, this writing, to judge by the pain in his face, but he forced himself to it. Never speaking his true thoughts freely in any other way, he always compelled himself to face the mark honestly, when he came to his diary at the end of the day.

He finished this work for the evening, blotted the last of the several pages which he had written, and then closed the book and returned it to its place in his luggage.

After that, he was about to go to bed, and was actually leaning over the lamp on the center table, to blow it out, when something stirred, with a whispering sound, at his window, and he turned quickly toward it.

What he saw was a fellow whose hat was pushed back from his forehead, and whose hair was gleaming yellow, his face thin, his nose like an eagle's beak. A gun hung from his hand, as he stepped aside from the window into the room.

"Hello, Chester," said Kinney. "Has everything else failed you? Have you taken to banditry, at last?"

"Not quite so loud," said Jack Chester.

"I've no reason to keep my voice down," said Kinney.

The intruder tilted up the gun that was in his hand.

"Here's the reason," said he. "If you keep on bawling out your opinions, as you usually do, I'll split your wishbone for you, Mr. Kinney. I don't know—perhaps it would be worth as much as the ransom to me, to see you down and kicking your last."

"Jack Chester," said Kinney, "I've every reason for thinking that you could be as good as your word. I'll talk quietly. What's brought you here, you rascal?"

"The fact that I'm a rascal brought me here," said Chester.

"You speak about ransom. What do you mean by that?"

"I mean the brat," said Chester. "I mean *your* brat. Is that clear enough for you?"

"That's clear enough," agreed Kinney. "I'm to suppose that you stole my lad from me?"

"You can suppose that," said Chester.

And he smiled, undauntedly facing the scorn and disgust that appeared in the face of Kinney.

Kinney nodded.

"You have the boy then?" he said.

"That's the idea," said Chester.

"A pretty business!" said Kinney.

"It *is* a business," said Chester. "That's the whole point. Back East, I've never had a chance at a proper stage. The cities are too crowded together. There are too many police. Out here, there's space for a man. I thought that I might as well come West and take a look around me at things. That was when I first called on you, cousin."

"Don't call me by that name," urged Kinney. "It may be that there's a faint strain of the same blood in us, but I don't want to be reminded of it."

"I saw that when I called on you," remarked the other. "I saw it so clearly that I decided on the spot that you were

153

a rich old Shylock, and that even sweeter than the money would be putting the screws on you. That's why I've done it. I've got you on the gridiron, and I'm going to see you dance."

"Go on," said Kinney. "Come to the point, if you have a point. You want the money, I suppose?"

"Yes, I want the money."

Kinney sighed.

"Suppose that I pay you down that money, how shall I know that I'll have my boy in return?"

The other grinned at once, very greatly pleased.

"That," he said, "you will have to trust, of course, to the honor of Cousin Jack Chester."

He actually laughed aloud, though very softly. Nothing could have pleased him more than this chance to refer to his "honor."

"I trust your honor? I trust in moonshine and water!" said Kinney.

"There's nothing else for you to trust in, is there?" asked Jack Chester impertinently.

"I don't suppose that there is!" groaned Kinney.

"Not even a King Bird, eh?" said Chester.

"What of him?" asked Kinney.

"Why," said Jack Chester, "I know all about how you've tried to get him as your agent for recovering the youngster."

"Do you?"

"Yes. You were stepping into hot water then. If I'd been really troubled, I would have put a bullet through the brat and finished him. D'you doubt that?"

"I don't," said Kinney, after a pause. "I think that you would."

"You're right," remarked Chester. "I've tagged him with lead already, when the little fool tried to run away from me."

"Tagged him with—you mean that you've shot him?" asked Kinney, his face gleaming with perspiration.

"Shot him down," said the other, with relish. "Shot him through the leg, just below the hip."

He laughed again, as he made the remark, and his bright eyes relished the horror and the pain that passed over the face of Kinney.

154

"You've never taken me seriously enough, Kinney," said Chester. "You'll know better, after this."

"There's to be an 'after,' is there?" asked Kinney.

"After I've trimmed you for a hundred grand for the boy? Of course there is to be an 'after,' if I have the brains to do it. I wouldn't mind squeezing you to the last drop of your blood and the last penny of your fortune. I like it. It amuses me. It's what I prefer to do in life. It's a career to me."

Kinney cleared his throat.

"You mean that he's badly wounded, still?"

"He's wounded so that he's a weight on our hands, and when the King Bird came after us, I thought that we might be too hampered. However, I've taken care of that now."

"You have?"

"Yes. I've given the King Bird, already, more trouble in a few days than he's had in all the rest of his life that went before. I've buried him alive, and nearly burned him, and finally, I took his horse and left him afoot. Just now, he's wandering about through the mountains, fifty miles from here. He's a persistent little devil, but I've taught him how the master hand works."

He laughed again.

"Now the King Bird would be a useful fellow to me," said Kinney. "If I had him here, he'd be worth his hire."

"He might be," said Jack Chester. "But to tell you the truth, I think that I'd be too much for him, with a knife, or a gun, or bare hands."

"Do you?"

"I do. The fact is, Kinney, that all of these Western desperadoes have been a good deal overestimated. Very few of 'em know how to handle themselves. They've never been properly taught to wrestle or box. As for their marksmanship, it's fair, but even there, they've never been properly schooled. In all those places, I have the advantage. I'd take this little game bird, this great desperado, and tie him in knots."

"Perhaps you would," said Kinney, "but I can't help wishing that you might have the opportunity very soon!"

"Thanks," said the other. "Now the money, Kinney?"

"If I give you money, I take your word that you'll return my poor boy?"

"That's all that you *can* get from me. But, I don't know— I might take the money right now, without giving you anything."

"Do you think that I'd be fool enough to keep a hundred thousand dollars in my room?" asked Kinney.

He smiled faintly, as he spoke, a smile vaguely similar to that which the King Bird often wore.

And Jack Chester, after studying him, finally shrugged his shoulders.

"Well," he said, "perhaps you wouldn't. In any case, I'd be glad to take the money, and give you my word about the boy. I know that I couldn't get *two* lump sums out of you. One of your brats would never be worth that much. You let the first one go without lifting a hand, didn't you?"

Without making an answer, Kinney stepped to the corner of the room and opened a small traveling case. Inside of the flap of it were a revolver and a small packet wrapped in oiled brown silk. Over a choice between these two his hand lingered, for a moment, but at last he let the revolver lie, and stood up with the silken parcel.

He laid it on the table.

"There's the money, Jack," said he. "Take that, and I'll take your promise in return."

"All right," said Jack Chester. "A hundred thousand from you and a bare promise from me—that's about a fair exchange, on the whole"

Kinney shrugged his shoulders.

"We'll say good night then," he said.

"I'll run a thumb over the edge of the stuff first, perhaps," suggested Chester.

"No," said Kinney. "You don't have to. The money's there. I don't lie, Chester. I have other vices, but lying isn't one of them."

"You're probably right," said the other, and dropped the packet carelessly into the side pocket of his coat. He added: "I'll send the boy in, within a day or two. Mind you, if

156

there's any attempt to follow me with the money, it will be worse luck for the boy."

Kinney said nothing. His face was white with disgust. His bright eyes burned into the face of the kidnaper. And it was at this instant that the King Bird, crawling noiselessly up the slant roof above the veranda of the hotel, came under the window of Kinney's room, and looked in.

CHAPTER XXVII

THE SAME TRAIL

CHESTER was saying: "You can imagine how much money you would have saved in the long run, cousin, by giving me the little lift that I asked for, not long ago, when I dropped in at your ranch! Instead of that, you threw me out. Called me a rascal, and threw me off the place. Remember that?"

"I remember everything," said Kinney. "And now I'd like to say good night to you, Jack Chester."

"Can't stand the sight of the viper, eh? Is that it?" Chester chuckled. "Well, Kinney, I don't bear so much malice toward you as I did. A hundred thousand dollars worth of malice less, as a matter of fact."

He stepped to the door.

The King Bird started. He had not expected that the fellow would have the courage to use the door and calmly walk down through the hotel. But for that matter, there was hardly a soul stirring, even this early in the night.

He pulled a gun, but as he drew it, Kinney unluckily stepped squarely between him and his target.

"Good night, and good-by, for the time being," said Chester. "If I'm ever out of funds, I may call on you again, cousin."

With another laugh, he opened the door, and shut it softly behind him.

The King Bird saw Kinney's head drop, as though he were relaxing suddenly, after a fearful strain.

For his own part, the young outlaw did not know what to do.

He would lose too much time, if he followed through the room of Kinney, perhaps?

No, it seemed clear that Chester would walk boldly out the front door of the hotel, and go to a horse.

On silent, moccasined feet, the King Bird stole over the shingles down the sharp incline of the roof until he came to the edge of it, overhanging the watering troughs that were strung out in a long line. There was no need for so many of them, now that the long freighting teams no longer went through the town of Elmira, but they stood there, a melancholy relic of the old days, gathering moss, and apt to be a bit slimy about the sides and the bottom.

There was only one horse at the hitch rack that ran above the troughs, and now the figure of Chester came straight out through the dim shaft of lamplight that streaked through the open front door of the hotel, and walked into the shadow toward the horse.

The King Bird rose to hands and knees, stood half upright, and leaped.

He shot straight down for the target that was to break his fall, his hands and feet extended, like a broad jumper. Jack Chester, though his back was turned, seemed to have a shadow of premonition whip across his brain, for he whirled suddenly, and that was the reason that the impact was only a glancing one.

Both men struck the ground, the King Bird far the worse stunned of the two by his fall. Only the soft dust, half a foot deep, kept him from breaking bones.

He got himself mechanically to his hands and knees and saw Jack Chester already up, and drawing a gun.

It was not a time for gunfire. Public attention was not what the King Bird wanted. His own weapon, he threw at the gun hand of Chester, and the heavy Colt knocked

Chester half around with its weighty impact. There was a slight clank, and the guns fell side by side in the dust.

Chester, grunting like a beast that makes a sudden effort, reached for them, but the King Bird was at him in a rush. He kicked the weapons farther off with his foot, and closed on the other man.

The King Bird was smaller. He had the advantage of his rush to give him weight, but even so he did not bring Chester down.

They whirled into the shaft of the lamplight. Neither of them wanted any public attention. In a dead silence they fought, and a thick white mist of dust boiled up around them. It would have been a spectacle to gladden the eye of Elmira, but not a soul was watching as Chester, true to his boasting, showed himself both a strong man, and a trained one.

His fist clipped the King Bird neatly on the point of the chin, and sent him staggering.

He stepped in, striking with deadly precision again, and the young man went down.

Jack Chester took a swinging kick with his heavy riding boot. It might break in the temple bone and kill his opponent. At any rate, it was reasonably certain to end the fighting.

But the King Bird rolled, and took the force of the blow on his shoulder instead of his head.

He came to his feet, half-crouched, as Chester came in once more. And so, side-weaving his body a trifle, he got home his first solid blow, a reaching right-hander that missed the chin of Chester and found his throat.

That clever boxer wisely leaped back, to prepare himself and steady himself against the next attack, but he was far too slow, now that the King Bird was in real motion. Chester only set himself in time to catch a harder and longer stroke that found the button, and turned him limp from head to heel.

When he wakened, strong cord was being whipped around his ankles and his wrists. A gag was thrust in his mouth.

And then he was dragged to the side of the old hotel, and dropped into the darkness of a shrub.

The King Bird turned and hurried for the room of Kinney.

He took the same way up that he had used before, a pillar of the veranda, and then the slanting roof.

At the window of the room, he could see Kinney seated at the table in the center, his chin on his hand, his despairing eyes fixed steadily before him.

An odd stroke of pity stung the King Bird to the heart as he watched the older man.

He tapped softly at the pane of the window. Kinney started up and came to him at once.

"It's not Chester, this time," said the King Bird. "But it's the money that you gave that rat. Here it is."

"The King Bird?" muttered Kinney, straining his eyes into the darkness beyond the window.

The packet of money fell upon the floor at his feet.

"Keep back from the window a little," said the young man. "You can't tell. It's possible that Chester has more of his friends along with him." He added: "I'm going to make him take me out with him to get your son. I've found out, I think, that the trail I was traveling before is the same as your trail, Kinney."

"You're going alone with him?" asked Kinney. "But he's sure to have more than one man with him. He's sure to have plenty of others. Wait, man. Wait till I've got into my clothes, and I'll be with you."

"No use," said the young man.

"I'm a fair shot," said Kinney. "I can play my part in the business, believe me!"

"No use," insisted the King Bird. "No matter what happens, one man is all that's likely to get close to that lot. They've been scared more than once, and they will be watching with their eyes open. Two men can't move like one, I tell you. And if there's a big alarm, the first thing they do will be to remove all evidence against them by murdering the boy. We must think of him."

"Young man," said Kinney, "it's a long shot that you're going to attempt."

160

"It's the only way," insisted the young man. "Good-by."

"Will you give me your hand?" asked Kinney.

"Here," said the King Bird, sliding it through the open window. "Good-by."

"And God bless you," said Kinney. "I——"

His voice broke off with what seemed a startled exclamation, but the King Bird, removing his hand from that of the other, was now rapidly gliding down the slope of the roof again.

He came to the place where he had left his prisoner, and removing the gag, sat the other up.

As soon as he caught breath again, Chester gasped: "You fool, you nearly strangled me!"

"That's the way you should have died," said the King Bird. "Maybe that's the way you *will* end up, one of these days. But a rope is more likely than a gag."

"Who are you?" asked the prisoner.

"Didn't you recognize me when we were playing around in the street together?"

"No."

"It's the King Bird."

"The King Bird!" exclaimed Chester.

He began to rock himself a little from side to side, to keep the rhythm of his whispered curses.

"It's not possible!" he exclaimed. "You were back there in the mountains cutting for sign. Garry *saw* you there. But Garry must have been bought to say that. You bribed the cur!"

"No. Garry may have seen me there. But I gave up that job and cut straight off for the town, here. I hoped that I'd be able to pick up the trail, here. But I never expected that I'd find you, Chester."

"Reach into my coat pocket," said Chester. "There's money there that'll be worth a split. I can buy my way out of this, youngster."

"The ransom?" said the young man. "I've given that back to Kinney."

A groan answered him.

"You fool," said Jack Chester. "We could have bled the tightwad white between us!"

"I'd rather bleed you, Jack," said the King Bird. "As soon as you're ready, you can show me up the trail to your camp."

"What camp?"

"Where you've got young Bobby Kinney, and the girl."

"The devil I will!" said Chester savagely. "You can brain me here and now, but I won't guide you a step."

"Won't you?" said the young man. "I've strangled you a little already, Jack? But how about a bit of fire treatment, such as you gave me back there in the ranch house?"

"You poisonous young rat," said Chester, "you were born to make trouble for me. The day'll come when I dress you down for it. If only——" His voice choked off in another groan.

"Stand up," said the young man. "There's your legs free. Now, mind you, brother—the killing of you is really sweeter than the saving. Watch your steps, one by one. I'll always be behind you."

CHAPTER XVIII

THE WOODED HILL

As THEY came over the hill, Jack Chester sank to the ground with a loud groan. He had been driven all the way from Elmira at the end of a lariat that was tied around his neck. His hands were tied, also, behind the small of his back, and there is nothing more exhausting than laboring over rough and smooth without an opportunity of swinging the arms as one steps out.

"Here it is—and I'm corked," said he.

The King Bird, mounted on the horse he had "borrowed" from his prisoner, now slipped to the ground, also, and sat beside the captive.

From the hill, he could look over a wide, starlit expanse. Range beyond range, the hills swept away toward the loftier mountains, and in the valley beneath them, he could see enough gleam of starlight to make out the progress of the river, as it slid down the decline, and then took a quick corner around a wooded hummock, and disappeared.

The night was so free from mist, and the mountain air so clear, that he could even see single trees at a considerable distance.

His captive nodded toward the wooded hill around which the creek disappeared.

"That's the place," said he.

"If I leave you up here and go to investigate," said the King Bird, "and then find that it's a wild-goose chase, I'll come back here and make it even with you, Chester."

"Why should I lie to you?" asked Chester.

"Because you have some partners down there."

"They don't matter to me," said Chester. "Not a bit. They're a mangy lot. They're all a mangy lot. I've had to do the thinking for the whole gang of 'em, and all that they'll give me is two shares of the clean-up. I ought to have half. That would be only about right. But two shares is all that I get—and they may try to knife that out of me."

"You could have held back part of the coin," suggested the King Bird.

"Yes, I figured on that," said the other. "I figured on keeping out seventy-five thousand of the hundred, before the split was made, and getting my right cut, that way. But it would have been a risky business. They're clever, some of 'em. Garry's a fool. But Jake and some of the rest are smart." He added: "Make me a cigarette, will you?"

The King Bird rolled one, accordingly, put it between the lips of Chester, and lighted it.

"Why can't you tie my hands in front, so's I could handle the cigarette for myself?" asked Chester.

"Because I won't throw away any chances with you," said the King Bird. "You're a tricky one, Chester. I'll play safe."

"That fool of a deputy sheriff might have had you—cold!" sighed Chester. "And then there wouldn't have been all this trouble."

"No," said the King Bird. "That would have finished me."

"You'd be cooling in jail, by this time," suggested Chester.

"Not there. I'd be in a darker place than jail."

"Dead, you mean?"

"Yes."

"You couldn't have put up a fight. Not when he had the cold drop on you."

As he spoke, the sparks from the end of the cigarette sputtered out, and showered toward the ground.

"I've never been in jail," said the King Bird. "And I'll never go there, alive."

"Oh, a jail's all right," answered Chester. "I've had a rest in a lot of jails. You're too proud, kid. That'll be the finish of you, one of these days. Pride. That's what hooks the biggest fish. That's what beats 'em! Get humble, King Bird—like me!"

He laughed as he said it.

"You're not worried just now, are you, Jack?" asked the King Bird curiously.

"No, I'm not worried."

"Why not? I'd be worried if I were in your hands, and helpless like this."

"Of course you would," answered Chester. "But you're too proud to take advantage of a helpless man. There's your pride again—always making a fool out of you."

He went on: "In the fight, you fought fair, like a fool. I would have kicked your brains out. I nearly managed it. But you wanted to fight like a gentleman."

He chuckled a little, and muttered, "Gentleman gun fighters, eh?"

"Why," said the young man, "I thought that there could be such a thing."

"There can't," snapped Jack Chester. "A man with a gun, a man that has been trained to use it, is the same as a tiger

164

in a jungle. He aims to kill—he doesn't care how, so long as he kills."

"I think you're right," said the King Bird quietly. "I've gone these years, thinking that I might find the right sort of fellows. But I've never found them. They're all on the side of the law—*all* of 'em!"

"You're a snob, too," Chester sneered. "It makes me sick to hear you talk, King Bird. Go on down there now, and stick your head in the lion's mouth. They're going to eat you, those boys."

"Are they a fighting lot?" asked the King Bird.

"Garry's no fighter. He's nothing but a mistake, the long, lean, drawn-out fool!" said Chester bitterly. "But the others can fight for their salt."

"How many ought to be in camp?"

"Five."

"And how is it guarded?"

"Two men on watch, and every other man sleeping on his guns, and ready to jump. They're a ready lot, I've got to say."

"Straight shooters?"

"They can shoot straight, brother. I won't tell you any lie. I picked 'em all myself—all except Garry. He simply sort of fell in our way. I never wanted him, but the best of the rest of 'em thought that Garry might do."

"Who's the best of the others?"

"The fellow with the saber mustaches."

"He's a fighter, too?"

"Wild cats. He's a pack of wild cats."

"Just where does the camp lie on that hill?"

"On the far side of it. That's all I can tell you. I don't know just where they would pitch camp. Just somewhere on the far side of the hill. They'll probably have a fire lighted. They have to, on account of that brat. His wound has to be washed with hot water and disinfectant every now and again; and then the girl puts lotions on him."

"What devil," asked the King Bird, "put it into your mind to get the girl as doctor?"

"Why," said Chester, "three of my men knew about her. She's taken care of wounded men before, and done it as well

165

as any doctor. And I thought that it would be easier to handle her. Besides, being a woman, she would make a better nurse for a kid like little Bobby Kinney. He's game enough, but he's only a kid."

"You might have thought of that before you dumped lead into him," said the King Bird.

"Yes. I might have thought of that. But I hated Kinney so much that I was sort of glad to spill a little of his blood, even at second-hand."

The King Bird shook his head.

"I'm wondering," said he.

"Wondering about what?"

"What they'd do with you."

"Where," asked Chester. "In jail?"

"No, in hell," said the King Bird.

He cleared his throat, and went on more briskly: "I'll have to tie you to a tree, brother. That's not comfortable, but I'll have to do it. Sorry."

"That's all right," answered Chester. "Your kind heart will make you come back here, before very long, and cut me loose again."

He even chuckled as he said it. He seemed to be iron, with the polished surface of a perpetual sneer at all the virtues in the world.

So he was tied fast to a tree.

"Now the gag," said the King Bird.

"Wait a minute," answered Jack Chester. "Don't put the gag in, partner. Have a heart about that, will you? I go crazy when I think I'm strangling; I'll strangle just on the scare."

"I nearly strangled back there in the burning house," said the King Bird angrily.

"Then you know what it's like!" exclaimed Chester. "But don't gag me, King. I'll swear on my word of honor that I'll not let out a yip. Not if I see a man walking within two steps of me."

"I don't know how far I could trust you," said the King Bird. "I'd rather peg your tongue to the tree with a knife, than trust you to keep still if you saw your chance."

"I'd rather have my tongue pegged with a knife," answered the prisoner instantly, "than to be gagged. I'd choke before you got back. I nearly choked back there beside the hotel."

"A gag is a horrible thing," agreed the King Bird. "And therefore it is exactly right for you. But I think that I might let you off it, Chester. "I'd hate to gag even a dog! Will you give me your word and as much honor as there is left to you, that you'll make no sound?"

"I'll make no sound," said Chester. "On my word of honor."

"I shouldn't trust you," said the King Bird. "If you howled at the top of your lungs, they could hear you down there on the hill, I think."

"They couldn't," said the other. "It's farther than you think. If they heard a howl, they'd think it was a mountain lion yowling. That's all."

"I'm a fool," said the King Bird. "As you pointed out before, I'm all sorts of a fool, but I'm going to trust your word and leave you here without a muzzle on, Chester."

"That's white of you, old man," said Chester. "That's as white as ever I heard of. I thank you very much!"

"You're laughing at me, in your heart," said the King Bird. "But what a fellow like you thinks is no great matter, I suppose. So long, Chester."

He went over the ropes again, testing their tautness with his forefinger.

"Those ropes will not cut into you, Jack," he declared. "They may make you numb, but I have to do that to be absolutely sure of holding you."

"Why, partner," said Jack Chester, "I'm as comfortable as a baby in a cradle. So long, and good luck!"

He was actually chuckling again, as the King Bird went down the slope.

CHAPTER XXIX

THE CAMP

WHEN the King Bird came to the foot of the slope, he paused on the brink of the stream, and examined with the greatest care the trees on the farther side, and the manner in which they were distributed over the ground. He closed his eyes, and printed the picture deep. He might need to know every bit of that lay of the land as well as he could possibly remember it.

He examined the creek, too. It was not a great flow of water, but it was serious as a crossing because of its great speed. Here it shot down through a polished flume, leaping along with a greater and a greater impetus, until it struck, here and there, a rock that rose like the fin of a fish, and threw out a bow wave of water on either side of it. By those rocks one could make the easiest crossing. There were two convenient places, one just to the right of him, and one a considerable distance farther down the stream.

He might need to know these things, in case he had to make a quick escape.

He now crossed the stream by the rocks, and again on one knee, his habitual position for rest, he scanned the slope that he had just left. A long-drawn sound grew out of the air. He thought that it was the distant voice of Jack Chester, crying, but it was only a hoot owl.

That shore behind him, he studied with an equal care, and then began to work his way around the edge of the water. He could go straight over the hill, and descend on the other side, but any one who has walked through brush and hills knows that it is not difficult to move quietly uphill, but almost impossible to avoid making a great disturbance coming down.

Therefore he went to the trouble of encircling the hill three quarters of the way around, before he saw, up the slope, the meager red eye of a small fire.

By that time, he was well-informed as to the lay of the land. He knew just what to expect in fleeing in any direction. But his grim expectation was that there would be no flight, but that he would have to battle it out to the finish against them all.

For Kinney's son was up there, helpless with a wound which the brutal Chester had given to him, and Helena Blair was there, also, caring for the boy.

He winced, when he remembered how she had tried to explain to him; he winced still more, when he remembered his foolish suspicion that she was with the thugs because she wanted to be!

Well, he would try to make that all square before this night was ended!

And so he started working his way up through the brush.

He took no chances. Before he made a step, he reached out with his foot and put down the toe first, and actually felt and studied the nature of the substance on which his stride was to fall.

He took no chances with places where twigs were thick, but got down on hands and knees, and wormed his way along like a four-footed animal.

Furthermore, he had to stop occasionally to listen, now with his head high, and now with his ear close to the ground. He had to take a deviously winding course, in order to avoid bits of ground too thick with brush or with fallen twigs. And so it was that he managed to draw close, after a long, long time, to that goal, the red, gleaming eyes of the fire!

He found the horses first. They were hobbled among the brush, and they were still grazing, in spite of the lateness of the hour, a sure proof that they were very hungry from the marches they had been making or because of the poor grazing which they had found.

Only one was lying down, and that, he guessed, was Molly. It did not take much grass to keep her up. She could live like a wolf, it seemed, on a mere mouthful a day, or a good bellyful once a week.

He managed to work his way around to her. It was folly to risk making a disturbance. It was insanity, perhaps, to waste time and brains and effort in this fashion on a dumb beast, but he could not help going to her.

He realized, as he crawled nearer and saw the silhouette of her raised head against the stars, what an empty spot had been made in his very spirit by her absence. And besides, there would be one bit of practical use in going to her before he proceeded farther.

That was to cut the hobbles that bound her, for he might need her suddenly and desperately, in the great pinch!

It was not difficult to work among the horses. When there are a number of them together, they are the least suspicious animals in the world. They have learned to depend, for too many centuries, upon the watchfulness of man, who keeps all enemies away.

Their feet moved close to the creeping form of the King Bird, but only once did one of them throw up its head with a snort, and a jump to the side.

Instantly a voice exclaimed, close by: "Who's there?"

The King Bird lay flat on his face, and waited.

"Who's there?" repeated the voice, more loudly. "That you, Jake?"

"I'm asleep, you fool!" said the angry voice of Jake. "I *was* asleep, till you had to start blattin'."

"I thought I seen something down there among the hosses."

"Don't leave it at thinkin'. Go down and make sure."

"I guess it wasn't anything. I'll go look, though."

A form strode suddenly near, stood lofty and threatening above the King Bird, not two steps away. He could hear the breathing of the man; he could hear the shoe leather creaking softly, as the big fellow shifted his weight from one foot to the other.

Then the man turned around.

"No, that wasn't anything," he said.

"Then shut your mouth, will you, and let somebody else sleep!" asked Jake, with increased irritation.

"Who are you to talk like this? You ain't the king of the world!" said the big man, with equal anger.

"You're goin' to argue, now, are you?" groaned Jake.

There was a rustling of blankets, and then another faint groan, as he strove to settle himself for new sleep.

The man on guard drew back. Still, for a moment, his head and shoulders were distinguishable above the upper line of the trees, against the stars. Gradually, they faded back.

The King Bird lay perfectly still, considering. He had known that the task would be a difficult one, but he had not been prepared for this catlike degree of watchfulness.

He moved on, inch by inch, and put himself beside the black mare. She swung her head over, sniffed at him, and made a lurch to get up.

One whispered word stopped her. He caught hold of her nostrils to keep her from whinnying.

And then, gradually relaxing that hold, he could feel the tremor of excitement that swept through her. She began to breathe as though she were running. Lying where he was he could see the thin lances of the starlight entering her eyes, and notice the flare of her nostrils.

The pricking of her ears, the eager, sensitive manner in which she stretched out her head to him, told him of her joy.

So he lay there for a moment, rejoicing like a happy child, and stroking her very gently.

Then he drew a knife, found her hobbles, and cut them.

But one horse would not be enough. He spent the next ten minutes in turning the hobbles of two adjacent horses into leads, and those leads he tied first together, and then to the halter of strong webwork which the mare was wearing.

After he had finished that, he paused, for he felt that he had merely covered the preliminaries, and that the main task lay all before him. He was on the verge of the danger, not actually entered into it.

When, at last, he began to crawl in the direction of the fire, he looked back, once or twice, and saw the head of the

171

black mare turned toward him, held high and eager. A mere whisper would bring her to her feet!

He came still closer to the fire, before he saw another soul-filling sight, and that was the gray stallion, standing in the glare of the firelight, with head down, grazing.

The stallion was kept there not by a hobble, but by a rope that connected with the hand of Dick Macey. For there sat the half-breed, with his flat, horribly white countenance. He was not one of the guards, for his head was bowed down on his knees, and in this fashion he was sleeping, his shoulders stirring a little, up and down, with the deepness of his breathing.

It seemed to the King Bird that the horror of that face gave the proper tone to the entire picture—low and savage brutality, in the midst of which he was to find the girl, and young Bobby Kinney.

He moved his head a trifle higher, staring to the side through the branches of the bush in front of him, and now he saw what he was working for—a thick pile of pine branches laid on the ground, and on this the boy sleeping. And beside him, her back against a sapling, and her head fallen on her shoulder in sleep, sat the girl.

CHAPTER XXX

BOBBY KINNEY

THE BOY wakened, suddenly, as those do who are in pain while they sleep. He muttered something, throwing out his hand, and the girl was instantly awake, also, and leaning over him.

"It's all right, Bobby," said she. "I'm here with you."

"It was all dark," murmured Bobby Kinney. "And we were on the move again. I'll die if we have to make another fast march."

"We won't have to make another," said the girl.

"D'you think that the King Bird will leave us alone now?" queried Bobby.

He put a hand under his head so that he could keep it lifted a little, and so watch her with more ease, and the King Bird saw a glint of reddish hair, and a sun-browned face, very drawn by the lines of pain.

"He probably will," said the girl.

"What makes him so hot after us? Did father hire him?"

"No. He doesn't do things for hire."

"I know," said Bobby. "He's just wild. He flies where he pleases. Now he's after this crew. Think of it, Brick! Think of driving six men, the way he's been able to do!"

Dick Macey suddenly rose from his place and stepped to them. He spoke not loudly, but with deadly meaning.

"It's the second time to-night that you gone and busted into my sleep. I gotta mind to cut the throat of both of you. You hear me?"

"Sorry, Dick," said Bobby. "My leg was burning up. It waked me, and——"

"I wish that Jack Chester had put his bullet through your head, instead of your leg," growled Macey. "It would 'a' done me good to see you flop, is what it would 'a' done. Now shut yer face and go back to sleep. You're bad luck, is what you are. There ain't good ever goin' to come to us, out of you!"

The boy was still. His eyes opened, glaring.

Macey turned to the girl.

"You, too. You're old enough to have some kind of sense. But you ain't got it. You're goin' to let the brat carry on and do what he pleases. What he pleases is goin' to collect trouble for him, is what I mean. If you had the brain of a half-wit, you'd know——"

"You half-breed cur!" hissed Bobby, with intense emotion.

"I'm a half-breed, am I?" said Dick Macey.

173

He struck the youngster with the flat of his hand, knocking Bobby's head onto his right shoulder. Then, with the other hand, Macey cuffed the boy's head across to the other shoulder. He would have struck a third time, but the girl caught his hand and clung to it.

He shook her away with such force that she went reeling back against the sapling.

"A beating, that's what the two of you need!" said Dick Macey.

"What's all this fool business?" asked the voice of Jake. "Ain't I goin' to get no sleep to-night? Is this here a dog fight that's goin' to go on till the morning?"

"The brat's been slangin' me," said Macey. "He's been callin' me a half-breed, and such. I'm goin' to cut his dirty little throat for him."

"He beat that—that helpless boy," said Helena Blair, choking with rage. "He *beat* him, Jake."

"He needs a beating if he can't keep his tongue still," said Jake callously.

"I don't mind the beating. I'll take that," said Bobby. "But he manhandled Brick."

"Hold on," said Jake. "Did you touch Miss Blair, Dick?"

"What if I did?" said Macey. "She was interferin'."

Jake, half-dressed, strode from the brush. He was smaller than Macey, but his wrath made him seem larger. With one hand he pulled at his drooping mustache. His other hand he laid on the shoulder of the half-breed.

"I guess you clean forgot, Dick," said he, "that you're in the Rocky Mountain States of America, and them kind of things ain't done. You take hold of yourself and remember it, after this."

"You ain't man enough to make me remember what I don't wanta," declared Dick.

"Ain't I?" said Jake softly. "All right, brother. Lay the tip of your finger on her, and see what happens."

"She's been and had a lesson that'll hold her for a while," answered Macey. "I'm sick of this here business. I'm ready to pull out, and take the gray along with me."

174

Jake answered: "You do what you please. Only, I'm telling you."

He turned back to the girl and the boy.

Macey retired to his former place and picked up the lead of the gray stallion again.

Compared to the great horse, he seemed a being of a lesser sort—like a monkey leading a man!

Jake was saying quietly: "Sorry he hit you, kid, but you gotta keep your mouth shut, around here."

"Not when they light into Brick," said the boy hotly.

"This ain't no Sunday school," answered Jake. "Miss Blair can take care of herself, all right, without you hornin' in."

He added to the girl: "I'm mighty sorry. Maybe it won't happen again."

She answered: "If the rest were all like you, Jake, this would be a happy little excursion. Don't worry about me. I'm all right."

Jake returned to sleep, but sleep seemed definitely banned for that night.

A far-off, recurrent cry was dwelling in the air, and the lofty, thin form of Garry now appeared on the verge of the firelight.

"I been hearin' something," said he.

"Tie up the flaps of your ears," said Dick Macey, "and maybe you won't hear no more."

"I been hearin' something, yonder," said Garry. "Listen!"

"Shut up and go to sleep," advised Macey.

"I ain't goin' to shut up," answered Garry. "I been hearin' something."

"It's a hoot owl," said the voice of Jake. "I heard it, too."

"Naw, it's a mountain lion," declared Macey.

"Hoot owls and mountain lions, they don't speak words," answered Garry.

"Words?" exclaimed Jake. "Dog-gone me, I gotta dress. There's something in the air to-night."

The King Bird sighed. The very devil of bad luck was following him everywhere, for now the entire camp was rousing.

"Listen at it," said Garry insistently. "Come up to the shoulder of the mountain, some of you gents, and hark at it, with me."

The air seemed to be purposely stilled, at that instant, and the distant sound came clearly home to the ears of all—the strain of a human voice, pitched very high, so that it would come to those far away.

"Kind of dog-gone ghostly," said Dick Macey, standing up.

Automatically, he laid his hand on the head of the stallion, and the King Bird watched the great horse move impatiently to avoid that caress.

It pleased the watcher to see that motion of repulsion. Far different was Molly, when the touch of his hand was on her!

Jake, fully dressed now, came across the dim red circle of the firelight.

"We'd better go up there and listen in, for a minute," said he. "Sure sounds like a man callin' out."

"Yeah, I got a pair of ears," said Garry.

"So has a jack rabbit," remarked Macey.

Two more men came striding in from the brush; the whole party of five headed up toward the shoulder of the hill, some distance above them, Macey leading the gray stallion, as always, behind him. It was plain that he valued it as he did his life.

And the King Bird, hardly able to believe in the sudden turn of good fortune, remembered the man whom he had tied on the opposite hill. Jack Chester, like the liar that he was, was breaking his plighted word and yelling at the top of his lungs to give warning. That must be the explanation. But the very warning he shouted was calling the watchers away.

Up the slope, Jake exclaimed sharply:

"Go back there, a couple of you, and keep your eyes peeled."

"What's goin' to happen?" asked Garry. "The girl goin' to carry the kid away?"

He laughed loud and jeeringly at the absurdity of his own suggestion.

176

The King Bird, at that moment, rose from the shadows, and stepped toward the bed of the boy.

"Who's that?" asked Bobby, in a quick, frightened voice.

"I'm the King Bird, Bobby," said the latter, "at least, that's what the boys call me."

"King!" cried the girl. "How—— You can't do anything. They'll be back in a minute. You won't make me go with you, King, and leave him?"

The King Bird leaned, and gathered the boy carefully in his arms.

"I'm taking both of you," he answered. "Bobby, this is going to hurt like the devil. I'm sorry."

"I'll stand it," said the boy. "But you're throwing yourself away. You *can't* get clear with me. You can't get——"

His voice stopped short on a gasp, as the King Bird lifted him, and the pain sent shooting agonies through the wounds of the youngster.

Right through the brush the rescuer carried that burden, and stepped over the back of the mare, couched where he had left her. She rose under him, as he said:

"Drag a bridle onto one of those others, Brick Molly will go without one. Have you got it?"

"Ready!" she said.

"Untie the lead. That's it. Turn that far horse loose. We can't use more than one. Jump on."

She was on the back of the first horse that he had attached to Molly in the dark, swinging up onto the bare back of the mustang with perfect ease.

Now voices came streaming rapidly back toward them, down the hillside, with that of Jake shouting:

"Get down the hill. He'll work up, not down. Shoot at anything that moves!"

They had heard the warning from Jack Chester, it was plain, that the King Bird was on the trail. And now they came with a confused clamor of angry voices.

But the King Bird was moving on the back of Molly down the slope, and the girl was just behind him, following the trail he picked out.

A faint groan came from the lips of the boy.

"Steady, partner," breathed the King Bird.

"I got my teeth set," gasped Bobby Kinney. "But sounds sort of come, anyway. It's all right!"

They were well started, now, when the mustang that the girl rode stumbled, and crashed noisily through a bush.

The heart of the King Bird leaped into his throat.

"Who's there?" yelled a voice behind them. "Stop!"

"Shoot, you fool!" yelled a second, and two rifles instantly spoke.

"Are you hurt?" called the King Bird to the girl.

"No! You?"

"No. We've got to move. God pity you, Bobby, because this is going to torture you. Hold tight. We've got to move!"

He spoke to the mare, and she glided into a trot.

Rapidly, then, they swung down the slope, with the yelling and the gunfire behind them.

It must have been exquisite agony to the boy in the arms of the King Bird, but he said nothing; only his panting grew harsher and quicker at the ear of the rescuer.

The moon was not up. There was that grace for them. But it would come soon, for there was a blunt pyramid of pale light forming in the east. However, they were spotted in the distance, and the bullets kept whirring, as they reached the bottom of the hill.

They rounded it at a gallop, every stride forcing a groan from the throat of Bobby. And as they reached the edge of the creek, they heard the mounted pursuit crash out into the open behind them, and come at full speed, the men yelling like frantic Indians.

CHAPTER XXXI

THE KING BIRD'S PLAN

"THERE'S where they came over—there's the ford on the right," breathed Bobby, pointing to a broad place in the stream.

"Good boy!" said the King Bird, and put the mare at the water.

The force of the current staggered her, but she steadied to it, and reaching the farther bank, climbed out as lightly as a cat. The King Bird looked back, and saw the mustang carry the girl rapidly out, behind him.

Still farther back, he watched the rushing, dark forms of the pursuers.

As the two horses stretched out in a gallop across the easier ground beyond, from the verge of the creek, rapid gunfire followed them.

That was not all. Three riders had gone straight through the water, without a moment of hesitation. The rest, pausing to pour in a few shots, in the hope of bringing down the enemy, immediately pushed through after the leaders.

"It's not good!" Bobby panted. "I can stand it, but it's no use. Molly can't carry double—not with the gray horse behind us. Look! Look! He's coming like anything!"

The King Bird did not need to look back. He could see in his mind's eye how the great horse must be plunging through the night behind them, and gaining with every stride. No, the mare could not carry double.

"Drop me, and go on," said Bobby. "Go on with Brick. Let me drop. It's as good as being saved, to me, to see anybody as brave as you, King! Let me drop, and go on!"

He actually struggled in the arms of the King Bird, and the latter exclaimed:

"Be still, Bobby. Be still, will you?"

He shouted, then: "Brick!"

Her mustang, though it was carrying only single, was barely able to keep up with the straining form of Molly.

"Yes!" she called, above the hoofbeats.

He looked aside at her, and relished the way she clung to the bare back of the mustang, and jockeyed it along.

"Brick, I'm steering for that wood, straight ahead. They've got us if we all try to go on. I'm dropping off there with Bobby. You catch the lead of the mare, and swing onto her back. Go straight in through the wood. They'll follow you till they see that only one horse is carrying a rider. They won't make that out till moonrise, perhaps, and they won't know where to look for us. Brick, I hate to ask you—but I think Molly can carry your weight and beat the gray horse. Will you try?"

"I'll do it!" cried the girl.

"Here, then—we're at it!" cried the King Bird, and put the mare straight in under the sweeping branches of a grove.

He was barely inside when he spoke the word that stopped Molly and as he dropped to the ground with the boy, the girl whipped onto the bare back of the mare.

"Luck!" cried the King Bird.

"Luck!" she cried, in answer, and shot away, pulling the mustang behind her on a lead.

It seemed to the King Bird, as he shrank back into a closer thicket where riders were not apt to sweep through, that not six heartbeats lay between her flight and the coming of Dick Macey on the tall gray stallion.

Behind were two more. Behind these, the last three, all riding at full speed.

With a roar like a storm, they struck the wood, and filled it with noise, and rushed out on the farther side, where their yells went tingling up into the sky.

Then, as though they had turned a corner in a street, all the sounds were shut off as they dropped down the slope beyond the forest.

180

On the rising ground beyond, the cry of the hunt came clearly back to them again.

So, in waves, it roared faintly and more faintly, and faded from the ear.

"If they catch her?" asked Bobby, in a trembling voice.

"She'll be all right," said the King Bird gruffly. "Can you stand some more pain?"

"Don't bother about me," said Bobby Kinney. "But about her—what'll they do?"

"Nothing but hard words—if Jake is with 'em when they catch her."

"But if Jake's away behind when they catch up—if Dick Macey and the gray catch her—what'll Macey do?"

The heart of the King Bird stood still.

He said stubbornly: "Macey can't catch her. It couldn't happen that way."

"What if Macey did?" persisted the boy.

"Stop it, Bobby," said the King Bird. "I'm not thinking of it—it couldn't happen!"

He had lowered the boy to the ground, but now he raised him again, and carried him out of the woods. He was not a light burden, for Bobby Kinney was solidly built.

And as the King Bird walked on, with short, rapid steps, he heard the boy muttering savage words of abuse.

"If Macey murders her," cried the boy, "you'll be worse than a yellow coyote. That's what you are! Let me go. Drop me here! You've thrown her to those wolves. That's what you've done!"

"I've tried for the best. I think the mare may carry her through," said the King Bird. "D'you see, Bobby——"

"You're a liar and a coward!" cried Bobby. "Let me down —let me be!"

He struck furiously at the face of the King Bird.

The latter bowed his head to avoid the blows, and panted:

"You don't know her, Bobby. She never would have let herself be the one to drop out, and be saved. And there was no other way. She couldn't handle you alone. It was this way or no way—or both of you gone to the devil! But she couldn't handle you, if I'd dropped her with you, here in the

181

woods. They'll come back and hunt to the line, Bobby. They'll search everywhere like bloodhounds. Only I've an idea how I can beat 'em!"

The boy closed his eyes, stopped struggling and lay suddenly still. His head fell back, and the burden bearer knew that he had fainted.

Still he did not pause.

For ahead of him, not far away, a voice was calling, at long intervals: "This way, boys. This way!"

That was Jack Chester, trying to guide with his hoarse voice any of his former companions who might be straggling back from the hunt.

And now, shaking with fatigue from head to foot, the King Bird arrived at the place.

The husky voice of Chester, worn out with shouting through long minutes, cried out one brief oath, and was still.

The King Bird, laying his burden on the ground, put his ear to the boy's heart. It was beating slowly, but steadily enough. And even now he stirred, and moaned.

The man rose and stepped to Chester.

"Jack, I've come back for you," he said.

"You've had some more luck," said Chester brazenly.

"You lied to me," answered the King Bird.

"I'd rather be a liar than a fool," said Chester.

"I think I'd put some brush around you and touch a match to it," said the King Bird, "but I need you. I'm going to make a litter for the boy there. And you're going to pack one end of it. I can't move him very far by myself."

"I'm a good pack horse, brother," said Chester. "You watch me work for my board and keep! Even liars come in handy, now and then."

His effrontery was a magnificent thing, mountainous and superhuman. The King Bird said no more to him, but with his hunting knife notched a pair of saplings, broke them off with some effort and more whittling, trimmed them of the larger shoots, and out of his shirt and underwear made a sling which he tied across the poles.

The moon rose to make that work more rapid, but it was an unwelcome helper. It made him glance eagerly over his shoulder, now and again.

Any moment, now, the stream of the hunters might cast off from the girl, and turn to hunt down the boy and himself.

Next, he freed his prisoner as to the legs, and secured his hands behind him, but left some foot of play between the wrists. After that, he told him to go to the head of the litter, and grip the sapling ends.

Jack Chester made one step, and fell headlong to the ground.

He turned to one side, and began to struggle to regain his feet.

"Just a little giddy, brother," he said, with the utmost cheerfulness. "A little numb. The ropes have frozen me a trifle, King, but I'll soon be able to navigate."

The King Bird desperately kneeled beside him, and massaged the muscles of the legs to get the blood back in circulation. It needed five priceless minutes before Chester could be trusted on his feet, but when he could manage, he took up his end of the burden willingly enough.

The King Bird laid Bobby in the sling of the stretcher. One piece of a branch, tied across at the head of the litter, kept the poles from working too narrowly together, and at the directions which the King Bird gave, Jack Chester marched off, his captor stepping behind him.

The boy, one hand under his head, was utterly silent, staring up at the increasing flood of moonlight.

It shone on his wan face, puckered in lines of tragic resolution and resignation. He was enduring his agony of body without noticing it, so much greater was the torment in his mind.

The King Bird, studying him, felt his own heart doubly pinched.

Half of his duty and his desire was to be here; but another and even a more vital half was flying down the trail on the black mare, like a shadow keeping beside the girl as she rode for her life, and the gray stallion hounded her closely.

But even he had been able to give the stallion work; and the girl was lighter—twenty—yes, thirty pounds lighter, or even more. Furthermore, she could ride as well as a man; she knew Molly, and the mare knew her.

So he arranged his hopes, but with bitterness in his heart he felt that, after all, not even the light weight that Molly carried, not even the skill of her rider, could keep the mare away from the prodigious strides of the stallion.

Now, lifting his head suddenly, he heard the pounding of hoofs, not far behind.

They were back. Some of them, at least, were already close at hand on the trail of the King Bird and the boy!

CHAPTER XXXII

THE RACE TO TOWN

THE GREAT gray horse was far too much for Molly at her best, even with such a light and clever jockey in the saddle. And when Helena Blair looked back, she saw the stallion looming behind her, more and more clearly.

It would not be long before her pursuers detected the absence of a rider on one of the horses. Already Dick Macey appeared to be close enough to have made sure. And now the gathering pyramid of pale light in the east sharpened, heightened, and the rim of the moon itself was about to glitter out above the hills, when the girl passed the narrow mouth of a ravine, and with the rushing hoofbeats of the gray not far behind her, she cast the mustang loose and gave it a cut to start it down the canyon's throat.

What she hoped for happened.

Dick Macey dared not pass the throat of that canyon. Neither did the men who swept up behind him. Inside it might be the deadly rifle of the King Bird to teach them manners if they were too hasty.

They had to stalk the mouth of the ravine, and it was

only a long moment after they got there, that they could make sure that the King Bird was actually not there, nor any one that they wanted.

By that time, she had ridden the black mare up a long and twisting ascent to the crest of a rise, after which followed a more gradual incline through a pass among the hills.

The gray had run very gallantly and well, and there was still a tremor in the girl's heart, but she knew that nothing on four legs could ever overcome a second lead such as she had built up with Molly.

On the top of the rise, Brick checked her mount, and even dropped to the ground so that the mare could blow a bit better.

Looking down, the girl saw the hunt come streaming out of the dark mouth of the lower valley. All was painted clearly before her. The moonlight through the thin mountain air seemingly drew up close the little figures of horses that poured out into the larger valley. She saw the bunch of them turn back, and go galloping the way they had come, leading with them the riderless horse which she had abandoned. But the great stallion, with Dick Macey on its back, had swung onto the farther trail, and was coming straight toward her.

Yes, as he came, she saw him brandish an arm over his head at her, a strange little gesture of that distant form, but one that filled her with horror. She had a feeling that she was chained up in the midst of a nightmare, and that she would have to remain there, entranced by that single glance which he had given her, until the silver horse had wound up the climb and come striding toward her bearing that horrible mask of a face in the saddle, that face that glistened as though it were all one scar!

She was freed from the numbing effect of that nightmare, to be sure, the instant the idea popped into her head. She got back to Molly, leaped onto the back of the mare, and sent her off at a good, reaching gallop.

They had gained invaluable time and distance. They had put behind them that exhausting climb up the winding trail.

185

Certainly nothing could capture them before Molly got into Elmira. So the girl, full of that conviction, rode the mare along easily, especially as they continued to work up the ascent toward the center of the pass.

She was almost at that crest when, looking back, she saw the stallion lurch up onto the trail and sweep toward her again.

Suddenly she went sick and weak—for suppose that her confidence in Molly were overstrained?

But as she let Molly out on the top grade of the pass, where the way was as smooth and level as a well-built road, and as the hills heaved up their big black shoulders and swept past her, she knew that Molly could not be overtaken. For a veritable gale of wind was raised by her gallop, and stinging the eyes of Helena Blair.

And so, looking back with a rather savage grin of triumph, she saw a thing that turned her heartstrings to brittle ice!

It was the gray horse, topping the rise behind her, and now thundering straight down the way toward them.

If, with one beat of magic wings, the stallion had smitten the air, and so risen without further effort from the valley floor beyond, to this height, he could not have been fresher for his running. He looked prodigiously high, and the vast black shadows worked in and out underneath him, collapsing and extending.

All the surety went from the girl then. She settled down to ride for her life. Looking back, now and again, as she urged Molly forward, she marked the distance shrink between the gray horse and the black, outstreaming tail of Molly!

They had still three miles to go, to get into the town of Elmira—three moonlit miles to get to that sleeping little town, and every stride that the gray horse made was a winning one.

It came like thunder through a blue sky, like a sudden avalanche roaring down a white mountainside, like the white horse of death itself.

Never had she seen a thing so beautiful, and so monstrous as that racing giant putting the dark hills behind him, and drawing gradually nearer.

Only gradually—of that she was sure, as she flattened herself lower along the back of the mare to cut into the wind. The incline of the trail, dipping down and down, ended, and there was a slight rise beyond.

As Molly flew up it, a gun barked behind them, and the girl heard the whir of the bullet. Somehow that loosened the freezing blood in her and gave her a new life and strength. She had known that Dick Macey hated her; now it was clear that he hated her well enough for murder.

She snatched out the little pearl-handled revolver that the King Bird had given her, and fired half blindly under her arm at the giant in the rear.

The answer was a screech that came hoarsely, like the cry of a sea gull down the wind. It was pure rage. There was not a chance in a thousand that she had hit him. Glancing back again, she saw Macey flogging the great horse with a quirt, and saw the gray shaking its head, as it made vain efforts to increase its speed.

But increase it the gray could not, and as they came out on the last long level stretch toward the shadowy town that crouched beyond, she made sure, with thanksgiving in her heart, that Molly had actually gained a trifle.

But she gained no more. The half-breed was no longer riding like an insane man, but crouching low, he jockeyed the silver beauty ahead, cutting down the girl's margin of safety bit by bit.

Then utter fear mastered her.

She began to fire over her shoulder, as Molly fled down the trail, not so much in the expectation of striking the monster who followed, as in hope that the noise of the gunshots would reach the ears of men in Elmira.

But what would random shots mean to those men?

A scream swelled in her throat and died there. Fear had closed her throat for the moment. Then the cry came, and tore her ears more than her throat.

She dared one glance behind her, and almost fell from the saddle, for the creature was close up, and the hands that extended along the neck of the stallion seemed to be reaching for her. Yet those hands were nothing compared with the deformed face of the half-breed. For the wind of the gallop fanned the brim of his sombrero straight back, and the moonlight glittered on his face, and in his eyes.

CHAPTER XXXIII

INEZ'S OFFER

HER SCREAMS were before her, in Elmira, now. They must be plucking at the ears of many a sleeper. Men must surely be rising, reaching for weapons. But how long would it take them to reach doors or windows? And how straight would they shoot, when the spectacle came before their eyes?

For it was plain that the devil in Dick Macey's heart would drive him to continue the hunt straight into the street of Elmira.

The houses, all silver and black under the moon, yawned apart at the end of the street. The mare shot through. And, looking down—she dared not look back!—the girl saw the monstrous shadow of the stallion galloping on the very ground where Molly strode!

What could she do?

Try to dodge, perhaps? It was risky work, without a saddle, and at that speed!

But she called out, suddenly, the word that Molly's master always used: "Whoa—hip!"

Then she gripped with hands and knees with all her might.

The black mare planted all four feet and skidded to a halt; and the girl, jerked from her place on the back of Molly by that sudden check, shot forward, gripped vainly at mane and neck, and rolled head over heels in the deep dust.

It had saved the life of the King Bird, that same night, this cushioning of dust. It kept the girl from being stunned, at least, and gave her wits to understand that the half-breed had shot by her, gradually bringing the stallion to a halt.

Now the gray horse was halted, almost, and swinging to make the turn, when an unearthly screech of rage came from the nearest house, and a rifle shot rang out.

Dick Macey howled; or the fiend that was in him yelled, as he put the gray horse over a fence top, and rode out of sight between two houses.

Out on the front porch of a cottage came a boy of nine or ten years old, trailing behind him the weight and length of one of those old Kentucky rifles that shoot bullets of sixteen to the pound.

His nightgown flapped about his thin legs. His tousled hair stood up in a pale fire about his head.

Helena Blair, leaning against Molly, began to laugh hysterically, as other people came running out, eager, excited men, all armed.

She heard the voice of the boy explaining:

"I seen it! I seen it! Me, Mickey White!—I seen it. There was a gent on the biggest gray hoss that you ever seen, chasin' her. And he reached for her. And her hoss stopped like a prime cutting hoss, and off she went, and that there gent, he missed her—and I shot—and he went back in that way. Get him! He ain't a man! He's a low skunk."

Cries of bewildered rage came from that group of men, as they broke and ran for horses to follow the trail of the brute. And the girl turning from the mare, steadier, but still a little dizzy, saw before her, half dressed, but always full of dignity, that worthy Spaniard—Señor Don Esteban Cuyas!

To understand Don Esteban's presence, it is necessary to go back not many days to the morning after the disappearance of Helena Blair from her home.

Inez Ramirez herself had ridden down the hill, and gone out to the little ranch house. There she found the old people going calmly about their work. They greeted her pleasantly, quietly, but there was death in their faces. And learning of their daughter's disappearance, Inez offered to do what she could—but what could any one do?

She could only say: "Whatever Helena did was done for the best. I know that. Everybody knows that."

They thanked her with pathetic smiles, and she went back to her house on the hill with ice about her heart.

Don Esteban surprised her. He was standing at the entrance to the patio, and he came up to shake hands, and say good morning.

"I thought that you'd be out of here," said the girl. "I thought that you'd be on a train, by this time. What's the matter, Esteban?"

"I forgot something that I couldn't go without," said the Spaniard.

"And what's that?" asked she.

"Yourself," said Don Esteban.

"Stuff and nonsense," said the girl. "You know what I am. You know what my family is. The whole pretty picture of us was presented to your eyes by that clever fiend of a King Bird, last night."

She added: "I'm glad he did it. I'm glad—I say it, and I mean it. I can breathe this morning for the first time in my grown-up life."

"I want to say some more things," said Don Esteban, "to you, to your father, and to your mother."

"Father and Ramon have gone out riding," said the girl. "They needed the air, it seems. Mother's likely right there in the patio. But she won't be glad to see you, any more than she'd be glad to see a picture of all her sins."

"If she's here, will you let me come to her with you?" asked the Spaniard.

She looked up at his long, ugly face, and the quiet strength of his voice was a very odd and new music in her ears.

"All right," she said. "We'll go find her, and talk a few facts."

The Señora Ramirez, as a matter of fact, was seated where the sun beat full upon her. It was her practice every sunny morning of her life, if time permitted, to spend at least one hour in this fashion, motionless, thoughtless, allowing the

190

sun to soak into her body, softening her soul, ripening her spirit, as it were, for another day to be spent in this animal world.

As she saw the two come into the patio, she did not rise to greet the Spaniard. She remained in her chair, as though she were a queen on a throne. She was as white, or rather as yellow, as carved ivory. In this strong light, all the wrinkles in her resolved old face showed with the utmost clarity.

Don Esteban kissed her hand.

And the girl said: "Esteban has something to say to the two of us. To the whole family, in fact, but I've explained that the men are out taking the air, or shooting rabbits, or something like that."

A gleam came into the expressionless eyes of Señora Ramirez. She turned her gaze on her daughter first, and then on Don Esteban, without speaking a word.

He endured that glance with a good grace. Then he said:

"No one wants to dwell on the past. One can't dress it to make a good salad, no matter how pleasant it may have been. For my part, I want to speak still about the future. I went to the hotel last night feeling that I should leave. I lay awake all night thinking not of departure, but of Inez. Now I have come to ask you all to reconsider me as a possible husband for Inez."

Amazement, suspicion, doubt, and joy, broke from the lady of the house in one exclamation. Then she set her teeth and looked at the girl.

Inez, for her part, blinked as though in the middle of darkness a light had been flashed in her eyes.

"Do you mean that, Esteban?" she demanded. "Of course you mean it. You're not attempting a joke. But I told you last night that I don't love you a whit."

"My dear," said her mother, "I pity you. I used to think that you had good sense even if you did not have good feeling."

Don Esteban paid no heed to that remark. Neither did the girl. The Spaniard said:

191

"I have finished courting you in one way, Inez. Why won't you let me start in another? You've been thinking of me as a stiffly starched empty-head of the Old World. Isn't that true?"

"Not as bad as that," said the girl.

"Well," went on Don Esteban, "I am not a clever fellow, and that is true. But perhaps I'm better than you think. I wish there were a way of proving to you that I'm not entirely removed from the New World. There's a great deal about it that I like already, and could like still more. If I could meet you on that basis, don't you think that you might be able to see more that's attractive to you in me?"

She put out her hand and gripped his, like a man.

"What a fine fellow you are, Esteban," said she, "and what a lot too good for me! I like you a thundering lot already. And of course I can like you better and better, but that may not amount to love."

"If I am allowed to keep hoping," said he, "I shall be happy. Do you permit that?"

"Of course I do," said the girl, "and thank you for coming like this."

"And if you could point out what can be done to bring us still closer together, so that we understand one another?" he suggested.

"I know what you mean," she said. "I've been raised in a world a good deal different from yours. I can't imagine you fitting into my life, or I into yours, unless I live a lie, all day long the rest of my years."

"That's what you fear, of course," said he.

Señora Ramirez leaned forward, with a sudden and keen interest.

"I'll tell you what *I'd* be doing right now," broke out the girl.

"Tell me, then," said he.

"I'd be spurring a horse to death on the trail of the scoundrels who got their hands on little Helena Blair. The King Bird is on that trail already!"

To the astonishment of both of them, Señora Ramirez exclaimed: "Good!"

Don Esteban answered: "If I know how to begin——"

"Throw yourself anywhere into the mountains, keep your ears open, and your eyes wide," said the girl. "I'll tell you this, Esteban—it's not much of a prize to offer you, but I'd marry at the drop of a hat anybody man enough to bring that girl safely home!"

He took in a quick, deep breath, and braced his shoulders back as he did so.

"I wanted to know something like that," he said. "Not that I can do so much. Not that I could succeed, say, where the King Bird might fail. But I would rather ride at his side, Inez, than beside a king, I think!"

And Señora Ramirez exclaimed: *"I've* been the fool! I never dreamed what a woman you are, Inez, or what a man you are, Don Esteban!"

That was the reason that Don Esteban's face was the first one that the eyes of the girl fell upon, as she turned from the panting black mare, there in the dusty street of Elmira. It had taken much riding for Don Esteban and a good deal of quick brain work, also, before he finally arrived at the storm center, around which so many happenings were revolving, as it were.

He took her hand, as she cried out at the sight of him.

"You remember me, Miss Blair?" said he. "Can you tell Inez Ramirez, some day, that if I didn't bring you back from trouble, at least I was ready to shake hands with you when you arrived from it?"

He laughed, with both pleasure and disappointment in his face.

"I'll tell her. I hope I understand," said the breathless girl.

Then, to the others: "We've got to get back down the trail—any good fellow who'll take a chance with his horse and his gun! Only Dick Macey chased me all the way to Elmira. The rest of 'em are back there—four men—hunting for the King Bird and young Bobby Kinney. Who'll go back with me? I'll show you the way! Who'll go back?"

Don Esteban was one who went.

Another was the elder Kinney himself.

A third was the Federal marshal, Jim Hampton. He had never entirely given up the trail of the King Bird, and it was he, as a matter of fact, who had found Don Esteban on the same trail for quite other reasons, and brought him into Elmira.

Aside from these, there were others. There were as many, in fact, as Elmira could horse and arm.

They streamed out of the town at a rapid gallop, with the black mare in the front, once more peerless, so long as the bright image of the stallion was not in the eye of the crowd.

Straight back up the trail she guided them. Of course they had no real thought of riding down Dick Macey. Not while the stallion was under him! But they might come up in time to save young Bobby Kinney's life.

And the King Bird?

They thought of him, too, and no one so much as the marshal. He had his face set in the hardest lines, as he rode his long-striding half-bred gelding at the side of the girl.

She, turning eagerly to him, was pouring out her tale of how she had been hired to nurse a wounded man, and how that had turned out to be the kidnaped boy, and of how that single man, the King Bird, had hunted and hounded the whole pack of them through the mountains, dropping on them again and again, as though out of a clear sky, and how they had used all their resources to stop him, and tried their murderous arts vainly.

Still the marshal listened, with a face as grim as before.

Finally, he said: "I ain't a judge and a jury, young lady. And besides, we ain't got either the King Bird or the boy in our hands yet. If we get the King Bird, and everything turns out well—— I dunno, though—it depends on what the jury will think that tries him. I reckon that it'll be a Western jury; and I reckon that it ain't goin' to agree! But don't you start thinkin' of the happy ending, till that boy and the King Bird are both free from this mess!"

CHAPTER XXXIV

DISCOVERED

WHEN THE noise of the horses came near the King Bird there was nothing to do but to take cover. The best place that offered was a tangle of brush, in which the grass had grown up tall, being protected from grazing by the dense growth of bushes. They went into that thicket at once, and the King Bird returned to the point where they had entered to straighten the grass they had beaten down.

When he stepped back to the litter, there was no sight of Jack Chester.

"Which way?" he muttered to the boy.

"Didn't see him go," said Bobby Kinney, with a shake of the head.

The grass waved near by, and the King Bird pounced with a long bound. He landed through the tall grass on the back of Chester, and dragged him back.

"That was a near thing," said Jack Chester, nodding his head. "Outside of nearly getting my back broke, I'm all right, and another second or two, and I could have been on my feet and running for it."

"I could have tagged you with lead," said the King Bird.

"And called 'em this way with the noise of the shot?" asked the other calmly.

He was perfectly at ease, the rascal. Neither remorse nor conscience ever had troubled him, it was apparent.

"Suppose that you were to deal with a fellow like this, Bobby," said the King Bird, "what would you do about him?"

"I'd put him in a cage," said the boy, "and I'd charge 'em

a nickel apiece to see something that looks like a man, and talks like a man, and isn't a man."

Jack Chester was the first to laugh, and rather loudly.

"One more noise as loud as that will be about the last you make, Chester," said the King Bird.

"All right, all right," said Chester. "But don't worry so much. They can't trail you by moonlight. It would be a hard enough job by sunlight, for that matter."

"Garry!" said the wounded boy. "Garry can trail things even in the dark, almost. He smells out trouble."

"Garry would do well under ground," remarked the King Bird, through his teeth. "I never knew a human with less reason for being alive than Garry."

"Nor I," said Jack Chester calmly. "He's a hound. There's no truth, honor, decency, or gentleness in him. He's an animal, not a man."

"What about Dick Macey?" asked the boy. He twisted a little, for his wound was tormenting him.

"Dick Macey?" said Chester. "Why, there's this about Macey. He's such a devil that he's interesting, but Garry's such a hound that nobody wants to do anything but kick him."

They were silent an instant, listening intently.

Then Chester sighed, for the sound of the horses was moving off to a distance, rapidly.

"Seem to be leaving you, Jack," said the King Bird. "I'd like to know one thing from you."

"Go ahead," said the other. "If only I could smoke a cigarette."

"I'd like to let you," answered the King Bird. "But it's too risky."

They sat on either side of the wounded lad. And Bobby Kinney looked up at the rising moon and wondered how long he could endure his present agony without screaming.

It seemed as though the nervous system of the King Bird extended to that of the lad, for he reached down with both hands, carefully, and adjusted him on the litter so that less pressure came on the torn leg.

196

The boy groaned with relief.

"You speak out, Bobby," said the King Bird, "when the pain is grinding you like that."

"I'm all right," said the boy.

"By the way, Jack," said the King Bird, "couldn't you have caught Bobby, when he started to get away from you? Did you have to go after him with a gun?"

"Sure I could have caught him," said Chester, with his usual cheerful air. "But I'd warned him before what would happen if he tried to run. It made me mad when I saw him sneaking off, as if I was blind. So I just up and let him have it. I like to live up to my promises," he concluded, "so long as I don't have to pay for 'em out of my own hide."

"I'd like to see you hang," said the King Bird softly. "That would do me a lot of good."

"I'll bet it would," agreed Chester. "I would have liked to see you burn, too. I thought I *was* seeing you burn, and I was a happy fellow. But you were only scorching a little. That was all!"

He actually sighed, as he finished speaking.

The King Bird chuckled. "I like to hear you talk, Jack," said he.

"People generally do," said Chester. "It's all that I've done to make a living since I started out for myself. Anybody can turn talk into money, if he doesn't care what he says. That's something for you to remember, Bobby, as you grow up."

"Yes," said the boy, "I'll remember a lot about you, because I guess you're pretty close to my idea of what's right, Jack."

"Got a mean tongue in his head, the kid has," remarked Chester indifferently. "Seems to think that I'm not all that I might be. But I've lived soft, Bobby. None of your nine o'clock to the office for me. None of your doughnut-and-coffee lunches, either. I've lived on the fat. A few lean periods, here and there. Like the one I was going through before I met your respected dad, Bobby. But on the whole, I've lived on the fat, and loved it!"

He meant what he said. There was enthusiasm in his voice.

197

"The King Bird's lived on the fat, too," said the boy, in answer. "But he's stayed decent."

"So decent that the Federal marshal wants to get him, and there's a price on his head?" queried Chester. "That's too decent for me, Bobby!"

"Maybe the law wants him," said Bobby Kinney, "but everybody on the range respects him."

"Aye," said Chester, "you know which side your bread's buttered on!"

He chuckled again. Then, raising his head, he listened hard. Far, far away, they could hear a horse snort.

"On the wrong trail," muttered Chester. "The blockheads! On a wrong trail, the fools!"

"They have time to work it out," answered the King Bird. "We're not moving from here till they've gone out of hearing."

"If Garry wasn't there," said the boy anxiously. "But he may put 'em right. He's a snake, the way he can find trails!"

"Only five of 'em," said the King Bird. "Remember that, Bobby—and I have two guns!"

The boy sighed, and said nothing. Even he, no matter how much he trusted the King Bird, could understand that five to one made terrible odds!

"If I live and grow up, King," he said, "I want to tell you something."

"Go on," said Chester. "Say you want to be like the King Bird, if you grow up."

"That's what I was going to say," answered the boy. "It doesn't make it any less because you snarl at me, Jack."

"Thanks, Bobby," said the King Bird. "That's the best thing that ever was said to me. But you'd better grow up like your father. He stays inside the law."

"King," said the boy, "I'd like to ask you something."

"Fire away."

"D'you ever do anything like this before—for a boy, I mean to say?"

"No," said the King Bird.

"I never could understand it," said Bobby Kinney. "I mean—when I'm a man, I hope I'd be able to do anything

I could for a friend of mine—a grown-up friend, but for a boy that I never saw in my life, I couldn't do it!"

"Neither could I," said the King Bird.

"No?" exclaimed Bobby. "But you've done it, King! That's why you're here, staked out for killing, like a steer, or something!"

"But I've seen you before," said the outlaw.

"You? When, King?"

"In the old days. When you knew me, too."

"When I knew you?"

The boy was silent, staring up at the moon.

Then he twisted his head up in both his hands and looked at the King Bird.

"D'you ever work on father's ranch?" he asked.

"I never worked on it, but I was there," said the King Bird.

"It beats me," said the boy, shaking his head. "But sometimes you've seemed sort of familiar to me—not your face or you, but your voice, sort of. I don't know how."

"I'm going to tell you how," said the King Bird. "Because we're sort of in the hole, and we may never come out. It's something that we ought to know together, it seems to me."

"Tell me!" said the boy.

The King Bird leaned, and whispered for a long moment at the ear of Bobby. The boy gasped. And Jack Chester, stretching his head forward, strained his ears, but could not make out the words. Then the King Bird sat upright again.

Chester could hear the quick, hard breathing of Bobby.

Then the boy said: "Will you give me your hand, King?"

"I will," said the King Bird.

He stretched it out, and the slim fingers of the lad gripped it hard.

Bobby closed his eyes.

"Nothing matters very much now," he said. "King, I'm——"

"Hush," murmured the King Bird. "There's something near us—a man or a snake, or something. Not a whisper out of anybody. Chester, get low!"

They flattened themselves, and as they did so, a horse snorted and stamped close by, almost on top of them, it seemed to all three.

CHAPTER XXXV

THE BLOOD TIE

JUST OVER them, out of the grass, arose the long, lean form of Garry. His voice screeched: "They're here!" And he lunged backward, toppling, and sprawling away from them in the grass.

The King Bird had half risen, gun in hand, but he sank down again, without firing.

Around the patch of thicket voices answered the yell of Garry, some near, and some far.

"You could have nailed Garry," said Chester quietly.

"I could," said the King Bird.

"Why not?" asked Chester sharply.

And Bobby Kinney said, in a voice shrill and high with emotion: "I know why."

"Tell him, Bobby," said the King Bird.

"Because he didn't have a gun in his hand—you couldn't shoot—you couldn't shoot!"

There was an exultation in the voice of the boy.

"The both of you are a little nutty," declared Chester. "Now, brothers, you tell me how you're going to get out of this, will you? They're stretched out all around you. They've got perfect cover. They can lie out there in the bright moonlight, boys, and pepper every inch of this patch with lead. You're the boy with the bright ideas, King. Let's hear what you're going to do about it?"

They heard the galloping of the horses, as Chester spoke, and voices shouting commands, particularly the voice of Jake.

"I like to hear you talk, Chester, most of the time," said the King Bird. "But just now you irritate me a little. I have an idea that I might relish lending you a gun, Jack, so that we could fight it out together."

"Yeah," said Chester, "you'd be that much of a fool, I suppose. But now I'm about to get up and walk away, King, and take the kid along with me."

"Are you?" said the King Bird, in the coldest of voices.

"I am," said Chester. "If they know that I'm in here, they'll give you another chance to be noble. They'll let me take the boy out with me—if you stay behind. How about that, King? Are you that noble?"

The King Bird had no chance to answer. It was Bobby who cried out:

"King, you can't do it. I won't go."

"You can't help yourself, Bobby," said the other. "Chester is strong enough to carry you, and you'll have to go. I'm sorry. Sorry to see Chester go, chiefly. I've wanted to kill men before, but I've never wanted to as I want to kill you, Jack. I'd like to do it with my bare hands. I'd like it better that way."

"Good old boy," said Chester. "Of course you would! I see that you can't, however. Too bad, King. A whole lot too bad. But you have to make sure that the brat's safe, don't you? You have to be noble. Oh, yes, that's it. For the sake of the blood tie, eh?"

He laughed again.

"The what?" exclaimed the King Bird.

"You fool," said Chester. "Don't you suppose that I've known from the first that you're Kinney's oldest son? Of course you are! I spotted that long ago. And now you'll prove it. Shall I call to 'em?"

"I won't go, Jimmy," said the wounded boy. "I won't go, Jim. Don't let him talk with 'em. I'd rather stay here with you. I'd a lot rather."

"Sound out, Chester!" commanded the King Bird briskly.

Chester shouted, rising to his knees.

"Jake! Oh, Jake!"

"Halloo!" came the answer.

"Get closer, Jake. It's me. It's Chester."

They could hear shouts of excitement in answer. And then the voice of Jake sounded closer by.

"Here I am, Jack."

"All right, Jake. It's Chester speaking."

"I recognized your tune, old son. What's in there with you?"

"The King Bird, and the kid, of course."

"Good for you. What's the news?" asked Jake.

"I take the kid out with me, and leave the King Bird in here."

"And what does the King Bird get for his share?" sounded the shrill voice of Bobby suddenly.

"He gets hell, that's what he gets!" howled Garry, from the near distance.

"That's it." Jack Chester chuckled. "A little hell is what the King Bird gets—for being so noble!"

He laughed aloud.

"You hear me, Jake?" he asked.

"I hear you, son."

"What's the bargain?" asked Chester.

"We got everything to win, on that, and nothing to lose," said Jake. "Mind you, though, the King Bird, he's gotta stay put. We'll handle him the way we please, when the two of you are out."

"That's all right," said Jack Chester, still laughing. "He's so noble that he won't say a word to that, if he can save the brat!"

"I won't go," shouted the boy in answer.

"You've gotta go, you little fool," said Jack Chester. "Don't spoil your brother's play. He's going to be noble, the fool. His life for your life, so you can grieve proudly over him the rest of your days—if you have many days, which you won't unless your tightwad of a father kicks through with some cash. His life for yours. That's the sort of stuff that they make music and poetry about, eh?"

He chuckled once more.

The King Bird knelt beside Bobby and said quietly: "It doesn't matter a bit, Bobby. The fact is, I've gone wrong. I've smashed up my life by running wild. The right way, the steady way, that wouldn't do for me. I had to go as I pleased. And that's why I'm cornered now. I don't mind. I have to pay all in one lump sum, and I'm ready. Bobby, steady up, and stop shaking—stop crying, too. Be a man. You've got to be a man in my place, now."

"I'll be—a—man," gasped Bobby, strangling, but stopping his tears.

"They haven't got me yet, either," said the King Bird. "And something tells me that I'll make 'em pay for all they collect out of my hide. That's one comfort. The other one is you."

"Don't speak about me, Jimmy," said the boy. "I can't stand it. I'm going to die. I can't breathe!"

"You're going to live, Bobby," said the King Bird. "You've got too many things to do for me. Understand?"

"I understand," said the boy. "You tell me, Jimmy. Oh, I wish I were grown up now—to do them for you—anything!"

"You can do them without growing up. One is about Brick. You can remember what I say?"

"About Brick? I'll remember every word. She's terribly fond of you, Jimmy."

"She?" exclaimed the King Bird, surprised. "Why, she does nothing but laugh at me, Bobby."

"Laugh? That's her way. She'd never let on. She'd rather die first. But all she did was tell me stories, and the King Bird was always the hero. I used to get almost tired of hearing about you—I didn't know it was you, Jim!"

"That makes everything harder," muttered the King Bird. "The fact is, Bobby, it makes it a little harder now—if Brick cares a whack about me. That's what I want you to tell her—that I was thinking of her. That about Inez—that was a flash in the pan. I had to be a fool about Inez so that I could get the range and understand what a lot of mileage there is between Inez and a girl like Brick. Will you tell Brick that?"

"I'll tell her," said the boy, beginning to sob.

He fought back the tears.

"I'm sorry, Jim," he said. "You go on and tell me."

"Pathetic, this is," commented Chester ironically.

"The other thing is about our father," said the King Bird. "I haven't had many kind ideas about him. But back there in Elmira, I changed my mind a little bit. He's a human being, like the rest of us, but his pride is that he won't show it to any one. You remember that, yourself, when you have dealings with him. You tell him that I wanted his forgiveness for the trouble that I've made. You tell him that I remembered how much thicker blood is than water, will you?"

"I'll tell him," said the boy in a choking voice.

"All right," said the King Bird. "That's about all. I'm glad that we've had this bit of time together, old fellow."

"Good-by, Jimmy," said the boy.

The King Bird picked him up in his arms.

"Good-by, old son," said he. "You'll fill my place. So long, Bobby. Here, Chester. Put your arms where mine are. Take short steps, because that hurts him less."

"I'll manage him, all right," said Chester. "Very touching, these family farewells. I'd like 'em a lot better if I were sure that we were going to nail you, though, King. Well, so long."

He walked steadily away into the moonlight, as the King Bird dropped back into the grass.

A loud howl of welcome greeted Chester. For they had won the prize they had lost, this day, and a lucky chance it seemed to them all.

The King Bird watched Chester and his burden disappear behind a rock. He would remember that, for wherever he shot, he would not fire in that direction. And, as he thought of this, the rifles opened.

The bullets began to whir through the grass, and beat into the earth close about him. Plainly they had marked well the spot where he had stood, so now he began to wriggle, snakelike, through the little thicket.

He reached a slight depression in the ground.

That would offer some shelter, he felt, and then, as he stretched himself out, he felt a bullet whir close by his head.

It was plain that they were proceeding methodically, and that they would beat every inch of the small thicket with their bullets. It was only a matter of time before they found him once, and then again, and again, while he lay helpless. If he worked to the edge of the brush and tried to fire back at them, the flash of his gun would be enough to bring an answering volley that would sweep him from the earth.

There was a better way than lying like a foolish rabbit, and that was to bring matters to a quick end—to jump up and rush them, and take his death in the front, like a man.

He looked up to the blazing misshapen moon, and then gathered himself to rise.

CHAPTER XXXVI

MACEY'S VENGEANCE

THE GUNFIRE ceased at that moment, as though his movement had been seen, and an order had been given. He looked out over the top of the grass, as he heard them yelling, and saw the cause for this excitement—a mere flash of a silver horse as it passed into a grove of trees.

That was Dick Macey back, of course—and what report had he of the chase of the girl?

If he had actually overtaken her, surely the black mare must be somewhere about? The King Bird heard the shouting run in a circle around the thicket he was in. It might possibly be that he could work out on the farther side of the place, while the reception of Dick Macey was attracting so much attention.

But in an instant a veritable roar of guns opened on the little thicket in which he lay. Some news that Dick Macey brought had made the others eager to bring their game to an end.

"Wait a minute!" shouted the voice of Jake. "Go up that tree, Garry, and you'll be able to angle down shots at him."

There was, in fact, a tall tree not far from the edge of the thicket. Now, with a shout of pleasure, Garry began to climb it, unseen by the King Bird, but heard as he worked up on the opposite side of the trunk.

In the meantime, the gunfire ended. Instead of scattering their efforts, Jake was establishing a lookout, who, from a safe position, could control the gunfire.

It was about the end for the King Bird, and he knew it, and accepted it as such. In the meantime, he had a hungry curiosity. There was no good reason why Garry should remain alive—there were excellent reasons why he should die at once. And the King Bird yearned only to be the executioner.

It would be a hard shot—something between sixty and seventy yards, and by moonlight; and he had nothing but a revolver to use. However, with a nice and practiced eye he made his calculations, and prepared for the shot, making those allowances which would have to be for height, and because this particular gun he would fire with carried a trifle to the right—not enough to matter at any point-blank range, but enough to make four or five inches difference at this distance.

A hand and whole arm appeared around the edge of the tree, but the watcher in the thicket made no attempt to take advantage.

"He's corked already, and the fizz gone out of him," said the voice of Chester, not far off, speaking from a nest of rocks. "That last pelting located him, I think, and there's nothing but a dead man in there."

"Garry'll soon tell," answered Dick Macey.

The King Bird looked up eagerly. He centered his attention on the first forking of the big tree, for Garry would have to be both daring and agile to pass that forking and work up along one of the two huge limbs that extended above it, and so screen himself in the foliage while he spied out the enemy.

But it was actually from well above the forking that the voice of Garry, sounded, shouting:

"King, d'you hear me? I see you, and I've got you in the holler of my hand!"

The wailing voice came with a howl against the ears of the King Bird. And, at the same time, he saw head and shoulders loom, dimly, behind a thin screen of leaves. He fired instantly.

The target disappeared. Then something loose, shaped like a great torn bag, dropped from the upper fork of the tree and struck the ground with an impact which the King Bird could distinctly hear.

It sent a faint shock through him, and it brought a yell of rage from the others.

"Leave him lay!" yelled the voice of Jake. "He's dead. He'll never move again. Leave him lay, and get the King Bird."

"Fire the grass," said the voice of Macey. "Why not fire the grass?"

"We can't get close enough for that," answered Jake.

"We can tie some dead grass to a stick, and light it, and throw it in. Or a piece of saddle blanket'll hold fire like a fuse."

"You're right!" cried Jake. "We'll smoke him out."

It was a mystery to the King Bird that they had not used that simple and effective expedient before. The night damp was in the grass—that was the only thing against it, that and the fact that the burning might make a low-rolling smudge through which he could run into the open.

There was still a hundredth part of a chance for him, he felt, when it seemed to him that he heard a far-away murmur, a pulse of sound that began to grow out rapidly into the drumming of hoofbeats.

"Hey, King, King!" shouted Macey. "Here goes for you, you hound. Here's the finish for you!"

A smoky streak darted through the air and landed in the edge of the thicket. The King Bird started working his way carefully toward it, but an instant later, a long, straight arm of smoke lifted up, white as milk, in the moonshine; under the smoke came the crackling sound of fire that was rapidly catching.

Now that it was started, he never could put it out. He saw the smoke column widen and heighten, and a chorus of cheers broke out.

That cheering ended as Jake shouted a warning; and after his cry, the hoofbeats that the King Bird had heard before rolled suddenly and heavily upon his ears.

"They're here!" shouted Dick Macey. "I told you that we didn't have no time. I told you that, you fools, and now you've throwed the chance away."

There was a definite sound of scrambling as they moved to get to their horses.

"Kill the brat!" yelled Macey. "Don't leave the kid for 'em. Kill him, Chester!"

"Leave him be," thundered Jake. "We've lost our hand, but we ain't goin' to throw the cards in the fire! Leave him be!"

The King Bird, lifting his head cautiously to the level of the top brush, saw now as pretty a picture as ever had graced his eyes. For as the kidnapers got to horse, here and there, and scurried away, off to the left came the men of Elmira, riding desperately hard, burning up the last strength of their horses.

In the clear moonlight he could pick them out, one by one—the girl on the black mare; a tall man beside her, riding very erect; and yonder a form that he could have picked from ten thousand—Marshal Jim Hampton! Who was that near him, a smaller man, but riding with a swing?

The King Bird looked again and then shook his head. Was that not Kinney himself?

208

CHAPTER XXXVII

GOOD ADVICE

THEY WERE shooting as they came, while the outlaws scattered wide before them. Chester and Macey alone paused for an instant—as though sure of the speed of their mounts —and vented their spite by firing back for an instant.

It was a luckless moment for Jack Chester, for a rifle bullet clipped through the brain of his mustang, and down went the horse, with the leg of the rider pinned underneath!

Straight down on him came a rush of vengeful men— capture, and death by the rope were settled for Jack Chester, in that instant.

Still, for a moment, Dick Macey hesitated, as though the last, despairing cry of Chester inspired him to seek for one stroke of vengeance. Again he fitted his rifle to his shoulder, and fired. And the girl who rode by the marshal's side dropped low in the saddle!

Macey, with an Indian yell of triumph, whirled the big gray, and streaked off into the moon haze. Those who were best mounted, with shouts of rage and horror, drove after him, but the rest gathered suddenly around Helena Blair.

"Brick's gone," muttered the King Bird harshly, rising to his feet. "The breed got her. Brick's done for!"

He saw the mare halted, and the men gathered around to lift her to the ground. He even saw how her head fell back limply and both her arms trailed toward the ground.

"She's dead, dead!" muttered the King Bird.

But even then he could not go in to make sure. Hampton. would hold him, hold him from the one task that remained to him worth doing—to run Macey to the ground and kill him with exquisite deliberation.

He shouted loudly, and as the cry rang in the air, Molly pitched about and headed for him on the run.

The smoke that came from the grass fire made no difference to Molly. She was through it instantly, and the master swung himself into the saddle.

There was a rifle tucked into the saddle scabbard, and he took grim and happy note of that. There might be some long-range shooting before ever he got his hands on Macey!

Out of the burning thicket, the King Bird turned Molly, and settled her into a steady gallop after the disappearing stallion.

"It's the King Bird!" shouted two voices from the posse.

"Every man stand fast—no shooting!" yelled Marshal Jim Hampton. "I'd like to ride that trail with him, myself."

The King Bird rode all the night, and thrice he had sight of the gray horse, always far off. He managed to stay on the trail partly by finding the sign, but more than that, by sheer guesswork. He knew that part of the country well, and he put himself inside the mind of Dick Macey well enough to hit the truth three times in a row when Macey had turned and twisted among the network of ravines.

In all that time, the King Bird was hardly an hour in the saddle. He had made up his mind, firmly and calmly, that he would devote the rest of his life to the hunting down of Dick Macey, if need be. But, as he knew, there never would be a better chance than the present, when he was actually sighting the fugitive.

He knew two things. The first was that the stallion was better-winded, more enduring in every way, and far fleeter than the black mare. But he also knew that Dick Macey would probably outweigh him by thirty pounds, and that the big fellow would never budge out of the saddle. It would be useless to ask an Indian to walk ten steps, when he could catch a horse and ride the distance! Not even to save his neck would Dick Macey think of running on foot!

And that would have to be made to tell against the gray

stallion, even as the King Bird had made it tell once before. Therefore he kept himself religiously on the ground.

When the pinch came, he would need nothing of his strength, probably, except enough to pull a trigger; the rest, he would burn up recklessly on the trail.

That night was a bitter test, and they entered the Mac-Mahon Mountains, big, rock-ribbed monsters, with the ribs showing through, here and there. After that, it was hard work, constantly, hard for him on foot, and hard for the mare, even without his burden in the saddle.

But he kept close enough to the half-breed in spite of all of those twistings and windings of the many ravines until in the red of the dawn, he came up the dry bed of a ravine, and reached a place where three narrow canyons slipped into it.

Up any one of the three the stallion might have been ridden. Eagerly he searched the mouth of each for sign, and found none. The stone was black and hard as basalt. One could hardly have knocked chips off it by using a fourteen-pound sledge. And the horse had left no trace.

The sun rose and found the King Bird still in his agony of indecision, when down the left-hand ravine came an old man, very tall, very thin, and so weak with age that he was bending under the weight of a small pack as though it had been a hundred pounds.

He stopped at the hail of the King Bird, put down his pack, and raised a face shaggy with beard, a face parched by time, but with a pair of burningly young eyes in it, that smiled at the young man.

"Howdy, partner," said the old man.

The King Bird briefly saluted.

"I'm looking for a fellow on a gray stallion," he said. "A man with a face as white as a scar. See him up that ravine?"

"No," said the old man.

The King Bird turned impatiently.

That removed one chance against him. Of the other two, if worst came to worst, he could make a blind choice, and know that fifty per cent of the chances were for him, and fifty against. But it would be bitter to go wrong. Scores

211

and scores of miles might be lost in that way, together with all of the hard labor that he had invested on this night.

He shook his head, half despairingly, hungrily eager to be off.

The old man was seated on a rock by this time.

"The way I do," said he, "is to set down and think things over calm and steady, when it comes to a pinch. When a gent's lost in the prairies, say, that's the best way. The first idea ain't ever any good. It just starts you around and around in a circle!"

The King Bird looked at him with a troubled eye; the advice of an old wiseacre was not what he wanted at this moment, but he could savor a point in the remark.

At least, while he paused there, the mare could graze on the quarter acre of sun-cured grasses that grew at the side of the ravine.

He tore the saddle from her, and turned her loose.

"There's a pretty hoss, partner," said the old man. "And she's made, too. She's made to last, and that's what I like best, in a hoss or in a man. Look at some of these gents what are built like a wedge, all shoulders, and then a long taper down to the heels. They're fine to see, and they're fast on their feet, and they might be fine in a fight, too. But when it comes to a long lug, gimme a gent that maybe ain't so pretty to look at, but has his weight spread out all even."

The King Bird hardly heard these words.

He said aloud, impatiently: "Where could he have gone? Which one of the two?"

"You gotta know what end he'd have," said the old man. "That's always the best way."

"No end at all—except to get away," answered the King Bird.

"That's an end," answered the other instantly. "That's where he's travelin', then—away. Away, that's the name of the town that he's headin' for."

The King Bird stared at him, suspecting that age and privations might have unhinged this mind.

"I mean," said the other, "that he's goin' to go where his wings are better'n yours."

"What you mean by that?" demanded the King Bird curtly.

"It's like this," said the other. "He's got a reason for travelin' fast?"

"His scalp, that's all," said the King Bird. "He's done a murder—he's murdered a woman."

There was a brief silence. Then: "It sort of takes the gloss off of the mornin'," said the old man. "I hate to start a day with a thing like that. Was she young?"

The King Bird gave a brief gesture of assent. He stared gloomily toward the two ravine mouths. Which one would be better to choose?"

"A girl, maybe?" said the other.

The King Bird nodded.

"One you was fond of," concluded the old man, "and that's why you're burnin' up the trail after him. That gent, would he have much of a chance agin' you in a fight?"

"He'd rather run than fight," answered the King Bird. "He's bigger than I am, if that's what you mean."

He answered casually, carelessly.

"And his hoss, it ain't likely, is as good as this mare?"

"Better," said the King Bird. "It's Dick Macey and his gray stallion that I'm talking about."

"I never heard tell of that," said the other. "Prospectin' here and prospectin' there, the most news that I get is likely to be what I chip off a rock with my hammer. But it's a better hoss than the black, you say?"

"It is," said the King Bird grimly. "Faster, stronger, more lasting."

He looked impatiently toward the mare. Her very content, as she worked at the grass, irritated him, but he knew the wisdom of letting her eat where the forage was so thick, and so good.

"Well, then," said the prospector, "if it's a bird with that kind of wings, it'll take the air."

"What do you mean?" asked the young man.

"Why," said the other, "ain't you ever seen a slow-flyin' bird take to the hedges to get away from a hawk? And a fast-flyin' bird would rather be up in the sky, as far and as fast as it can go—so's it'll have more room for shiftin' and dodgin'. Ever watch a hawk droppin' at a bird, like that, and missin', and boundin' up into the high spots ag'in, and then stoopin' once more, like a rock throwed out of the blue top of things, and bouncin' up ag'in? And a hawk and a wild duck, that's a sight for sore eyes.

"I recollect seein' a wild duck hammerin' through the sky, and a big hawk mountin' above it, and chasin' that duck straight toward the mountain where I was sinkin' a bit of a shaft through quartzite—which the devil made quartzite to break the hearts of miners. And I laid off work, and watched, and that dog-gone hawk, it kept footin' through the air, and lettin' drive at the duck. A duck can fly, too, and that duck was sure hittin' the high spots, and tryin' to get higher and faster, and shiftin' this way and that.

"Right in the valley beside the mountain, not more'n a hundred yards from me, that hawk, it turned over in the air and come down, and hit that duck such a whang that I could hear it, like two hands beat together. And the hawk tied to that duck, and the feathers flew, and I seen the head of the duck hang down, dead as a rag. And so the pair of them went sifting down through the air, and down into the shadows in the bottom of the canyon, where I couldn't see no more. It was a kind of a fierce thing, and a grand thing, too."

The young man listened impatiently.

"Partner," he said gently, "will you tell me what that has to do with Dick Macey and the gray stallion—and me?"

"Why, it's got a good deal to do, I suppose," said the other.

"I don't see it."

"Well, you wanta get that murderin' Macey, don't you?"

"Yes."

"And you wanta know where he's gone to?"

"Yes."

"Well, then, I been pointin' out what birds'll do when they're hunted, and the fact is that birds and men, they're just about the same. Animals is all the same, too. A mule deer likes mountains, because it knows how to run upgrade. And an antelope, it likes the open, and lots of it, because it knows how to bust a hole in the breeze. Ain't I right?"

The King Bird nodded, frowning a little, for he began to see a point in all of this.

"And there's your man with the murder red on him—and the fine hoss under him—ain't he goin' to go and get into a place where he can see far and have a chance to burn up the ground?"

The young man nodded. "He's likely to do that," said he. "He wouldn't keep on running forever; not if I run him out of the mountains."

"Is his hoss big or small?"

"Seventeen hands, if it's an inch."

"Then it ain't for mountains," said the old man. "It's for the open, and I could tell you where that gent has headed to."

"Tell me, then," exclaimed the King Bird eagerly.

"You wanta tie into him, all right," murmured the prospector. "You wanta tackle him, and make one murderer less in the world, I can see. Well, that's all right. Only you wanta be sure where he is, and I'm goin' to risk tellin' you."

He jabbed at the ground with his heel, muttering:

"Here's the MacMahons, and yonder's the Flander Range, and yonder's the desert. Why, that's the only place for him. Look, partner—where'd you start after him?"

"Know a town called Elmira?"

"A dead town, without no blood in it?" asked the prospector.

"That's it. It wasn't so very far from there."

The prospector half closed his eyes, and then exclaimed:

"Why, it's dead sure. He's been drivin' for the desert all the way. He's been hammerin' hard for it. The big basin is what he's aimed at, where he can get plenty of goin'. Comanche Basin is what he's dived into, where there's water enough—for them that know how to find it—and grass enough to feed a hoss, spotted here and there, and rabbits enough to feed anybody that's got a rifle and a mighty strong stomach. Comanche Basin is your place, brother. Know your way to it?"

"I know my way to it," said the King Bird. "You're right —I guess he's gone to the Comanche Basin."

"Sam Tucker has got a shack right in the mouth of the pass, and day and night, nothin' goes by that Sam don't see it. You could ask Sam, and maybe they's one chance in five that he'd answer you, if he was feelin' pretty good. Go and try him!"

"I'll go and try him," agreed the young man.

He gripped the cold, hard hand of the prospector.

"Thanks," he said. "I never would have worked it out that way."

"Time tells," said the old fellow, wagging his head. "Time tells, but it takes you closer and closer to the end of the road, too. I reckon we all know a lot, when we get to the steppin'-off place."

CHAPTER XXXVIII

THE SILENT MAN

To the top of the pass, the King Bird struggled steadily along on foot. But from that point, where the ground sloped away before him, he mounted the mare and rode down.

Before him, the mountains opened like a funnel and gave him a prospect of the great basin beyond. Comanche Basin was obscure with a yellowish mist that seemed to promise that a sand storm had blown there, not long before.

Could the fugitive half-breed have ridden into this desert? It had seemed that he undoubtedly must have done so, when the old prospector was opening his mind on the subject, but now the King Bird had increasing doubts.

A hundred canyons had opened their mouths temptingly to receive a fugitive, between this point and the triple working of that ravine where the prospector had talked with him. Into any one of these the half-breed might have turned, no matter what his first goal in the flight might have been.

So there was doubt, and grave doubt, in the mind of the young man, and under the burning noontide sun, he turned aside to the cabin of Sam Tucker.

He was more generally called "Silent Sam." The nickname he earned most industriously by rarely parting his lips. He made his living by serving coffee and meat and pone to travelers to and from the Basin. Even the price of his meals, which were served under a lean-to outside his cabin, were generally written on a slip of paper, and not named aloud.

He was sitting in the shade of this lean-to, as the young man approached. The King Bird dismounted, and watered the mare at a little pool which Silent Sam had hollowed in the rock, and which was constantly filled and refilled by a slender trickle of water which, winter and summer, flowed down the rock. Then he turned to the keeper of that wayside inn.

Silent Sam was so ugly that he is difficult to describe, and almost difficult to think about. The four essential gifts of eyes, teeth, hands, and feet had been bestowed upon Sam in such excess degree that he could have divided his measure in half and still have provided more than enough for the average person. And all of him between eyes and feet was provided for in the same handsome manner.

Those eyes were buttressed around with great, massive bony structures. A mule might have broken its hoof, kicking Silent Sam in the eye, but he would hardly have fractured the skull of that giant. There was not much nose. A nose is an easily injured appendage of the face; as for the essential part, the nostrils, Sam had two big flaring ones, but there was no middle section to his smelling apparatus. He did not need to lift his head in order to turn up his nose at any one. His nose was permanently turned up.

Below the nose was a wide mouth. The lips did not amount to much. Nature remained strictly utilitarian in her provisions for Sam, and the lips were devised solely as an entrance for a great mouth. They formed, therefore, merely a straight slit that almost divided the face of Sam into two halves. Beneath that mouth there was a chin of granite,

217

rudely but durably built; under the chin appeared the neck of a gorilla that swelled with no sudden line of demarcation into a vast chest, big as a barrel, and solid as a barrel loaded with well-packed cement.

The understructure of Silent Sam was fitted to uphold such a formidable top, and his arms reached almost to his knees. All of Sam was therefore made according to the most generous pattern, except above the eyes. And there nature had stopped. Literally stopped. That is to say, there *was* no forehead. There were the shaggy eyebrows, a thin interim, and then the hair began.

Sam's forehead did not slope sharply back. It simply did not exist. And that was why he always wore a hat, even in that white-hot summer weather, because he never had found a hat so devised that it would not cover his eyes with the hatband.

There were two benches and a stool under the lean-to, but the ground was cooler. Therefore, Sam was seated cross-legged on the ground.

"Hello, Sam," said the young man.

Sam shrugged his right shoulder, and stared.

"Kind of hot," said the King Bird.

Sam shrugged his left shoulder.

"Many people been passing?" asked the young man.

Sam shrugged both shoulders at the same time.

The King Bird leaned against one of the rough-cut saplings that upheld the roof of the lean-to, and made himself a cigarette.

"Have the makings?" he asked.

Sam proved the words had meaning to him. He extended a vast hand and held it steady while the papers and tobacco alighted in it. For the slim package of wheat-straw papers he had no use. Instead, he took out a sheet of cheap paper, tore it in half, and emptied the remainder of the sack of tobacco into this homemade device. A few swift movements and he had framed a cigarette that had the dimensions of a cigar.

The King Bird made no protest. He merely held the match by which that huge smoke was lighted.

Silent Sam drew in such a long breath of smoke that the end of the cigarette flared out a brilliant yellow-white, and burning bits of the tobacco and white wisps of paper ash fluttered down to the ground.

"Not many people go by, this time of year, I suppose," suggested the King Bird.

Silent Sam exhaled a powerfully driven blast of breath and smoke that reached the body of the King Bird, and furled out against his person.

"What I most want to know," said the King Bird gently, "is if a fellow with a white face, a white, flat face, went by on a big gray stallion. D'you know?"

Silent Sam inhaled another big breath, and regarded the young man with the contemplative eye of a pig who sees a red-cheeked apple.

The King Bird smiled.

"The fellow I'm referring to isn't pretty," he said. "He's good-looking compared with you, but he isn't pretty."

A slight thrill—it could not be called a start—passed through the enormous body of Silent Sam.

"He looks," said the King Bird, "like a higher order of ape, that's all."

The body of Silent Sam straightened by several inches. He did not rise and he did not speak. Half his cigarette was consumed by his enormous inhalations, and he looked regretfully at the remainder, as though he might soon be forced to abandon it.

Said the King Bird: "A good many people have gone by this way, Sam, and they've all been treated in the same way. Most of them thought you were too big to handle, but I see that you're nothing but a big four-flusher."

Silent Sam choked on his inhalation which was going forward at that moment. He choked, and then coughed and spluttered.

The King Bird went on: "My idea is that I'll teach you manners, Sam. And all that's left of your face when I'm through with you will talk civil language, when the next man in a hurry comes by to talk with you. Understand?"

Silent Sam groaned—then regarded his cigarette as he was in the act of rising, and postponed his decision.

His color had changed. He had grown fiery red, mixed with white spots, his breathing was rapid.

"As a matter of fact," said the King Bird, "you've been sitting out here for quite a while trying to raise a reputation by never speaking. I understand the reason. It's not that you're even a grouch. It's because you don't know anything beyond words of one syllable."

Silent Sam regarded the cigarette again. Then he put it down, with care, on the edge of the table, and without the aid of his hands, he rose to his feet—a thing worthy of mention, considering his two hundred and fifty pounds of bulk.

He rose to his feet, and as he did so, the King Bird flicked the fat cigarette from the edge of the table, and ground it into the earth with his heel.

A brief, wordless howl issued from the mouth of Silent Sam, and he reached with one hand for the small man. The King Bird avoided that hand, and on the granite chin of the other, he struck twice with each hand. Compared with the size of Silent Sam, it seemed that such a small fist could accomplish absolutely nothing, but it is true that a tack hammer, if it hits the right spot, will eventually crack a boulder.

Silent Sam stepped back and shook his head, and made a gesture before his face, as though to brush away a fly.

While he was in the midst of that gesture, fists hard as iron, and driven like the end of a snapping whiplash, cracked against his mouth, his left eye, and his button of a nose.

From mouth and eye and nose, little trickles of blood commenced.

Silent Sam opened his throat and roared. The roar was stopped short, for two long-range punches, perfectly timed, landed in the middle of his mouth, and loosened several teeth.

But Silent Sam was a man without any more pride than a grizzly bear. Fairness in fighting tactics was nothing in his worthy life. This young stranger had become annoying;

wherefore Sam gathered up the homemade stool that stood at the end of his dining bench, and leaped for the enemy.

He might as well have struck at a wraith. The King Bird jerked aside from his line of vision; the heavy stool smote the air in vain, and the long, blue barrel of a Colt revolver hit the head of Silent Sam.

He dropped, very slowly, to his knees.

The King Bird laid the muzzle of the Colt against that crag of a chin.

"Brother," he said, "did you see a man go by on a gray horse?"

"Yes," said Silent Sam. "Mister, don't shoot."

"Was it a stallion?"

"It was," said Sam.

"Was the fellow an ugly mug?"

"He was," said Silent Sam.

"As ugly as you are?"

"Yes," said Sam.

"You lie," said the King Bird.

"I lie," said Silent Sam instantly.

"When did he go by?"

"An hour ago."

"Did his horse look fresh?"

"Strong, but not fresh," said Silent Sam.

"All right," said the King Bird, stepping back. "Stand up, Sam. The next time I hear of a man being rubbed with the rough of your tongue, I'm going to take a minute off and come up here to teach you more lessons in manners!"

CHAPTER XXXIX

A DESERT CRIME

HALFWAY down from the rest house of Sam to the bottom of the Comanche Basin, the King Bird paused. He had found a little meadow covered with long grass, which was covered with dust. The dust was bad, but the grass was good. It was the best bunch grass. The King Bird looked at it wistfully, then dismounted and turned the mare loose to graze.

It was a bitter shame to lose time, but in the end a well-fed horse will beat a starved one. He began to prepare himself against the future. That is to say, he got down on his knees and began tearing up the deep-rooted bunches of grass, and shaking the dust out of them. He collected a good fifteen pounds in this manner; it would be the equal of fifty, he felt sure, of any other sort of fodder.

With that wrapped in the slicker that had been rolled behind the saddle, he went down the slope again.

It was not a sprint. It was, in a sense, not even a distance race, but one in which time entered, and the endurance of two horses, and the brains of their riders.

The half-breed had one vast advantage. He was in the lead, and he could say just where the contest should lead. And it was not long before the King Bird discovered how great an advantage that was to be.

He picked up the trail at the bottom of the pass, as he entered the oven heat of the Basin. The big, round, unmistakable sign of the stallion led straight out into the desert, and for five miles, through the oven heat, the black mare followed, with her master going along swiftly on foot, beside her. Their companionship was never more clearly to be seen, as they turned their heads to one another, now and again, he with a smile, and the black pricking her ears a little.

Five steady miles he ran, with the sweat dripping on all his body, and turning to a salty incrustation before it had trickled half an inch, such was the dryness of the air.

They reached the first water hole, at the end of those miles, and they needed it badly.

What they found was a mudhole!

Nothing is more sacred than a watering place on the desert; men may have gauged their lives and the lives of their animals to an hour, so to speak, aiming at a watering place. But this one had been deliberately fouled. The sand had been beaten in around it, and in place of water, there was only a wash of thick mud.

For no more than this, many an old desert rat would have voted the gallows for Mr. Dick Macey.

The King Bird regarded the thing for a moment. Then, with a piece of board lying near—left from what camping party, new or old?—he scraped out a trench in the sand just at the edge of the hole. He made it two feet deep, and by degrees the water began to seep into it slowly. But it was a pure water, far purer, in fact, than the liquid in the original water hole.

Minutes were passing, in which the sun incinerated him. Even the labor of running seemed worth while, for the wind that he raised in his face. But still he had to wait until the trench was sufficiently filled.

Then he drank himself, filled his canteen, and let the mare have a good draft.

She had been standing with head down, now and again pushing her muzzle against him, plainly begging for leave, but not until she had word from him would she touch the water. Then he watched her drinking, with a queer love making his heart gentle, and saw the boluses of water slithering down her throat.

He used that pause to take a wisp of the bunch grass and with it rub her down thoroughly. More of the grass was laid before her, and she ate it thoroughly while he groomed her.

A good grooming, it is said, is worth half a feed. It supples the muscles of a horse and opens the pores.

But still he did not use her.

He preferred, when they went on down the trail, to run on foot. Straight on they went, a twenty-mile grind, to the next stop, another watering hole, and man and horse needed it again.

It was the same story over again, except that this was a larger pool of water, making a dark spot in the midst of the glare of the sand. But it had been thoroughly fouled by the same endeavor on the part of the fugitive. The King Bird, bitterly regarding that work of ruin, took up again the bit of board which he had kept with him, and mined another trench in the sand.

He was half blind, and sick with running, but he delved the trench three times as long, and wider and deeper, and it began to fill at once with a crystal-clear liquid. It was alkaline to the taste, but some of the evil had been filtered out of it.

Again the mare had a little of the bunch grass, a good draft of the water, the canteen was filled, and then they went on.

But this time he rode.

For he could see by the trail that the gray stallion was being kept at a trot most of the time. Yet the sign was fresh before him, the fine sand running down still into the depressions which the heavy hoofs had cut and beaten into the desert surface.

The stallion was being sent on at a round pace, but he had not gained much distance. The halts at the water holes must have been rather long; perhaps the delay to foul them so thoroughly had taken even more time than the trenching of the sand to drain off drinkable water!

And now he saw, far before him, the gray and its rider.

There was no doubt about it, from the direction in which the horseman was traveling and the fact that there was any rider at all before him.

Instantly, the King Bird dismounted and struck off at a brisk run, weary, sun-beaten as he was. For the horse was

224

the thing, far more than himself. He must save in the black mare that essential reserve of strength. Also, by going on foot, he reduced by one third the size of the silhouette which he and the mare made against the sky line. He could get that much closer without being observed.

So, drawing upon his nerve force, summoning his strength, he put forth his best efforts, and managed to maintain a steady gait.

He was drawing nearer, too. His own speed was just a trifle more than that at which the half-breed was jogging the stallion. He pulled within a mile, within a half mile, he was in long rifle range when he distinctly saw the stallion itself turn halfway round and throw up its head.

That was the warning signal!

As before, in that first long chance, the horse proved more alert than the rider. And off went the half-breed and the gray at a dazzling rate.

The King Bird swung into the saddle and followed, but not so fast. Molly was an excellent worker in sand like this, that slipped a little under her with every stride she made, but the King Bird had no desire to burn her out. He knew the abnormal qualities of the gray too well. Brains must beat the stallion, human brains, not the value of the horses.

So he kept Molly to a steady lope, which she could maintain half a day.

He ground his teeth as he saw the stallion draw away, dwindle to a spot of mist and almost vanish, but he kept the mare steadily to that gait. It was that or nothing!

The stallion drew clearer again; the horse had stopped, and now the King Bird could see that the half-breed was out of the saddle. But in a moment off they went again.

He found the reason for that halt, when he came up—another watering hole. And this time Dick Macey had not had time to foul it. The mare could drink at once, while her rider stood beside her, and sloshed water over her, and then rubbed her down vigorously and then used more water to cool her off.

He washed out her nostrils. He opened her mouth, and

225

washed the sand from her lips and the remnants of bunch grass from her teeth.

Then he started on again—at a mere jog. When a horse has taken on water, it must be pushed cautiously. Everything is up-hill, after such a time.

Once more the gray stallion was a mere bubble, dancing on the horizon. The King Bird dismounted and punished his aching, weary body again. And again, after long hours, he saw the enemy coming back to him.

That day he would never catch the other. The sun was drawing down toward the horizon, and Dick Macey, after heading for the promising and cool blue of the mountains, angled off again toward the heart of the desert.

And the very soul of the King Bird leaped.

For it was as the old prospector had said. The fugitive, fleet of wing, was trusting in the strength of its pinions against the hawk that pursued it!

He turned in the new direction, and gave the last of his strength to a final burst of running afoot.

CHAPTER XL

PURSUIT'S END

THE SUN set. The dark pulled down over the desert, and not till then did the King Bird stagger to a halt, and swing into the saddle again.

Before him, the form of the fugitive was small indeed, and almost swallowed with darkness; but never again, all that night long, could Dick Macey bring the gray away from the pursuer.

Now he trotted. Now he galloped. But always the black

mare was close behind, keeping the objective against the horizon line that was spotted dimly out by the stars.

The acrid smell of the desert rose into the nostrils of the King Bird. Twice he pulled up his belt, for he had had little sustenance for many days. He was starved. His body was starved until it was light. His soul was starved, and nothing but pain remained in him.

He had a strange surety—that this was the end of everything. And always, with a nightmare regularity, the picture of the girl returned to him, as she had been that day when he found her riding fence, and again, as he had seen her head and arms fall back limply after Macey fired.

What devil could have made him do it? Why were such people as Helena Blair put within the range of rifles, in the hands of beasts like Dick Macey? Why was such a horse given him to ride, also?

But this was the end. The stallion simply could not draw away!

Twice and again, the King Bird dropped to the ground, and ran ahead, to save the mare. She was tired, very tired. But so was the stallion. It was tired to death. It had not been saved as the mare had been saved. The gray had not been both watered and fed with such regularity. It was hollow—and the demands made on it were a furnace that burned out all the remains of its strength.

And the King Bird felt, now, that no thoroughbred in the world could have maintained the pace as the tough mustang blood of the mare sustained it, that blood which had been disciplined through four centuries of privations on the great ranges of the New World. Her blood was as good—the old Barb and Arab blood of the horses of the *conquistadores*. It had not been bred so fine for speed, but the blood was there, and now it told for sheer endurance even over that priceless king, the gray stallion.

For Macey, as the King Bird had guessed, had never left the saddle except at the water holes. He would hardly have believed his ears, if it had been suggested to him that the reason the mare kept up was because her rider was not goring the flanks of his mount with spurs or beating him

227

with a quirt, extracting the last ounce of effort through pain, but burning the life out of his own body with tireless effort, running on foot.

And spurs were not needed. A word would make the gallant little black lay down her life, striving.

But this was the end. The King Bird knew it, as the gray of the dawn began. If he allowed himself to relax one instant, fatigue of body and mind overwhelmed him; the flat land swirled around before his eyes; the far-off mountains, brown and blue, waved together, and grew tall, and then shrank small. He had to keep his jaws set until they ached.

Then, as the morning light increased, he saw the fugitive more clearly, slumping far forward, his hands on the pommel of the saddle.

The King Bird began to massage his right arm and wrist. Very soon, he would call on the mare for the last ounce of effort of which she was capable, and then the final test would be made. He must have that right hand ready for the crisis—and it astonished him to find that the fingers were shaking, the hand was shaking, the whole arm was uncertain!

Such a thing never before had happened to him. Was it possible that he had overtaxed even that well of limitless nerve power that had always been there in him, to be drawn upon unendingly?

He put up his hand and touched his face.

The skin seemed as hard as wood. It was drawn. It pulled on the corners of his mouth, and he felt that he was smiling without wanting to.

Then the sun came up suddenly, and the mare stumbled.

He looked down at her with amazement.

But it was true. She was almost beaten. Her head dropped. Her hoofs scuffed through the sand. He leaned out, and she swayed weakly with the motion—he could see that she was badly tucked up. The feel of her beneath the saddle was a different thing, because her back was humped, as the backs of cattle are bowed when they have stood long in a strong, cold storm.

And the stallion?

He could not see so well, for he had no side view. He only knew that that glorious head was down, and that the hoofs kicked up dust at every step.

He drew out the rifle and leveled it. But the horse and the rider danced so wildly into the sights and out of them that he knew he could not be sure of the mark. He might as well strike the horse as the man. And that he would not do. To shoot the horse was murder; to shoot the man was justice, performed only too late!

He sheathed the rifle again. A second thought made him snatch it out and throw it away. Every ounce told now. For the final effort had to be made.

He pulled out his revolver for the left hand, and abandoned that, also. Fool, fool that he had been to carry the extra weight so long. That would have told now. Every ounce would have told against the terrible strain of the night's work.

And then, aloud, he called to her, and she responded with a trot, and then with a canter.

It was not the old, flowing gallop that he knew so well. It was like the gait of a hobby-horse, going up and down, covering no ground!

Was this all that was left of her—this hollow mockery?

He looked bitterly ahead, and saw the gray roused to a trot, saw the white, frenzied face of the half-breed turned toward him.

Then the spurs went home to raise the gallop that would leave the mare far behind.

The stallion jerked up its head. Its ears pricked with honest effort. But its hind quarters swung to the side, and the King Bird saw the great round patch of red where the spurs had been thrust home, again and again.

And still there was no gallop—even the gray horse, that hawk of the earth, could no longer gallop. He could only trot, shuffling his hoofs through the sand, raising a trailing cloud of dust.

Steadily the mare was overtaking the gray. It was beaten, beaten at last by brains, not power of body.

It was true then—this was the end.

The King Bird drew his last gun. There was nothing under the hammer but an empty chamber. Five bullets were all that he dared to load for a gun that was fanned by the swift flicking of his thumb.

Five bullets—but one would be enough!

Closer they drew.

Then he heard a frightful cry before him, and saw the head of Dick Macey turned. Yes, horse and man had turned, and swept suddenly back at him.

To meet that last demand, the stallion had raised a gallop, perhaps the last that ever it would be capable of in this world! But gallop it did, to meet the gallop of the mare. The gray's ears were back, to prove that only pain drove it forward to the limit.

So they closed, and as they neared, Dick Macey was firing from an unsteady hand. Every shot flew wild. It needed only a glance at the wavering of his hand to show that only by chance could he hit his target. So the King Bird, point-blank, raised his hand, and fired.

He looked, but the other rode on, straight toward him.

Amazement seized the King Bird. The rifle might fail him, but never the Colt, at this range!

Again, again, again he fired, and still the half-breed sat his saddle, unharmed!

What enchantment had fallen?

The magic of weariness and totally broken nerves. That was it! As the hand of the half-breed shook with exhaustion and with hysterical fear, so the hand of the King Bird shook with weariness alone.

Two masters of their weapons, and yet every shot had missed its mark!

The King Bird saw the larger man looming suddenly big before him, and saw Dick Macey rise in his stirrups, and lean out and forward.

The young man glimpsed a hideous mask, not a face—a contortion, not human features. Then the arms of the half-breed closed around him, and the pair were jerked out of their saddles by the contrary motions, and dropped to the ground.

Hand to hand? Well, that was equally good for the King Bird; better, even!

But when his mighty will commanded his body, the body lay inert.

Sick amazement held him. He was like water in the grasp of Macey, and he understood the shriek of incredulous joy and disbelief that welled out of the throat of the other.

He, the King Bird, could only slowly master the weight of the gun he held, and twist the muzzle of it upward, toward the body of the enemy.

He saw Macey, mad with joy, hysterical with it, whip out a knife and raise it high above his head.

He saw the knife flash down, and as a heavy impact struck all light from his eyes, blindly he pulled the trigger of the gun.

It was long hours afterward before the King Bird roused himself feebly, and rising upon one elbow, looked at the thing that sprawled away from him on the sand, with the death agony still dimly printed on its face.

He felt that it had been no act of his, but the judgment, working through his helpless hand.

And the depths of that moment would never pass out of the mind of the King Bird.

A wet muzzle nudged his cheek. It was the black mare, nosing him, her ears hopefully pricked, her knees still bent with exhaustion.

He threw up a hand, pulled down her head, and pressed his face against the salt and dust of her forehead.

The stallion was not ten feet away. It had not moved because it could not, for it stood with bent knees, trembling from head to foot.

The King Bird got feebly up, steadied himself, saw with amazement the height of the sun in the sky, and then went drunkenly, unsurely, toward the great stallion.

Beaten, utterly gone was the gray. Its body was covered with terrible welts. In scores of places the cruel lash of the quirt had bitten through the skin and drawn the blood, and on the flanks were hideous red sores. The shoulders were even ripped, and the belly, where the brutal rider had raked his mount fore and aft with needle-sharp spurs.

The King Bird looked suddenly away, sick at heart.

He returned to Molly. She was badly spent, but not too spent to follow him, with uneven step. She had the greater reserve, after all, and for that reason, the stallion should have the canteen of water which the King Bird had reserved for the crisis of crises.

Toward the end, the red madness had made him forget it, but he remembered it now, and the small flask of brandy that he carried at his hip, in a metal case. He uncorked the canteen, poured in the brandy, and returning to the gray, stood before the hanging head.

It was a dead weight that he lifted. He got the head of the horse to his trembling shoulder, then pushed it higher still, for a moment, thrust in the neck of the canteen, and let the contents run down the throat.

He had never made a prayer in his life, that he could remember. Now he prayed, out loud, and instinctively: "God save him! He's too good to die!"

CHAPTER XLI

BACK TO ELMIRA

SOMEHOW the King Bird got both horses to the water hole; somehow he managed to get them there. Toward the end— all through the last mile—he had the reins of the stallion tied to the saddle of the mare, and she pulled valiantly, while the King Bird walked at the side of the great horse and cheered it on.

It seemed that the gray hardly knew the meaning of a

caress. But it learned. It would lift its ears a little, and a faint light would come in its eyes.

But they got to the water, at last, and drank, and then the young man worked, sloshing water on them, and rubbing them down, until the horrible shuddering in those limbs of gray steel ended, or almost ended. Then he started out of the Basin.

The gray was almost dead, that morning, but it was the gray that he rode up the slope, past the shack of Silent Sam, who stood with his hands on the table under the lean-to, and stared at the apparition that went up the trail.

So much the stallion had in it of recuperation that, as they reached the top of the grade, it tried to shy at a wreath of dust, whirling in the wind.

There the King Bird changed, and took the mare on through the next stage.

He headed straight back for Elmira. At least they would pay the girl the honor, for her gallantry, of taking her body to Elmira. His father, to be sure, was a grim man, but he would see to that.

So the King Bird rode straight to Elmira. It took him three days to get there, though he worked the two horses as much as they would stand. It was not until the third day, in fact, that they both began to lift their heads.

The gray, by that time, had learned to come to the call, and Molly had grown so jealous that she would run alongside, when her master mounted the stallion, and nip at his leg, and try to make him dismount.

The King Bird tried to laugh at her, but laughter was an art that he had forgotten.

He stopped at the first house outside of Elmira, and asked for two things—food for himself and the horses, and a razor to shave himself.

The old sourdough provided what was wanted, and as the shaggy beard came off the face of the King Bird, and he turned at last toward the old fellow, the man said:

"You know what I thought, when you came up? I thought that you was the King Bird, with a beard growed. But he's only a kid, and I see you're a gent of forty or so. I thought

233

you might be him, and that these two skinny nags might be the black mare and the gray stallion!—certainly is funny, the way a fool idea can come into a gent's head."

The King Bird ate what he could force down his throat, swallowed much hot coffee, paid, and rode on to the hotel.

The one-legged cook was on the veranda, peeling potatoes.

"Jumping Caesar!" he exclaimed, and letting the pan of potatoes fall, he sprang up and hobbled into the hotel.

Marshal Jim Hampton was in the hall, talking with several men.

"There's something out there that looks like the uncle of the King Bird," said the cook. "And he's got the shadow of the black mare, and the ghost of the gray stallion along with him."

Jim Hampton turned. The King Bird himself stood in the entrance to the hall.

He was saying calmly: "It's all right, Jim. I'm giving myself up. You can put the handcuffs on me now, if you want. I've only got one favor to ask of you."

"I ain't got any handcuffs," said the marshal, staring. "Is he—is he dead, King?"

"Yes, he's dead," said the young man with the old face. "I've got one favor to ask you, Jim."

"Asking ain't poison," said the marshal, never stirring.

"I'd like to see the grave, first," said the King Bird.

A frozen audience stood before him. It amazed him that not a gun was drawn—and he, the King Bird, helpless before them, too weak really to put up a fight, even to run for it!

"What grave?" asked the marshal.

"*Her* grave," said the young man.

"Whose?" said the marshal.

The King Bird tried for the name, but could not bring it to his lips. He made a vague motion.

"Hers," he said. "The girl's."

"You mean Brick?" gasped the marshal. "She's lying in bed in the first room to the right, head of the stairs, with a plaster around her forehead, that's all. You need a plaster the same place, it looks to me!"

The King Bird raised his hand and touched the place where the knife of Dick Macey had glanced from the bone.

"You don't understand, Jim," said the King Bird patiently. He found the name, and used it. "I mean Helena Blair. I want to know where she's buried."

At this, a tall man walked through the shadows that half covered the brain of the young man, and his face took on the features of Don Esteban. He put a long, strong arm under the shoulders of the King Bird.

"This way, señor," said he. "Let me show you the way. One glimpse of you will be enough to make her laugh; already she is safe for life."

He helped the King Bird up the stairs.

The marshal turned to the others in the hall.

"Well," he said, "there's a price on his head. Any of you boys can go up and collect it. There ain't any more fight in him."

The voice of the King Bird came down to them from the head of the stairs.

"I know you. You're Don Esteban. What I mean to ask is, Cuyas, can you show me the grave?"

"He's all in," said a hard-faced young cowman. "Did you hear that?"

"I'm asking who wants the reward," said the marshal. "Any of you boys wants to climb those stairs?"

"Don't be a fool, Hampton," said the hard-faced fellow. "Nobody wants to be lynched. You gotta go and do the arresting yourself—and may Heaven help your unhappy hide!"

"Hush," said the marshal, "that's the youngster. Kind of choked, ain't he, but happy! A game kid, is Bobby, I'm here to state."

"Nobody would say no," declared the hard-faced cowpuncher. "Nobody but a half-wit. You wouldn't think so, though, to hear him cryin' right out loud like this, would you? But he's only a kid."

"It seems to me you look kind of watery around the eyes yourself," said the marshal.

"I got a cold in the head; don't be a fool," said the cowpuncher.

No one smiled.

"How did the mare ever catch the stallion?" asked some one. "That's what I'd like to know."

"You didn't take a look at the King Bird's face," said the marshal.

"He ain't the King Bird no more," said the hard-faced man. "He's done with all that. Marrying and settling down is the next thing for him, all right, as soon as the Blair girl is able to be out again. Yep, he's James Oliver Kinney, now, thank you. But there's old man Kinney. He's just found out. Listen to him! You wouldn't think that nothing could make that old skinflint holler like that, would you?"

"Hush up," said the marshal.

A door opened.

"That'll be the door of the girl's room," said the marshal.

He raised his eyes with a contemplative look.

"Listen to that!" he said. "Listen when a good woman pulls the door of her heart wide open. You don't hear that so often. About once in ten lifetimes, is all, I'd say. I guess there's more room in the street, boys, than there is in here. Things seem to be pretty private, up there."

He led the way onto the veranda.

"There's gotta be a lot of fool letters written now," said Jim Hampton. "That's the worst of it. Letters to the governor; letters to Washington, too. Signed petitions, and the whole range wanting to write its name down on the petitions. It's goin' to be a whole lot of trouble."

"Listen," said the hard-faced man. "Listen, will you?"

"I'm listening," said the marshal. "What of it? Didn't you never hear a man called 'King,' before?"

"Yeah," said the other. "I've heard a gent called 'King' before, I guess, but I never heard it in that tone of voice. I'm goin' to move along. I feel kind of homesick. I dunno for what!"

THE END

236

THE UNSHAKABLE, UNSTOPPABLE, UNKILLABLE CAPTAIN GRINGO IS BACK IN:

RENEGADE #2, BLOOD RUNNER
by Ramsay Thorne   (94-231, $1.75)

They're waiting for a man like Captain Gringo in Panama! In this soggy, green hell where the French have lost a fortune in lives and francs trying to build a canal, the scum of the earth —and their scams—flourish. Every adventurer with a scheme, every rebel with a cause wants a man like Captain Gringo—running guns, unloosing a rain of death from his Maxim, fighting Yellow Jack. Indians, army ants, even the Devil himself if he stands in the way!

EVERYONE WANTS TO LAY HANDS ON CAPTAIN GRINGO

RENEGADE #3, FEAR MERCHANT
by Ramsay Thorne   (90-761, $1.95)

In this revolution-wracked land where the man with the guns is king and those who grovel before him conspire behind his back, no one can be trusted. With his eyes wide open and his Maxim at the ready, the Captain is primed for action: in the bed of a Chinese girl whose eyes are startling grey, at the challenge of a general who has only one eye, at the silent command to murder in the cold gaze of a high-born lady, at the demand for love in the hot, savage stare of an Indian girl. For no one can fight and no one can love like Captain Gringo.

NO MAN CAN HANDLE
CAPTAIN GRINGO IN
COSTA RICA!

RENEGADE #4: DEATH HUNTER
by Ramsay Thorne   *(90-902, $1.95)*

In these cool and quiet nights Captain Gringo trails the highlands with his profile low and his Maxim ready. It's been a year of hell fighting his way through three revolutions and a U.S. court-martial. He's wanted by the U.S. Cavalry and even more by certain ladies. For now, all the Captain wants is some drinkable beer and serviceable women. But before Captain Gringo's vacation ends, he will have a job—masterminding an attack on three of the world's major powers.

"THE KING OF THE WESTERN NOVEL"
is MAX BRAND